W9-CEI-501

PARTHOLON

D. KRAUSS

Rebel ePublishers
Detroit New York London Johannesburg

Rebel ePublishers
Detroit, Michigan 48223

Partholon

For information regarding permission, email the publisher at rebele@rebelepublishers.com, subject line: Permission.

ISBN-13: 978-0-6158758-8-0
ISBN-10: 0615875882

Cover design by Damon
Interior design by *Caryatid Design*

ACKNOWLEDGEMENTS

Stella and Mark and Sara made it better. EJ and Jayne and Cat made it happen. Good on ya, mates.

For Terry, who endures.

"And it is there that Partholon died, five thousand men and four thousand women, of a week's plague on the kalends of May. On a Monday plague killed them all except one man..."

The Lebor Gabala Erren [Book of Invasions]
Irish Texts Society
http://www.ancienttexts.org/library/celtic/irish/lebor.html

1

Stutter roll, stutter roll, stutter ...

John straddled the bike and gave the pedal a kick, watching the tire spin then catching it on the pavement. Let's go, let's go. Yeah, in a minute. Kick, spin, catch.

Still dark. Should take advantage of that. Be invisible, be silent, dodging the cars and wreckage, tire hum only eight, ten feet in front, so he'd be on the dogs before they knew it. They'd start, confused, trying to spot him while he saw them so clearly, lit up like day in the goggles. Raise a threatening pistol and they scatter. Instinct.

So let's go, man.

No. Don't want to.

There. The thought. He relaxed, actually smiled. Yeah. Didn't want to. He just didn't want to. Stupid to go. Gonna get killed. Gonna get shot. Gonna gonna.

Call in sick.

He laughed. That's a good one. Start shouting now. Maybe someone'll hear.

Sick. Wouldn't be a lie. He must be sick, must be crazy, going to work like this. No one goes to work. There is nothing to work for. There are no bureaux or chiefs or coordinators or patrol officers or dumbass students crying 'cause someone stole their laptops out of their rooms, which they left open while they went to eat and make phone calls and they trust everyone on their floor and this is just unbelievable and what kind of campus is this and what kind of lousy cops are you anyway?

Well, that was one advantage. He didn't have to hear

that stupid crap anymore. That made for a bigger smile. And that made him push, finally, off.

The hardest part was getting started. Once done, things settled into rhythm pretty quick and he actually enjoyed it. That was true even pre-Event. How many times, say, he'd just sit in the living room dressed in his dobok, fingering his black belt and coming up with hundreds of reasons not to go to practice. Too old, too tired, too late, just wanna finish this movie then Theresa would say, "Are you going or not?" and he would and when he got there and got warmed up and did a couple of falls and started teaching the beginners about holds and pressure points he'd be into it and glad he came.

But see, there was benefit to that. What's the benefit here? He wasn't being paid. That was the fuck of it. It's easy to justify the dumbest of jobs if you're paid for it, even if you're not paid well. This arming up and leaving when it's still dark and using night vision and changing routes, so no established pattern and shooting at suspicious movement and outrunning the dogs was all effort uncompensated.

So why do it?

He stopped at the end of Harwood, where it emptied onto Old Keene Mill, and considered holing up, living furtive, sneaking out for groceries or medicine or ammunition like a scared rat. Nah. That was dying by inches. Not his style. He wasn't going to go in measure – he was going all at once, in a blaze of unknown glory. So that's one.

Two. He was tired of losing. He'd already lost too much. Vandals weren't going to pick his bones and sell him at the Gate. He was going to leave a mark here, a sign of his passing, not of his succumbing.

No three. Two were good enough.

There was panting and clattering and snuffling behind him but he didn't react. Lupus came up to the bike and nudged his hand off the handle and he reached into his pocket and threw him a Snausage. Hairbag stood off, as usual, watching and John waited. Presently the sheepdog shuffled near arm's reach and John figured that was close enough and threw him one, too. Lupus watched it sail over but wouldn't interfere. He loved his partner too much.

"You boys keep an eye out," he ordered them, "and don't devil Snuffy."

They looked to see if, somehow, the morning ritual would change and he would throw more. Hope springs eternal. "Get," he said, signaling the end of that hope and they both turned and barked a couple of times, and romped off. John smiled grimly. A little taste of meat and, hopefully, they'd run down some deer today.

Damn deer. They're like big furry fleas.

He coasted to the bottom of Daventry and kicked in the electric motor to help with the steep climb into Springfield. "Good morning, Mrs. Vanderbilt," he said, as he always did, to the fur-coat-wrapped grinning skull leaning against the Cadillac's window across from the 7-11. Not her name, he was sure, but he wasn't interested enough to dig through her rotten purse to find out.

She was the only one in a position to grin at him during the morning ride so she deserved some kind of greeting. And if she had tried to get away while wrapped in her precious furs, well, then she should get a wealthy honorific, too.

He reached the interchange and stopped. Which way today? Probably should use 395 then parallel on Van Dorn to Beauregard when it gets a little lighter, maybe get back on at Route 7. When was the last time you did that, four days ago? Should be okay. John checked his harness, ensuring the mini-14 was tight across his back and the .357 was riding high enough on his hip. Slap the tanto and the .25, all in place. He headed up the ramp and, last minute, decided to use the HOV lanes, which meant dodging all the dead cars facing him. Disconcerting. And it was harder to get onto Van Dorn, no ramps, but it had the advantage of being a little unexpected.

Bundys think everyone thinks like them and chooses the path of least resistance. It would give him an extra few seconds to spot them.

He coasted down the ramp and got into rhythm after passing Edsall, turning off the battery to save power. Not really necessary because he was carrying a spare but it was always good to have a little more juice for the last leg. It was still dark by the time he passed Gallows and he was in good humor. Riding always did that to him, even Before. In the blackest of moods, he'd pull out the Bianchi and go tooling up the Parkway and, about a mile into it, was thrilled and smiling and wondering why he'd been so pissed off. Just love to nurture our hurts, don't we, sitting on the couch and toasting our grudges. Entropy. Takes an effort to put the drink down and shake the mood by doing something productive, mow the lawn, fix the fence, kill some Bundys, although he didn't really need a lot of push to do that.

The world was green. It was a clear night, although a little cold (spring, waddya want?), and the stars were firing up the goggles. If he looked up, the Milky Way would dazzle, overwhelm. You could see every faint star and nebula with the goggles, so fascinating and beautiful that he would lose control of the Zap, staring at a green universe in open-mouthed wonder.

So don't look up.

He watched the road and shoulders instead, seeking movement. The cars were clear and green and dead in the goggles, skewed, off angle, most of them crashed into the car in front, here and there settled on top of each other. Evidence of frustration: drivers plowing into the jam that prevented escape while the cloud of death crept

4

up behind.

A few were overturned and burnt, whole families of skeletons spilling out of the windshields and windows. Skulls grinned at him from behind steering wheels or lolled in passenger seats or, occasionally, bunched all together, as if they'd decided on one last group hug. Several had big holes in them, evidence of something other than the Al-Qaeda Flu.

But, overall, not that many bones here. Most people had just abandoned their vehicles and walked. The bone pile-ups started more towards Woodbridge, as the weakened refugees stumbled then stopped and, wheezing for air, huddled miserably under whatever shelter they could find, a truck, a tree, an overpass. The 95 rest stop was damn near impassable because of the bones. He supposed things had evened out from there with a better distribution of bones all the way to Richmond. Hell, all the way to Charlotte. Not that he was going to look.

It was kind of fun dodging in and out of the wrecks. Motocross, something he had never done but sure looked like a hoot. You had to be quick and sharp at this speed to make it through without collision. If he kicked in the battery, it would be a lot more hair-raising but he wasn't sure he still had the reflexes for that, so no. Besides, it was too distracting. Couldn't look for ambushes while playing skull chicken.

It took about an hour from Edsall to reach the Pentagon and he was a sweatbag. Hell, he was a sweatbag before he got on 395, even with the collar undone and the tie loosened. That's why he always brought another shirt. Even with the electric motor, this was a helluva workout, considering all the weight he carried. He was a profuse oozer under the most benign of conditions, anyway – simply watching others work out was enough to get him going. A natural for that old Mitchum commercial.

That's why no body armor. Forget it. He'd die of heatstroke before he made the Route 7 exit. The high calibers everyone's using made armor somewhat futile, anyway. That thought made him peer hard at the shoulders, looking for someone wielding a rifle. Nothing.

It was a bitch of a climb to the top of the 110 ramp but he looked forward to it because of the long descent down the other side past the Pentagon, where the jet had smashed into it. They'd almost completely repaired it. The rubble had been carted off and the breach sealed but there was still some curtaining around the wound and blackening about the edges. A lot done for the little time they had, but, given things, just as well they never finished. It was now a shrine, a monument to the first blow of the war. That it was abandoned was evidence of the second.

But not today. A Cobra suddenly swooped over the ramp and John almost upended, braking hard and ducking under the overpass. He cursed. How do you not hear a helicopter? Must be some trick of acoustics because rifle shots were heard miles away now, so the damned Cobra should have sounded like the Second Coming.

John unholstered the .357 and, cautiously, inched the Zap down the decline. At the edge of the overpass, he leaned the Zap against the wall then slowly poked his head around the corner. The Cobra was gone although he could still hear it. Sounded like it was on the other side of the Pentagon. He watched, patient.

Ah. There.

Movement along the parking lot, some more on the lawn opposite the breach. Big yellow suits and big self-contained breathing units.

CDC.

Had they seen him? John tensed but no one headed his way and the Cobra stayed off, so probably not. Didn't

6

mean he was safe. They probably had some guys scanning the area just waiting for someone like John to do something they interpreted as threatening, like breathe, and then waste him. Or worse, take him. John gripped the pistol. No friggin' way.

A couple of CeeDees had paused in front of the breach and were staring at it. Tribute, John supposed, although it was highly unlikely either of the moonsuits had been anywhere near the Pentagon when it happened. Doubtful they were even military. Just because they had emergency authority and widely expanded powers and weapons systems and patrols and itchy trigger fingers, didn't make them club members and didn't give the two moonsuits the right to render honors to people they wrongly considered brethren. The CDC was as far away from the principles those Pentagon people died for as their doctors were from compassion. So they were just tourists. He set his jaw. He should shoot them.

So what was the CDC doing here? He took a risk and craned his neck to see more but couldn't really tell. Odd place to do air sampling and you weren't going to find a lot of test subjects running around the place. Most Survivors avoided the Pentagon because they believed there were arcane security devices, like mines and lasers, scattered all around it. Same reason they avoided Langley. John knew those stories were crap, probably sowed by the military to keep Raiders from breaking in and selling their dirty little secrets at the Gate. More likely, the military kept a security team in place with orders to kill all trespassers, although he'd seen no evidence. Didn't mean they weren't there. Maybe he was now seeing that evidence, a relief unit.

A transport helicopter, a Chinook, roared over the side of the Pentagon and hovered above the roof. John watched as a large cable dropped down with what looked like a pallet attached to it. He couldn't see much from this angle so he waited and, about ten minutes later, the pallet went back up loaded with hundreds of boxes.

Well. They finally decided to collect their dirty little secrets, did they? 'Bout damn time. Shoulda done it when they first emptied out DC, but, better late than never.

Which meant they weren't CDC, but military. So maybe he should drop the bike and run across the lawn and say, "Hey! Hey, I'm one of you! I'm a retired captain, take me, take me!" How many rounds to the chest would he get for that – twenty, thirty? Forty if he acted as if he was going to tear their suits. He chuckled grimly. Yeah, they'd take him, all right. Straight to the Atlanta labs.

He grabbed the Zap, moved to the opposite side of the overpass and checked the area. He watched the Chinook as it spun off and then looked at the CeeDees but they weren't paying attention. And no Cobra, so go. He whipped the Zap past the wall and hauled it over the railing, sliding down the steep decline and almost killing himself at the bottom, which had such a sharp angle he was afraid, for a moment, he'd bent the tire rim. All this while clutching the .357. Pretty good. He held his breath but no shots rang out so he'd given them the slip. Or they weren't going to reveal their position for somebody obviously running away.

He pulled the Zap up the next incline and over the set of railings, puffing and panting and resetting himself and yes, wiping away the sweat with a pocket handkerchief. Okay, have to travel the outbound lanes of 110 now to avoid the CeeDees, which meant a long haul past Ft. Myer. He was definitely going to be late.

2

The trumpet blew and Collier groaned deep in his blankets. Gawd, who did they get this time, some 12-year-old slick sleeve? No one, even in their most drunken state, could confuse that caterwauling with anything approaching Reveille. Maybe that was the point, make it so bad everyone would leap out of their bunks and charge the Quad intent on murder.

"Rise and shine, rise and shine, another beautiful day in the Provos," Davis griped from the top bunk and Collier smiled. Same thing, every morning. So he knew Davis was all right.

Collier kicked the bottom of Davis's mattress and heard a satisfying "Oof!" and Davis rolled off and pounced on him and they were wrestling in the middle of the floor, Davis more technically proficient but Collier with the weight and leverage. Collier got him in a headlock and held him until Davis tapped out, saying "Dammit!"

"That's three this week," Collier noted.

"Yeah, yeah, jerkwad, you ain't gonna win. There' s still tomorrow."

Collier smiled and let him up and started making his bed. He would win. He wanted Sunday off, no KPing the room. He'd make it up to Davis next week, losing four of the five matches, but not this week. Ah, Sunday, sleep late, spend time on the lacrosse field shooting goals, maybe barbecue on the parade field, if they could find meat. Grab some guns, grab Davis when he was done with the room, head into town and look for pussy. Or trouble. Plenty of both in Waynesboro.

They KPd, grabbing clothes and books, squaring chairs and desks and folding laundry from last night and then Davis took the bathroom first. One of the privileges of company rank: your own bathroom. Suffer, peasants, he sent the uncharitable thought out to the Quad.

"There, by the grace of God," leaped into his head in Dad's voice and he felt a momentary shame. You're right, Dad, you're right. He sent an apology out to the quad, too.

He lit a candle to dispel the murk and opened his copy of the Federalist Papers. If he didn't pass American Government, then he wouldn't graduate, although they'd let him walk, and he'd have to do summer school. Not a bad idea; it would hold off his draft for at least three more months, give him time to finish his negotiations with the air force.

But Dad would be peeved and the army might just say enough is enough and send a Draft Gang to collect him. The last time they tried that, they got their asses handed to them, so, this time, they'd come heavier. He had no doubt Fishburne would repel them, but at a much higher cost than the twelve they lost last time. And they might end up getting him, anyway. Pass the course. Do Dad proud. Besides, should have an answer from the air force by the end of May. Or June.

Davis burst out of the bathroom yelling "Next!" like, who else would it be? Steam followed him out and raised the temperature in the room about four degrees, which was nice. The staff turned on the boilers at 0400, which usually gave enough hot water to shower the Corp and raise the classroom temps to at least the point where you couldn't see your breath before they shut them off again at 0800. Thank God it was spring; soon the problem would be cooling the rooms and, since the four-hours-a-

10

day of electricity wouldn't do the job, everyone would end up sleeping on the Quad or under the overhangs, if it was raining.

He closed the book and slipped past Davis, who was air-guitaring the bass line from "Smooth Criminal," Alien Ant Farm version, "DododododoDO, doDO, Do," and getting it wrong, of course. Man had no sense of rhythm and Collier picked it up in his mind as he closed the door. Yeah. Music from 2001, Before the World Ended.

Shit, shower, shave, not necessarily in that order but with the special urgency three years at Fishburne had instilled and he was out in seven minutes, all three tasks accomplished to his satisfaction. He kissed the (illegal) poster tacked to the back of the door – Brooke Burke standing in water with a come hither look over her shoulder. "Brooke, Brooke," he muttered, "come away with me."

"Your dreams," Davis commented, eating an illegal corn muffin. The man ate continuously but managed to lose weight. Tapeworm.

"Cadet or Provo today?" Collier asked.

"Cadet."

Good. Collier reached for the grays, the day uniform because there was no parade scheduled, just drill, so he could be a little more informal. He dressed quickly, was tying his shoes when the first bell sounded.

"Here we go," Davis said and they squared each other and eyed each other and Collier punched Davis in the shoulder and he ball-slapped Collier in return, causing him to gasp and hunch over. "Bastard!" he said, with his remaining breath.

Davis grinned and placed the loaded .45 in his holster. "You betcha."

Collier grabbed his own pistol and they both strode onto the landing. Cadets scurrying by dodged them while saluting, some, at this late moment, running from the shower. Collier shook his head. Never make it, so they'll end up braced later this afternoon.

They both looked down in the Quad, still dark because sunrise had not yet climbed past the mountains surrounding Waynesboro. Captain Bock was a silhouette there, clipboard in hand, legs apart, the sleeve over his missing arm dangling, a statue, a rock. Davis and Collier squared each other one more time and waited.

Bong! Officer of the Day rang the ship's bell, "First call!"

Doors slammed and the sudden uptick in mutter and scuffling and motion meant the corp was moving, most of it, anyway. In the early morning, it was a gray mass on black, defined only by the two field torches that threw just enough light to make out figures. The gray tide flowed around the quad, the companies finding position.

"See ya later," Davis said and hit him on the shoulder as he walked away. Davis, as adjutant, would stand with the command staff. Collier watched his own corner and saw that most of Alpha Company was there. Good. God help, though, anyone who was late.

Briskly he turned and walked to the cement landing, smoothed and grooved down the middle by thousands of boots over the past 120 years, and marchwalked his way down to the first floor. Cadets saluted him, saying, "Sir" and he saluted back. He reached the grass and made his way to the front of the company. Farley, his first sergeant, was already there.

"Sir," Farley saluted.

"Everyone here?" Collier asked.

"Paulie and Jones and Stick aren't."

Collier snorted, "What a surprise," and they both grinned. Collier walked back to the milling group, slapping shoulders, straightening uniforms, adjusting equipment. The boys were respectful and saluted and thanked him. "Morning, sir," Hendricks, one of the privates said, "Did you hear from your Dad?"

"Yep. Last night. I'll tell y'all about it later."

"Thank you, sir." Genuine gratitude, from him and others who leaned in to listen. Hearing from a dad was gold.

"Assemble!" the officer called out and the gong sounded and Collier straightened and stiffened and marched to the head of the now formed company. Farley marched up and saluted and just grimaced, confirming those three idiots were late. Out of the corner of his eye, Collier saw Stick stumbling off the landing and falling into place. Other movement told him the last two were racing down the stairs.

You boys just bought yourselves an afternoon of tours. "Put 'em on report," he told Farley.

"Ten ... HUT!" Davis called out from the arch and they all hit it. The battalion commander and his staff marched to position and the sun broke the horizon somewhere beyond the brick walls, the sky turning fiery with the early morning clouds. Collier glanced up. Maybe it would be a warm day.

3

Made it. John stood the Zap at the top of the Key Bridge. What a pain in the ass going by Ft. Meyer. Easily added another twenty minutes to the ride, although the long hill from the Route 50 gate down to the Bridge ramp was a joy. But an out-of-the-way joy, tempered by the steep climb up the ramp itself.

He was in the middle of the complicated intersection next to the Rosslyn Metro. A breeze blew, kind of cold, but nice against his sweat so he stood off the seat to enjoy it. The traffic light above him swayed and pieces of odd paper and cloth rattled and moved threateningly, causing him to jerk around every few seconds; a pain-in-the-ass survival instinct, but one that kept him alive.

There was a huge pile up of cars here. DC had made all the streets and bridges one way out when the evacuation was in full swing, so the pile up was mostly facing him. A given population includes enough incompetent and selfish drivers who can't maneuver a straight line on the best of days, much less during a panic, so had no hope of negotiating the Parkway/Moore St/110/66 exits and entrances which all seemed to pipeline right here. Result? The inevitable wall of cars, some of them on top of each other, little different from 395. Bones here, bones there, everywhere a bone bone.

He picked his way through and out the other side where it was, strangely, almost clear all the way to Georgetown. He stood behind a pickup truck and looked but there was no movement so he made a sudden dash to his favorite wreck, a Chevrolet Caprice down on its rims and turned sideways at the crest of the bridge. He patted its hood as he peered through the busted windshield towards Georgetown, "Saved my life, bucko," he said, as he did every day since the Hellacious Firefight, or, as it was more formally known, *Meeting Metro PD for the First Time After.* He spotted movement at the end of the bridge. Yep, there they were. Almost reassuring, now.

It was what, 'bout a year After when the Caprice saved his life? Something like that. He'd been back to work for a while and everything seemed pretty quiet, so he was completely unprepared when he crossed the Key midspan, looked up and saw a patrol car barricading the end of the bridge. Behind it were three black-leather clad and white-helmeted MPD officers, bristling with MP5s and AR-15s, bringing their barrels down on him.

He'd dumped the Zap and rolled behind the Caprice as they opened up, pinning him with a lead hailstorm and blasting out the car windows, tearing off the hood and all the tires. Thank God. That's what protected him from under-car ricochets. Gang, he first thought, fuckin' ass Gang waiting for me. Or maybe he'd thought, Raiders. It was, after all, transition time. He had the shotgun that day, so it was on. They threw enough rounds at each other to qualify for a small war.

Fortunately, the MPD guys weren't very good or they would have stitched John in about three minutes, especially since he had to reach over the ruined hood to fire. John, by contrast, was damn good, but fortunately for them, was using .00 which just didn't have the range (although, right after, one officer said he got sprayed pretty good at least twice). John had since switched to pumpkin ball. Lesson learned.

This is it, John had thought, going out in the proverbial blaze of glory, wonder if Collier will ever find out

15

what happened to me, when he heard a bullhorn. A bullhorn? Intrigued, he stopped shooting and listened. "Metropolitan Police Department!" An amplified voice, and then something about emergency decrees and John was in violation of weapons, trespass, disorderly conduct, whathaveyou statutes. "If you don't want to die, then throw out the gun and approach with your hands up now."

Yeah, right. MPD. John hadn't seen MPD since the Event. Other than CDC thugs, he hadn't seen anybody in uniform. "You're full of shit!" he yelled. "You're a buncha goddamn Gang members!" Or goddamn Raiders, something like that. "I'm the law! You surrender to me!" Like he would have taken them alive. It was just a dodge he hoped they were stupid enough to fall for.

There was a pause. "You're the law?" Bullhorn couldn't hide his astonishment.

"Yes, asshole, and you're under arrest!" John had a good command voice so no problems with being heard. Besides, the acoustics at the end of the bridge were great since there was no more traffic.

Another pause. "What agency?"

"American University Police!"

"What?" John wasn't sure if Bullhorn didn't hear him or was just incredulous.

"I said, 'American University Police'!" yelling that with everything he had, enunciating every word so there was no misunderstanding, jack offs.

They started laughing, which just burned him. Yeah, yeah, yeah, Special Police Officer, rent-a-cop, wannabe, security guard, call me what you usually do, fuckers. May be true for most, but not in John's particular case. This was his retirement job. He'd been a *real* lawman, an agent, you hear that, you cackling bunch of hyena fucks? A door-busting, gun-toting, maggot-grabbing, ass-kickin', hard-drinkin', woman-lovin', iron-fisted rampaging Viking of a lawman for twenty glorious years. He ran murderers, rapists, drug dealers, burglars and general assholes to ground, tore them up, beat them half to death, stuffed 'em, cuffed 'em, and hauled 'em to Leavenworth before the three idiots chuckling at the end of the bridge were even born.

He really, really should just shoot them.

"Show us a badge," Bullhorn again, laughing.

Bastard.

"Don't shoot!" he yelled, fishing into his vest.

"We're not going to shoot. Just stand up and show us your badge."

Like hell. "I'm not standing up!" he yelled and started waving his big gold Captain's badge in their direction so they couldn't get a bead on it, just in case they decided to become marksmen. There then ensued about twenty minutes of negotiations that finally culminated in John advancing, arms out, badge out, coat off, shotgun on ground and .357 beside it, cursing himself for a fool and convinced they would start shooting when he got within ten feet and he'd have to pull the .25 and shoot back.

He'd lose, but he'd get a couple of them.

They didn't, and he didn't. And they didn't because they believed him when he refused to stand up – only a cop would do that. Someone pretending to be a cop would have leaped to full view, convinced the badge was holy, protective, and always fooled the stupid pigs. Boom, surprise, you can't fool cops. Just stop trying. But he never forgave them for laughing at him.

And for not passing the word. You'd think they'd have done so, after he'd explained what he was about. But no, there were a few more corollaries to the Hellacious Firefight before MPD finally caught on and stopped shooting at him. A little mention at shift change, fellas, would have saved everybody a lot of grief and ammunition.

17

He hadn'tt seen Larry, Moe, and Curly again, a shame because he wanted to bitch-slap them. They were probably dead but he wasn't going to ask. He didn't even know their names. MPD didn't wear nametags anymore and, the one or two times he'd tried introductions, there was stony silence. Some super-secret government vibe here, probably having to do with the New Order. But, please, be reasonable. Make up a name. At least try to throw off John's suspicion that they really weren't MPD at all, but Something Else.

What, John, what? CIA? NSA? Disney-A? He chuckled and watched the checkpoint carefully as he waved at them. Motion stopped and he saw helmets and sunglasses turn his way and then someone waved back. Okay, now he had only a fifty per cent chance of being shot instead of one hundred. He pedaled down and engaged the drive and started coasting towards them.

Usually they just waved him through onto M Street and watched as he canted onto Canal Rd and down towards GU. His back always itched at that point, like a bullet would be splitting it any second. But, occasionally, they acted like real cops and told him stuff – some nonsense around the reservoir or some particularly weird Vandals making the rounds on Wisconsin, so watch your ass. Downright stunning and those were the occasions he made the mistake of asking names because, well, if you're going to act normal, then he'd do something normal back. Got the silent treatment.

Which was a lesson. They were not friends, they weren't even compatriots. They'd just grown used to him. They were hard-eyed men who shot first, leaving bodies where they fell. John guessed he was a hard-eyed man, too, but that didn't create empathy. It did create inertia. They didn't shoot John because … well, why? He was no threat. His showing up every morning of the workweek had settled into routine.

18

Besides, history militated against friendship. SPOs and cops didn't like each other. Virginia and DC didn't, either, and he lived in Virginia. Hell, even Before, he'd had lots of arguments with MPD because they just didn't want to take campus crime reports, like an assault on a student or a credit card theft, especially if it happened towards shift change. And they generally dropped the ball on the ones they did take so John ended up running the cases himself for no other reason than self-satisfaction since the DC courts never prosecuted anyone he caught anyway. MPD, hell, the whole District, was pretty incompetent back then, and he had, on a few frustrated occasions, voiced that opinion. Not that any of the present group would know that, but attitudes remained.

Best he could hope for was respect. Prove yourself an asset in this war and even your most recalcitrant allies will give you props. And he'd seen a growing, albeit slow and grudging, acceptance, ever since the punk firefight.

That had been a good one. He'd been walking the rear ball field, checking his stashes, when he'd heard some commotion towards the main Quad, an acoustic 911 that, obviously, he had to check out. He'd unslung the 14, rushed up through the south complex, which gave a lot of cover, and crept along the McKinley Building until he could see.

Three or four punks stood in front of the Hurst building. They had piled up a bunch of classroom furniture on the front stoop and were pouring gasoline on it. True punks, the mohawked, purple dreadlocked, all leather, eyes blackened, chains attached-to-everything types.

John had moved to cover and cut loose, immediately taking out the guy with a pump shotgun and two of his pistol-waving buddies. Six shots, about two-and-a-half seconds, and all they'd got off was exactly one wild round from the fourth guy, who ran like hell. He supposed it wasn't much of a firefight since it was all one-sided, but he was still pretty proud of it.

MPD, stunningly, had responded, drawn by the noise. They'd looked at the bodies and looked at John and debated whether to kill him or not, further proof the checkpoint guys weren't passing along intelligence. John had his badge out but, hey, SPO, unimpressive to these guys so he gave them his pedigree. They'd still debated, until he pointed out there were now three less punks to deal with. That, and the slow realization they didn't have to patrol the campus anymore, won the day. They'd swung their MP5s away, got into their cars and driven off (wonder where they were getting the gas?), but not before one patrolman gave him a wink and a box of .223. "In case anymore show up," he'd said.

Since then, the patrols came by from time to time to see how he was doing, tell him about more weirdness, just BS for a bit. John looked forward to those infrequent drop-bys. So many casualties, so many things gone, and, out of all that, one of the things he missed most was simple, old fashioned, wasting time. Jawing, goofing off, gold bricking, coffee break, whatever your name for it, gone.

Five minutes shooting the shit with MPD officers, aloof, murderous, apparently with some hidden mission, was like a cold beer on a summer afternoon. John was grateful. He repaid the kindness by showing them where the good tools were. "Have at it, boys. Better you get it before Raiders do."

He rolled to a stop near the kiosk and a young one, a newbie, stepped out, eyes wary, looking at John's 14 strapped so prominently across his back. "What are you doing here?" he asked.

Figures. John clucked his tongue in annoyance and looked at an older guy with sergeant stripes, familiar face, who stood idly in the shade of the kiosk. "What, you didn't brief this guy?" The sergeant just shrugged and looked away.

"I know you're up on the campus," Newbie said, smartass, "I just wanna know why."

"Why, are you?"

"I ain't at the campus."

"No shit."

Newbie's eyes narrowed and he got all tense and John smiled inwardly. They always think they're tough. Well, John was a lot tougher than he looked, something punk ass here was about to find out.

The sergeant was now interested and turned his attention away from the empty buildings behind them to watch.

"Hey," Newbie said, "you know how dangerous it is out here?"

"Yep."

"So why don't you stay home?"

"Why don't you?"

"I got a job to do, Mister."

"So do I."

Newbie colored and John prepared his template of answers – "You're too old." "Yeah, wanna go a couple of rounds?"; "You don't know what you're doing." "I know more than you. I've been doing this longer than you."; "You're gonna get killed." "Haven't yet. And I'll damn sure take a lot of them with me."

John waited.

"You're crazy," Newbie said.

John considered that. He'd had a long debate with himself on that very subject some months ago and had concluded he wasn't. A crazy person wouldn't realize the futility. He did. He wasn't delusional, either, thinking that, somehow, he was creating a small patch of goodness or hope or some such rot. He wasn't fixing anything, wasn't putting things back the way they used to be. That was impossible. He was just finding something to do.

"And what are you?" John asked.

"Huh?"

"If I'm crazy, what are you?"

Newbie blinked and glanced at the sergeant who was grinning. Newbie shoved his chest badge towards John. "That's what I am."

John snorted, "Mine's bigger. Wanna see?"

"Look, old man," Newbie was clearly frustrated, "I'm here to protect the city. That's what I do."

John stared a moment. "I was doing that before you showed up."

Newbie said nothing. What could he? John was back into it before MPD was back into it, and that meant John's motives were their motives, and if theirs were pure (still open to question), so were his. Even if, as Newbie so graciously pointed out, he was too old or an interloper or, as Newbie graciously implied, less capable. Whatever, he reflected them.

All Newbie could do was shake his head, try to give John a hard-eyed look, and step out of the way.

John nodded to him and to the sergeant, adding a return grin for his benefit, and stroked the pedal.

4

"Cadet Major Rashkil!"

Oh Lord, Collier thought, frozen for a second by Captain Bocks's harsh call. What did I do now? "Sir!" he responded and double-timed from the front of his company up to where Captain Bock stood with Spangler and Davis and the rest of the command staff, slight murmurs of sympathy following him.

It was mid-morning, the entire corps assembled on the parade field, even a militia unit from the town. Useless bunch of dumbass civilians, but mandates were mandates.

He hit attention and focused his eyes about an inch below Capt. Bock's patrician nose. Out of the corner of his eye, he saw Davis suppressing a smile and he made a mental note to smack the jackass later.

"Major," Captain Bock's cold, raspy voice, "what kind of a fuck up are you?"

Great, just great. He'd missed something. Not the inspection: his company garnered fewer demerits than the other two and his and Davis's room had been gig free, as usual. Not school: he'd been prepared, for once, in Algebra II – well, enough to avoid making a complete fool of himself and, besides, Davis had pretty much taken over the class, distracting Mrs. Lord. Must be one of his boys … Stick, stole some food, missed a class, went AWOL, for God's sake. Stick's fuck up was his fuck up, so there was nothing to do but make the best of the situation.

"A Fishburne trained, Colonel-West-Captain-Bock-forged kind of fuck up, sir!" he responded with normal command inflection.

A snigger ran through the staff and Captain Bock's eyes widened and it was all Collier could do to keep from grinning. He figured he was dead, anyway, so make it memorable.

Captain Bock studied him a moment and then said, "Well, do you think a Colonel West trained fuck up like you can march this scurvy bunch of criminals around the parade field and bring them back here in something resembling a coherent unit?"

Collier's jaw dropped and the staff just lost it, busting out laughing and even Captain Bock had to contain himself. "Uh," Collier said, a most unmilitary response, but, hey, waddaya want? My God, what an honor. He gathered himself. "Yes, sir!" he saluted and stepped up to Spangler's position, who smiled and saluted him in.

"Nice," Davis whispered as he took position and Collier warmed.

He faced the battalion. "Right!" he roared and the order was echoed down the commanders' and first sergeants' positions. He noted Farley had taken his post and Cropp had filled Farley's when he was called out and they were executing as if born to it. His trained fuck ups.

"Face!" he completed the command and the battalion snapped, even the militia following in more or less proper manner.

Wow.

5

Foxhall. John coasted past the oh-so toney mansions and townhouses up to the half-completed Field School, where an overturned dump truck still blocked part of the road, spilled asphalt piled around it. He stopped and scrutinized the wreckage.

No movement, so he got off the Zap, crept up, his .357 ready, and peered around the truck. Nothing. There was usually nothing, just the occasional dog or deer. He had to check, though, because it was a good ambush site – skirting the asphalt put him dead in the middle of Foxhall within rifle shot of another abandoned work project, some kind of embassy they'd been building across the street.

If he saw anyone, he'd just shoot. No questions. Everything of value had already been stripped from the sites, so why are you here, Jack, unless you intend mischief? Well, he'd give them a second before shooting. That's about how long it took him to distinguish between Loner or Bundy, the former getting a wave, the latter a bullet. Wouldn't be Raiders; they were off pillaging the houses now and pretty much ignored John when he happened by because he pretty much ignored them. Outside his jurisdiction so, have at it, crapheads. Just stay off the campus.

Funny how they plundered the construction sites before the obviously expensive houses on either side. Difference between a riot and Armageddon. Tools and materials were the first things on most Survivor shopping lists. Raiders were now making up for that initial oversight, but riches were still secondary. Want expensive paintings and furniture? No need to cart them off, just move in. The owners won't complain.

John hitched the Zap over the pile, remounted, balanced everything, took another long look, pushed the pedal and began his coast, pistol ready. He was more concerned about dogs than Raiders at this point, although dogs weren't such a big threat anymore. Most of them had retreated to the woods that stretched from Foxhall all the way back to Rock Creek Park. There was a lot more prey out there in the numerous overgrown walking trails, but packs have long memories and may just acquire a taste for human again, so be wary.

Dogs had been everywhere the first few months and you'd think they'd be sated with all the bodies. But, no, they're hunters and it didn't take long before they were looking for something fresher. At first, it was smaller and weaker dogs (and cats of course), squirrels, other rodents, but then the wolf in them emerged and they formed packs, pretty dangerous ones.

For months, John had dog fights – around the house, out with the Pathfinder, later, from the Zap. He'd gotten real good at shooting them on the fly. That had made him good at shooting Bundys and Vandals on the fly, so he supposed the dogs had served their purpose. Training aid.

It had been a while since his last real dog fight, a couple months or so ago, at the house. Hairbag and Lupus had started a ruckus over by the woods and John had grabbed the 14 and met them about halfway down the street where they were challenging a fairly big pack emerging from the Old Keene Mill side. He'd emptied half a clip, indiscriminately taking out as many of the lead dogs as he could, making as much noise as he could.

26

The pack broke, scattering back across the highway and John followed them through the Harwood extension, shooting even after they were long gone. Keep running, boys.

He had rewarded Lupus and Hairbag heavily for their service, even Snuffy, who had kept up running commentary inside the house while all this was going on. The only good dogs left in the world. The rest were enemy.

That was about the last time he'd engaged a Bundy, too, at least while traveling. Some punk on 495 yelling at John, standing on a car hood and hefting a rifle. Roll, hold, sight and squeeze from the left side, crossing his body with the .357 one-handed and getting sight picture in .5 seconds, both rounds in the stomach.

The Bundy'd still been alive when John rode up. "What the fuck, dude?"

"Fuck you, lawman," Bundy'd gurgled and died. Lawman? Disturbing; John shook the lifeless body hoping to get a little spark going so he could ask how the hell he knew that. Pointless, and he'd been extra wary for at least a month after, trying to spot surveillance. Nothing.

He even searched for cameras along his route although he did not credit Raiders, let alone Bundys, with that kind of sophistication. CDC, yeah, army, definitely, but not these yahoos. He'd finally concluded the Bundy was anomalous because there'd been very little bothering of him since.

He didn't know if he'd killed one of the last so inclined, or if he just wasn't worth bothering anymore. That didn't make him complacent. If there was any constant motive in the hearts of men, it was the desire to bother others.

He coasted slowly past the embassy, the Ruger barrel following his shifting eyesight. Dead silent here, like everywhere, but there was a special irony in it. What a fuss the neighbors made when the Field School began construction. Old men and women dressed in their wools and furs, manning tables by the side of the road waving signs protesting the traffic the school would bring and asking commuters to stop and sign petitions. Be careful what you wish for.

He could avoid it, this ghost town. He could go up Wisconsin and cut back down Mass. instead; forget this dead section of DC where the lawyers and lobbyists and diplomats and SESs and heads of committees all bought their fabulous brick mansions, with fabulous DC addresses, neighbors to other Very Important People, whose wives drove Volvos or Infinitis and whose kids all attended Sidwell Friends or Georgetown Day and who knew more than John and smiled indulgently at John and were so intent on making his life good and righteous and meaningful with their legislations and ideas and plans and ever so civilized diplomatic efforts ... he could.

But this was the way he drove to work Before, and he wanted to see the ghosts, the translucent gibbering shades of good intentions standing on the silent corners in bewilderment. See what happened?

He got to the end, made a right on Nebraska, a left at the Parkway, a quick right and then coasted slowly up to the Public Safety building. He stopped at the bridge and examined the halls looming over him to the right. Everything looked okay so he nudged the Zap onto the bridge and began weaving between the barrels he'd set up. Silly precaution, that.

Years ago, when the university was connecting Public Safety to the main campus at the third floor with this bridge (because the lower half of the building was below the hill and very hard to reach), someone made an offhand comment that it ought to hold up a truck. So it was built to do so, buttressed with cement columns and iron, and was even wide enough for a truck to enter and drive right across and smash through the front door.

John had worried about that and placed the barrels. But who had gas to drive a truck anywhere, much less down the bridge? Just MPD and CDC, and if those guys wanted John, all they had to do was shoot him.

But at least it made him weave and that was a good precaution in itself. A punk had set up a sniper's nest on the side of Anderson facing the bridge a few months ago, about the same time as the 495 Bundy. He would have had a perfect shot of John framed in the bridge; it was the weaving that delayed the shot and a stroke of pure dumb luck that saved him.

John happened to glance up mid-weave and noticed the torn-away window screen and he did not hesitate, leaping off the bridge as the punk fired, damn near killing himself in the fall and doing the punk's job for him.

He'd cut down the steep bank and made it around the Hamilton Building and across to the back entrance of Centennial. It took John about two hours to find the guy, who'd left the room and set up on the Anderson stairwell, no doubt anticipating John's approach from there. Obviously, he hadn't known about Centennial connecting to Anderson, across the second floor mystery rooms, which was another stark lesson in thorough reconnaissance. John shot him in the back of the head as he peered down the hall the wrong way.

The guy was a punk but not one John had seen before. Dressed all in black leather, like a Nazi uniform, he had strange tattoos – rank markings, chevrons or Hell's Angels' wings, something earned. They reminded John of Egyptian symbols, so many of them John couldn't tell if the punk was a light skinned black or a dark tanned white guy. Weird. And he had planned this out pretty good, too, just that the gods intervened. Too damn organized to be a Bundy, too decked out to be a Vandal, so he had to be a Raider. A Raider acting alone? Bothersome.

No ambushes since that period, and John had lost the expectation of attack, a dangerous attitude, he knew, but one fed by the many weeks of relative quiet. Why mess with him? Only a Bundy would try anymore and there were still enough of them out there to cause concern, but in the same way you were concerned about snakes. John's presence on the campus was pretty much ineffectual, anyway.

He went home at 1700, so just wait him out.

6

Each day, John found new depredations. Something disappeared or was smashed sometime overnight. Annoying. It was an indictment of his efforts.

At least once a week, someone carted off a few computers or tools from Physical Plant. He couldn't figure out why the computers were taken when all a looter had to do was waltz into Radio Shack down on Wisconsin and help himself to something still in the box. Maybe they thought a university computer had spiffy programs and didn't need a lot of configuration.

At any rate, the systems were walking. The tools made more sense because Physical Plant's were industrial grade, all laid out and easy to choose from. John had done a little liberal borrowing among them himself. He got the arc welder from there, as well as some choice hammers and drills. But he was a university employee, the last one, it seemed, so who else had a right?

Useful stuff disappearing he understood, so he treated it like a misdemeanor and didn't get that upset. Someone came in one night and took a lot of books out of the library and he didn't even make a report because that was downright edifying. There was at least one good soul out there wanting to expand the mind or at least keep it sharp.

He couldn't fault that because he'd taken quite a collection from the Fairfax County Library himself. He was a county resident, so why not? And he didn't really keep the books, just had them out for extended loan periods.

When he tired of something, like *Adam Bede*, he'd take it back for anyone else who dropped by. 'Course there'd been no evidence of anyone dropping by – his stack of returned books lay undisturbed on the checkout desk – but you never knew.

Vandals bothered him the most, and for more reasons than the aesthetic. They were just mindless, and anyone who would destroy stuff for the sheer spite of it would love to capture and torture good ole' John out of that same spite. So, when he found them, he killed them.

Since the punk firefight, though, confronting Vandals had been somewhat rare. He assumed the word was out, an odd thing given the lack of communication. No phones except cells and those were limited, no local TV broadcasts and the satellite stations went into fits ignoring the Zone, which was such a bummer of a place to talk about, man. No radio, although sometimes you could get a pirate broadcast if the atmospherics were right. Yet, people knew not to come up here and mess around while he was patrolling. Grapevine, best source of information.

And what a contrast from when he first started back to work. People were all over the campus, Bundys and Vandals and Gangs, oh my. It was like school was open and the student body had collectively decided to rape the place. Well, he wasn't going to have that and if he didn't shoot two or three a day back then, he was slacking off.

Damnably easy work, too. He'd park at the building, check in, heft the rifle or shotgun and head out to the Main Quad because that's where all the action seemed to be. Sure enough, as he rounded the library or the McKinley Building or, if he was feeling particularly sneaky, the Battelle Building, there they'd be.

If they were just sauntering along minding their own business, that'd be fine because the university had an open campus policy and Loners rarely started anything. But, inevitably, there'd be a Gang loading up a truck or Vandals breaking a window or burning something. He'd give the Gang a chance, call out, tell them who he was, this was private property so take the stuff off the truck, leave, and everything will be fine. But they wouldn't. One of them would make some smart remark and reach for a gun and that was too bad, because John was faster and a better shot.

He'd put the bodies inside their truck, drive it across to the Nebraska Lot and drape them over the hood as a warning. They're still there. Vandals he just shot outright, no warnings. They were Bundys. They deserved no less. He dragged them across the street and threw them on top of the hedge. They were still there, too.

They tried to get him. Vandals set up ambushes about four times, but he expected things like that and those guys were screaming amateurs, so he spotted them before they knew he was there. Hedge ornaments. The only one who ever came close was Mr. Tattoo, now also decorating the hedge.

So what would he find today?

Loners probably, which was fine. Unorganized Neutral Good, Cat 1. Fellow travelers and he always wished them a silent *mazeltov* as they strolled along the campus not bothering anything. John kept a wary distance, waved, got a return wave, and moved along. Don't bother them, they won't bother you.

"They?" More accurately, "We." We don't start trouble but will fight if pushed, seek maximum security and minimum detection, only go out for supplies and are generally law abiding, at least conscious of the law. We shun company. We have seen where company leads.

John was the only Loner actually working that he knew of, which probably made him his own category – maybe Unorganized Neutral Good, Cat Negative Zero.

It definitely made him someone to avoid. Having a job was one step away from the CDC or the army. A giant step, to be sure, and one he would never take, but no one else knew that.

Some Bundys, Unorganized Evil Cat #1? Probably not. Their day was pretty much over. Right after the Event, the sudden loss of authority brought them out in droves, like taking the cross off Dracula's coffin. But there'd been a rapid downturn in their fortunes.

It's not like they were the savviest to begin with, not the A-Team, like Bundy himself or Ramirez, pick your favorite serial killer. They were mostly wannabes, held in check by their fear of capture, which, of course, went out the window when everything collapsed. The bench took the field, sadists and rapists and murderers, all. John found their work more than he found them: a raped and disemboweled woman left rotting on a trash heap, a child burned to death while tied to a pole, that sort of thing.

But they were clumsy and obvious and made the mistake of going up against their betters. The Zone had rapidly become a shoot-first society – even kids were heavily armed – and the Bundys didn't stand a chance, especially against Families. Especially alone.

Which was why Bundys evolved, er, devolved, into Vandals, UEC #2, or, as John liked to say it, Yuk Number Two. John hefted the 14 at the thought and swung it through an arc, aiming back at the campus and making *pow pow* sounds. Yeah, fucking jackass Vandals. No doubt, he'd run across a few of them today.

Good.

Two or three Bundys banded together for mutual protection and what do you have? Multiplied chaos, of course, and the damage just one Vandal group could do was amazing. John lost the Osborne Building and Kay Chapel to them. They had a high old time in the Chapel, defecating on the Bible and the Koran, vomiting in the wafer plate, setting the place, mercifully, on fire with whiskey they had brought along for the fun.

Half the building went up and it was now an open, burned shell, one wall remaining with some kind of pagan ankh tag spray-painted on it. John would love to catch the jerks who did that, see how they liked a whiskey fire. John patted his flask affectionately through the jacket.

Probably would never catch them, but no matter. Someone would. Vandals were episodic, like tornadoes – forces of nature that came in unexpectedly, wreaked havoc, and disappeared. Unlike tornadoes, though, Vandals made a lot of mistakes, a lot of noise, left trails easy to follow, fell asleep drunk at the foot of their latest burning, killed each other, and generally self-destructed.

John found them in various conditions all over the campus and dispatched them unmercifully. No trials, no arrests, no plea-bargains, just kill them. They were Bundys, they deserved nothing more. The Families agreed with John on that point. He was sure the Loners did, too.

John smiled grimly. So let's be about it.

First things first.

John sat down at the Customer Service desk, the Daily Reports stacked on one side, the Security Observations on the other. He read the last four Observations. Yeah, he wrote them, he knew what was in them, but, if there was one thing he discovered early in his career, a set of fresh eyes on an old report could do wonders. Some innocuous forgotten little tidbit will suddenly leap out and presto, a whole new case. So, always review.

The Observations were narratives with a Findings and Recommendations area, not for distribution. Wouldn't do to advertise the vulnerabilities, would it? He used them to spot trends and make the necessary adjustments. Say he noticed someone attacked the left side of the Watkins Art door with some kind of pry bar, if something similar happened somewhere else, he'd link them because he had a good cop's memory for the small, odd details. Figure the pattern, like day of the week, and lay a trap with a timed or trip-wired Claymore. Might end up killing some innocent Loner, but hey, the cost of doing business.

Without him intending it, the Observations had become documentation of the local disintegration ... hmm, that's kinda catchy. Even just a casual read disclosed the decay and downward spiral. Wreckage, theft, anarchy ... what's next? Pagan sacrifice and demon worship? He chuckled grimly. That may not be far off.

He didn't bother with the Dailies until the end of the day, writing them in a stylized format with headings and Roman numerals, the more ornate the better, a sort of Book of Kells for the end of the world. If he was huddling in his monastery while the Vikings ravaged the land, he might as well make the product look good. Besides, the flourishes fooled civilians, made them think the bulleted, brusque, maddening language cops love so much actually said more than it really did. Understatement, short, sweet, and to the point, the things not said, communicating volumes to other cops while baffling outsiders. Cop style, developed in reaction to defense lawyers' penchant for isolating one word out of a report and making a big and irrelevant deal out of it, like rhyming "fit" and "acquit." So, the fewer words, the better.

Not that anyone was reading his few words. He didn't have a website to post the Dailies and he certainly wasn't going to spend a few hours stapling them to bulletin boards. He left a stack in the roundabout located next to Dispatch, putting the latest one on top before quitting time. Somebody wanted to read 'em, they could come get a copy.

Yeah. Right.

He used to print the Observations on separate pages for comparison, or split screen them, using dates and building names as markers. Great tool, but with the scarcity of viable gas, he only ran the generator long enough to charge his Zap batteries, certainly not to run the computers. So he was back to the good ole days, when all the reports were typewritten. In triplicate. With carbons. Ha, he was back even before that. You couldn't find a typewriter anymore, much less a set of carbons. His reports were a hand job now, yuk yuk.

Things, left to themselves, deteriorate. Some kind of physical law, that; maybe one of Newton's, or was it that Ontogony, Philogony phrase he could never remember? Should read up on it, but no need. Since the Event, John had ample and redundant proof, starting with the power grid.

The electricity stayed on far longer than he expected. That was good, on one hand, because he'd enjoyed the amenities of civilization for quite some time, but bad, on the other, because it meant automatic heat pumps kept running.

That had resulted in several unpleasant surprises when he started burying everyone on his block. But there was no way in hell the power would last and he had to do something before it died, so John went to Home Depot and picked up five Coleman Powermate 6250s, still boxed.

It took him three trips, three or four days and a strained back to get them home and set up. It was winter and cold, and trying to put those blasted things in strategic places where they could run without detection, was a real bear. He worried the electricity would go off and leave him stranded mid-installation, but that didn't happen. It stayed on even through his switch to the

Magnums, God bless Virginia Power.

Made him feel like an idiot, after working so hard to get his own systems ready, to see the streetlights coming on every night. But, one day, *phffft*, gone, leaving him pretty smug about his foresight.

Smugness came later, though. In the beginning, he felt like a dolt. It quickly became apparent the Colemans weren't going to work. They were small, too small to run a house. They had two 120 volt outlets and one 120/240. Three plugs, that's it. Try to run a refrigerator, a couple of air conditioners or small space heaters (depending on the time of year), microwaves (forget the stove, it's gas), the computer, satellite, phone charger and some lights on that. Forget it.

Worse, he had to place the Colemans around the house, close enough to doors and windows where he could run cords from them to whatever. That meant gaps, which let in more cold air than the space heaters could overcome, not to mention inviting dogs and other critters to nose around.

He thought about drilling through the walls to get the cords in and out, but never got that far because just running the Colemans was causing him headaches. They had five-gallon gas tanks and would go about 10-11 hours on one fill-up, which is damn good for occasional use. But he needed them every night and that meant about 15-20 gallons a day, which is a lot of gasoline to store, something with its own problems.

Also, one Coleman is silent, two give off a low level hum, but five? He couldn't figure out how to muffle the engines so no passing Raider would hear them. Then, of course, there was the exhaust, a real problem because it wafted down the block. Even the most stuffed-up Bundy could smell it.

So he went back to Home Depot and rummaged around some more and found a couple of Onan RS-

12000 Home Generators. True power plants, stand-alones that could hide behind the house and hook directly into the circuit box. They put out 11 kilowatts and about 80-90 amps. So, okay, he couldn't run the entire house, but could keep a lot of stuff going, including the pool.

The Onans didn't need a concrete pad or any kind of hard foundation; set them down, hook them up and flip a switch. There was even a video in the box explaining how to install them and it looked pretty easy, even for a klutz like him. Little victory dance right there in the aisle.

He was calculating how to get them home when something on the box stopped him cold. They ran on natural or LP gas. Natural gas was out, too volatile and pretty much shut off by that time. LP gas, please. He didn't know anything about LP gas, how long it lasts, how to store it, volatility, all that. And where in the world was he going to get that much of it? He stopped dancing, sat down on the floor and said, "Fuck."

Stumped. Destined for a quasi-eighteenth century life, running the Colemans every once in a while to keep the fridge and pool going (if he could ever figure out the pool) and maybe catch the news sometimes. Oh well, better than nothing, so John resigned to it.

But, a few weeks later, he was driving around the Newington Road industrial complex just to see what was back there when he topped a hill and, chorus of angels, saw them – a long row of yellow Magnum MMG12 Standby Mobile Generators, sitting in the back of a huge VDOT parking lot, along with backhoes and snowplows and dump trucks. He couldn't believe it. He knew what they were, having seen a few during his air force days. He smashed open the gate with his bumper and pulled right up to one. Please don't use LP gas, please, and … they didn't. They used diesel.

He did the victory dance and then towed two of them home.

Wasn't theft. He filled out a piece of paper with his name and credit card number and taped it to one of the remaining Magnums. For all he knew, the slip was still there, unread, because he'd never seen a sudden charge for power generators appear on his statement. He figured they go for about 14 or 15,000 each, so it would be interesting if some VDOT bureaucrat came along one day, found the paper, and hit his account. There's no way he could pay it; a shame, because he liked American Express. They'd been real good to him, keeping the account open although he barely used it, even enclosing a note every once in a while in the bill, keep your chin up, that kind of thing.

John ordered a book or CD for Collier over the phone from time to time, charging the account, and then sporadically pay for it through his bank, also over the phone. AE didn't give him a hard time about due dates or late fees or anything like that. Sometimes they even told him not to worry about the charge, consider it a gift. Real good people, but probably wouldn't remain so if $30,000 suddenly appeared. He'd have to work something out because he didn't want to stiff them.

Of course, some Raider could find the paper and start tapping his account. If that happened, he could claim fraud and get out of the payment all together. But then he'd be no different than a Raider, would he? He wondered if there was some way to get the charge placed on his equity loan. Maybe the finance company could send him another foreclosure notice, ha ha.

After he got the Magnums home, the real work started, more than necessary, of course, because John was scared to death of electricity. Pre-Event, he would shut down the entire house just to change an outlet, something Theresa thought quite hilarious.

He couldn't help it; electricity gave him the willies and hooking up the Magnums kept him on the edge of a nervous breakdown. Couple that with his natural clumsiness and an almost pathological stupidity when it came to home repairs ... slow going.

It took him about a month to puzzle it all out, put slot A into Tab B, all that crap. When he thought it was finally ready, he cringed, held his breath and threw the switch on the first Magnum, fully expecting to blow up the house and fry himself at the same time. It didn't and he didn't and he was quite pleased with the result, although, of course, he didn't have a fully powered house. That was a bit beyond him. All the necessities and some luxuries were running though.

It was a jury-rigged system. He went back to Home Depot and took one of the 200-amp transfer panels from the Onans and hooked it to his circuit breaker box. Onan's manual was real clear on how to link the two panels, and had enough hints about connecting to the power source that he didn't have too much trouble wiring to the Magnum. There was a lot of drilling and praying involved, but it worked.

He wasn't sure Onan would be too happy about his mixing the components, but, their Board, if there still was a Board, should be proud of the product.

He had to play with the panel to figure out which systems were going to run and he ended up shutting down some parts of the house because they just wouldn't draw the current very well. Those were mostly upstairs; Theresa's sewing room and Collier's bedroom, but he didn't use them, anyway.

Only one outlet worked in the master bedroom but despite that, he still slept there, using one of the floor air conditioners or a space heater to keep him comfortable. That is, until it was too hot or cold for those appliances, then he'd wrap himself in a blanket (or stay naked) and groggily trudge down to the fully powered basement. Had to be pretty extreme, though, to force him out of his beloved bed.

All the lower rooms closest to the panel were running great. Some vital things, like the refrigerator and the pool pump, worked fine too. Just upstairs gave him trouble. One day, he was going to pull some books about wiring and figure out what's wrong.

The Magnums were his antidote to the eighteenth century life. They had a lot of features, primarily a 57-gallon fuel tank which he could run about two days straight before refilling. Because he didn't run them all the time, just when home, one tank lasted about a week. They had safeties built in, too, like an automatic disconnect if he, or someone else, lifted the lug box. The box and power panel actually locked, but he couldn't find any keys when he stole (bought) them. There was an automatic shutdown if the system detected an engine problem and a kill switch he could easily get to if something went wrong.

There was even a "low oil" light and one to replace the air cleaner. That could be a problem because he didn't have any spares, unless he went back to the yard and raided the remaining Magnums. Neither light had come on yet, so he'd worry about that later.

He ran one Magnum all night long, mainly to power the security system and the air conditioners in summer, space heaters in winter, pool pump all year, and all the other stuff he needed. On a schedule, he shut the main one down and fired up the other – that "things left to themselves" law.

He even ran the Colemans on a schedule for a few hours. They were a much bigger pain but you never knew what would happen – the Magnums might die, the diesel might go flat, the wiring might break, and then suddenly the Colemans were critical. If he didn't maintain them, they'd crap out when he needed them most, which was another law. He figured the whole set up would last a few more years. What he was going to do after everything inevitably broke down, he didn't know. Maybe Virginia Power would be back by then.

Ha.

Why worry about mechanical failure? He was going to suffer fuel breakdown before the Magnums went, anyway. He had poured hundreds of bottles of gas stabilizer into the diesel tanker as a precaution, but he had no idea if that stuff even worked on diesel, so it may have been a waste. In time, he'd know.

He'd thought about hauling a Magnum up here and hooking up the office. Be better than the Coleman, better than the crapped-out-not-worth-fixing Public Safety backup generator sitting like a beached whale in the back. He remembered that thing firing up during power outages Before, sounding like a 747 on final approach and pouring fumes through his office window. Same thing with a Magnum, so forget it.

He'd had a devil of a time dropping the noise signatures at home to about a half a block, the undertone from the motor's vibrations carrying much farther than that, almost down to Daventry. Nothing he could do. Diffused enough, though, so ambling Raiders couldn't immediately tell where it was coming from, which should give him enough time to arm up before they figured it out. Especially since they'd be led next door.

That's where he'd sited the primary Magnum – inside his neighbor's house, hidden from sight and mostly sound. It had been a struggle of epic proportions getting that monster through her patio door and into the living room. He had to rig a block and pulley system and maneuver it into place because the thing was so damn heavy, almost two tons. He took out the room divider between her dining and living rooms, but, overall, not too much damage.

He'd worried her floor couldn't handle the weight but she didn't have a basement so what would be the worst outcome, a drop of a couple of feet onto the foundation slab? No big deal.

Her house acted as one gigantic muffler. It also acted as a gas chamber. Running the Magnum sucked out the oxygen in about ten minutes and he had seriously considered using an oxygen mask to go back and forth, but that had its own problems so, instead, he knocked a hole in her ceiling and vented the fumes through a hose out her attic. It was still dangerous but at least he wouldn't fall over dead in about three seconds when he walked in to shut it off.

Of course, that created the same issue as the Coleman fumes, but venting them out the top of the house seemed to spread them to the point where no one could get a quick bead on him, especially on windy nights. During the summer inversions, the diesel hung like a cloud over both houses and he'd go a couple of days on the Colemans until it finally broke. Irritating, but it beat fending off Vandals.

The second Magnum was buried next to the pool, an even bigger epic of installation because John had no idea how to operate the backhoe he borrowed to dig the hole. Hell, he had no idea how to drive the 18-wheeler he also borrowed to get the borrowed backhoe to the house in the first place.

Both had been sitting in the same VDOT lot as the Magnums, the backhoe on a flatbed already hooked up to the tractor and raring to go; that is, after he got the battery recharged and figured out how to start the damn thing, all of which did stead when he went back for the diesel tanker. OJT in gear shifting, driving a hinged and way-too-big truck down a highway crowded with wrecks. Actually didn't do too bad, hit maybe four or five cars, one or two guardrails. Didn't get hung up. Then, OJT on starting the backhoe, shifting its gears, driving down the trailer ramp without putting it on its side, maneuvering it through the fence (which meant spending the next day putting the fence back up), figuring out how to place the braces, and then digging the necessary eight-foot hole.

Oh, don't forget lifting the Magnum with the backhoe and placing it in the hole. Never had he cursed so much, been reduced to frustrated tears so much, and hurt so much afterwards.

He wished his brother, Mr. Fixit, Mr. I Can Drive Anything, had been here. Woulda taken Art what, an hour, two, to do all that? Took John four very frustrating days. Embarrassing. Art would have laughed his ass off – big brothers are supposed to be All Powerful, not blithering incompetents. Hey, what could he say, Art had inherited all those handyman genes from Dad. All John got was a penchant for alcohol and moroseness. And beatings, yes, lots of beatings. So had Art, for that matter.

He remembered their last conversation. "Art, look, this is bad, real bad, you've got to get out."

"Shit, John, don't I know it? Wurrmi gonna go?"

"Go north, take 295 up to 17 then the Thruway, go up where it's real cold, where I was stationed once, Plattsburgh, remember? You can hide there."

"I hate the cold."

"So fuckin' what? Jesus, man! You gotta save Belinda and Chris."

"How the fuck do I do that? 295, the Parkway, the Turnpike are already jammed. And I'm already coughing. So are they."

"Ah, fuck, fuck, fuck."

"Yeah, man. We're fucked." He'd paused. "So are you," and he hung up.

Oh, Art, man, you were always the master of under-

45

statement. Respected you, man, always, even when I was giving you Indian burns. One day, he knew, he'd have to make his way up to Pemberton and bury them all.

He sat still, fingering the Observations and suddenly feeling very, very small. He tossed them with a flicker of contempt and stood. Fuck this. He grabbed his rifle, slapped his backups and strode to the door. He took in a breath, deep, exploring. Yes, the ever present mustiness of moldy bodies, moldy buildings, but underneath, the coolness. Spring. He remained in silhouette, stupid, but daring the bullet.

Kill me, motherfuckers.

Please.

He shook himself and stalked up the bridge, dodging barrels.

Time to patrol.

7

"All right," Colonel West stood at the front, resplendent in his dress uniform, his black eye patch more baleful than his good eye. Collier thrilled. Loved this class. "Someone tell me, what was the purpose of the Saudi invasion?"

"Payback," Litton snarled.

You got that right, Collier thought.

"Ah," Colonel West raised both eyebrows, which was a bit comical, "but Mr. Litton, didn't the nuclear destruction of Mecca serve that purpose?"

"Not enough," Litton snarled again and there was a murmur of agreement throughout the room, which Collier joined.

"I see," Colonel West stepped around the desk, head lowered, a sure sign they were getting it wrong and he was about to lead them to a West Truth, one of those rare gems of knowledge that often altered the course of history. Collier thrilled again. "You're saying the massive logistical nightmare and expense of withdrawing from the Korean peninsula and assaulting the Red Sea was motivated by mere," and he turned a patrician hand upwards, "revenge?"

"Couldn't stay in Korea, anyway," Hardesty piped up, "it was nuked."

"Well, yes, Mr. Hardesty, that is true, neutron radiation has the effect of making large areas of land somewhat uninhabitable. A very unfortunate aspect of the Pusan perimeter defense strategy, even more unfortunate for the Koreans," here the class snickered, "but, the wholesale abandonment of Japan, the Philippines," he paused, "Taiwan?"

"They can take care of themselves," Booker muttered from the back where he was playing with a paper airplane.

"Can they? And, Mr. Booker, please put that away. Japan might beg to differ, what with China consolidating Taiwan, insurgency or no. Facing the Dragon themselves, *tsk*," Colonel West shook a mournful head, "abandoning allies is not a thing done for light reasons, and revenge, gentlemen, is a light reason. Could there be another one?"

They all looked at each other and Collier considered challenging the Colonel's assertion about revenge. Pretty good motive to him, but the Colonel was a master of debate and Collier didn't particularly feel like a humiliation, especially after the compliments about his marching. He kept silent, always wise.

"What is Saudi Arabia famous for, gentlemen?" Colonel West idly examined his fingernails or, given his eye patch, half-examined. Collier giggled inwardly. He'd have to tell Davis that one.

"Sand," Litton snapped.

"Oil," Collier said over the laughs.

Colonel West pointed at him, "Exactly, Mr. Rashkil, exactly."

Collier felt satisfied, even when Hardesty whispered, "Suck up," in his ear.

"Think of it, gentlemen," the Colonel whipped the map down from its roll, slapping a scaly hand over the boot of Arabia, "almost one third of our refining capacity, all on the East Coast, suddenly gone. Of course, one third of the population is gone, too, but among those remaining are the people with the intelligence and training to compensate for the lost capacity. With Israel down to its last breath and a ravening Russian bear looming over the oil fields, what else could we do but assure a future supply? It is the one thing," and the Colonel raised an emphatic finger, "the only one, this ever changing and forever reorganizing government of ours," said with much contempt, "has done right."

"Who's the president this week?" Hardesty asked brightly.

As one, they all, including the Colonel, turned and pointed at him, "You are!" in unison and they all laughed and high-fived, the Colonel making it a point to slap-hand Collier. They never tired of that joke.

"All right," the Colonel brought them back, "so we have a tenuous toehold around the major oil fields, a meat grinder, our dwindling technology against the screaming Muslim hordes. The nuclear barrier keeps the Iranians off us, but for how much longer? They are sinking more of our tankers than we can replace, and the French have a half-ass blockade on our Florida ports, citing the 'fear,'" and here the Colonel made finger quote marks, "'of worldwide contamination' but it is, after all, the French."

He let the laughter die down. "All these things pile up, though, gentlemen. So, I ask, how long can we maintain the toehold?"

It was perfectly timed. The silence his question evoked let them hear the far off rumble, the slight tremor of the floor emphasizing it. As one, they all looked at the picture windows framing the distant Blue Ridge, all of their brows furrowed in curiosity. As if on command, they all walked to the windows and peered out, but at first saw nothing. Slowly, a smoke cloud formed over the mountains, malevolent, roiling.

"What the heck is that?" Hardesty asked.

"Mr. Rashkil?" Colonel West said from his position on the center window, straining with his one good eye to make out distance. "Would you kindly go down to CQ and find out?"

He didn't need telling twice and bolted out the door, evading Hardesty's clumsy tripping attempt. Get him later. He ran down the concrete steps, so expert at it by now he never stumbled, and launched himself toward the portal. Several agitated privates were running back and forth. Collier grabbed one of them, young, maybe 13, Beamis, yeah, that was his name, dressed in parade whites, so he must be the Duty Orderly. "What happened?" Collier barked.

"I don't know, sir."

"Well, why aren't you on the radio finding out?"

"Sir?" Beamis looked stupefied.

"Ach," Collier threw him aside and stalked into the Duty Room. Another baby private in whites, Dole, yeah, that was his name, was at the radio, headphones on. Well, at least this one had some presence of mind. He looked pale, shaken.

Collier thumped him on the head. "Well?"

Dole goggled at him. "It's hard to tell, there's a lot of calling back and forth, but ..."

"Yeah?"

"Well, it sounds like ..." Dole stopped, his eyes widening.

Collier lost his patience and shook him. "Tell me, dammit!"

"They just blew up downtown Charlottesville!"

Collier's jaw dropped, "What?"

Dole stared at him, pale, trembling; a kid, just a kid. "It sounds like ... like it's all gone!" he sobbed.

Collier stepped back, letting Dole go.

Oh my God.

8

John stood on the hill behind Watkins, gazing over the ball field. It didn't look like a ball field; it looked like an archaeological dig, an abandoned archaeological dig at that. Most of the yellow tape marking the place off, fell down long ago but through entropy, not intrusion. Bundys, Vandals, even Raiders, were afraid of this field. John had to admit it gave him the willies, too. Arsenic piles and cyanide tended to do that.

During WWI, AU tested chemical weapons for the army and, well, in those days, you just threw your leavings out the window. Fifty years later, college kids were traipsing across the dumpsites and, every other month or so, stumbled across something noxious out here. One time, an officer picked up a canister sticking out of the ground near the soccer goals and brought it back to Dispatch, setting it right up on the counter as a paperweight. John came diddlybopping in, took one look and said "Evacuate." Mustard gas grenade. Bomb Squad said it was inert but imagine!

A bit trivial now.

At some point, the Army Corps of Engineers got wind of these shenanigans and showed up and started poking around the field and went, "Oh my God!" and shut the field down in 2000 and then went absolutely nuts digging it up. Everybody flipped out.

The always-sensitive students shrieked and implied the long buried and now forgotten chemicals had somehow seeped into their bloodstreams, damaging fragile, very precious internal systems. Children of trial lawyers, no doubt.

The faculty got up in their usual high dudgeon, aghast that a place so venerated, so filled with love and peace and the spirit of learning, could have once, gasp! worked for the Aaaarmy! The student newspaper wrote a lot of self-righteous and quite revisionist editorials about AU's Responsibility to the Community. Everybody felt very noble. If you're a bleeding heart screaming leftist pinko, that's all you need. No facts. Just sincerity. Tinged with irony.

Speaking of which ... John grinned. He wondered how many of those emotionally damaged students, given the choice, would prefer Arsenic Field over the Event. They'd probably wallow in the dirt in gratitude. One-hundred-year-old cyanide deposits ain't so bad now, are they?

Arsenic Field's fearsome reputation was an advantage – no one was going to mess around out here. John had taken advantage of that. He peered hard at his stashes, but they looked undisturbed. No need to walk over and verify, nothing was out of place and Raiders weren't too concerned about him discovering their handiwork.

Riches, Collier. Your future assured. Not cash or something stupid like that, but old rare books, sealed and buried, quasi-famous paintings by dead up-and-coming artists, William Faulkner's papers – all absolutely priceless. AU had some rather good stuff in the archives, didn't they? And, at home, a map inside John's quick-release handgun safe; fireproof, Flu proof, and theft proof; well, as long as no enterprising Raider found it.

"Collier, I gotta tell you something." A conversation a year or so ago.

"I thought you were."

"Yeah, but I'm only going to tell you this once, and you are to listen and remember and never ask me anything about it again. Understand?"

"What?"

"Do you understand?"

"Yeah, I understand! Geez, you think I'm stupid?"

"Stop that," John had gotten mad. Collier was too damn sensitive, like all teenagers. "Listen. Do you remember where we used to roast chestnuts?"

"Yeah, in the ..."

"Don't say it, don't say it. You know people are listening."

"All right, all right, what?"

"You know where I'm talking about?"

"Yes, yes, okay, I get it. What?"

"If you ever get back here. If your children ever do, or your grandchildren ..."

"Gotta have a girlfriend for that to happen, Dad."

"Stop interrupting," John said, irritated, "this is important. You have to look in there. You have to look real good."

"Where? In the ..."

"Don't say it!"

"All right! What am I looking for?"

"You'll know it when you see it."

"Okay. Great. That's real mysterious."

"Also, remember this. Two times at two and four, once at three. Say it."

"Huh?"

"Say it."

"All right! Two times at two and four, once at three. What does that mean?"

"You'll know when you see it. Don't ever forget it. Ever. It's really important."

"Okay, okay, you know we're coming up on curfew. So, two times at two and what?"

"Four! Two times at two and four, once at three. Remember that, dammit! Christ, Coll! You memorized

53

every scene of *Ghostbusters*! This should be easy!"

"All right, all right, all right! I've got it! Would help if you'd tell me what it was about!"

"No."

"Okay. Fine. Be Dr. Strange."

"And Coll?"

"Yeah?"

"When you get back here, when your kids do, bury me next to Mom. In the front yard."

A long silence. "It's curfew, Dad. I gotta go." And he hung up. Even though it wasn't curfew.

So Coll, if the Flu mutates into something else, or if immunities develop, come on back, dig through the wreckage and find the safe on the inner ledge of the downstairs chimney. Hit the quick release combination and you'll not only have the map but your Mom's jewelry, including her one carat antique diamond, and some of Grandpop's gold coins. And the book.

Legacy.

Find it, Collier, otherwise the only legacy is pain and sorrow, war and death. The future is shrouded in a long pale winding sheet and if you, Collier, can fight your way out of it, if you can find a safe place, then you stand a chance. Live free, but do it in some unknown place because, Collier, freedom stirs envy and others want to take it from you.

Take it from you.

John stood for a moment. A spring breeze searched him, chilled him, but he wasn't so sure if it was the cold or a premonition. He shook himself.

Time to patrol.

9

John stood outside the Cassell Center frowning. The breeze shifted and there was that smell again. Great. Things have a geometric ability to get worse, and only a linear ability to get better. Cop's motto.

He shook his head. Trying to keep up with the overnight thefts, trying to keep most of the buildings from being torched, not trying to shoot a perfectly innocent Loner, all that was hard enough. This, he didn't need.

Obviously, someone had croaked inside the building. What the hell was someone doing inside this craphole in the first place? Cassell was condemned even before the Event, a dark, dreary and musty confusion of warped rooms and rickety stairwells and sudden alcoves that made just the perfect deathtrap. AU had, unbelievably, insisted on using it for classes, night classes at that. Daft.

Cassell was out of sight and out of mind, across the street from the main campus, isolated and dilapidated, the perfect place for rape or murder. That rape and murder had not happened there was beside the point; the place was too scary even for rapists and murderers. Not for artists, though. The campus poseurs and wannabes set up their personal studios in the abandoned moldy rooms, even, in a few cases, moving in. Public Safety left them alone. They were all crazy.

And so was whoever had died in there. Or maybe he was just curious why a university had actually spent time and money to keep such an obviously awful building viable. Had to be something real valuable or interesting inside, right?

Dumb Loner or, if John was lucky, dumb Bundy. Suffered the cat's fate. Probably fell in the legendary half-filled-with-algae pool in the legendary basement filled with legendary rats. John had never gone down there, even Before, the legends sufficient for him. This schlub had never heard them, obviously.

Okay. Get this done. John unholstered the Ruger and pressed it forward from the doorjamb, ready to shoot. Cassel was the perfect ambush site, so he let his eyes adjust before snapping through the doorway and settling against a corner wall in the foyer, sweeping the gloom with the barrel.

Oh. Good. Lord. John gagged and then frowned. He had become quite the connoisseur of the various rotted-body smells, having received initial training at autopsies and crime scenes Before. Breaking into the neighbors' houses and dragging out the corpses for a decent front yard burial After, had truly honed his palate, so to speak. This wasn't the sickly sweet, cloying smell of the naturally dead, gasses vented and flesh drying, wormfood. This was the sharp metallic smell of rotted blood.

The smell of violence.

He listened and stared, looking for even the slightest twitch. Violence begat violence, and whatever had happened here might attract an encore, someone waiting in a shadow for him to move first. That's what comes from not doing your job, idiot.

John hadn't been out here in a week or so. Let them gain a toehold, had he?

He was against the wall in the narrow hallway that opened into the weird foyer with the even weirder winding stairs that went up to the inappropriately placed bathrooms. Halls shot out from the foyer in three directions and he could be picked off at leisure should he step out in the wrong direction, so he hesitated, squinting at the gloom.

The odor was overpowering so it was not coming from the halls or wafting from the evil basement or even from some depth of the building. It was close. Upstairs.

He closed his eyes and ratcheted his hearing. Need to adjust sight so, ears, take over. If there was just one creak, he was going to cut loose, but, no, nothing and, counting down two minutes, he opened his eyes.

Okay, better. He could see a way down the halls now. Anyone who popped out of a side room would be silhouetted and he could blast and roll and shelter and blast again. Could be fun. He crouched and took a decisive step into the foyer. And slipped.

What the hell? He caught himself, dropping to his knees and bobbing back into the doorway, putting a lot of strain on the hamstrings but nothing that some Ben Gay wouldn't fix. He focused on the hallways, ready to shoot. No movement. There was something slippery on the bottom of his Rockports and he reached a finger, bringing it back to his face. Immediately he gasped and rubbed his finger vigorously on the wall.

Shit. He had stepped in shit.

Dogs? Nervously, he cocked the Ruger and peered hard in the gloom. That would be odd. Dogs stayed in the open now and besides, would have rushed him the moment he came blinking in. Wolves? Silly thought and no, for the same reasons. So, what ...

Grimly, John reached into his pocket and pulled out the penlight. If there was an ambush, this would spring it. He snapped on the beam, holding it low and ready to return fire, but no one shot. He gave one last hard look at the hallways and then swept the beam along the ground.

Feces. Piles of feces. Human feces. A lot of them.

John stared. They were arranged rather well, not haphazard, like one or two guys moving as nature called them, but like lots of people had decided, collectively, to

57

drop their drawers and do a mass dump right here in the middle of the foyer. A shit minefield. Was that the purpose, make him step in it, have a good laugh at his expense?

He didn't think so.

The piles were maybe a week old, and it seemed like they were all done at the same time. How extraordinarily weird. John played the light toward the staircase, noting the piles were clear of it, like a trail inviting someone to step this way. He wondered if they'd found one of his Claymore traps and set it on the stairs, then used the feces to guide him into it. *Boom.* No more John. He examined the stairs but didn't see any trip wires. Silly. They could have done that at the door. No, they weren't inviting him up the stairs.

They were letting someone come down.

Slowly, he played the light up, stopping at the first twisted landing, then following it. Almost to the top, his beam caught something. Suspended in the air; something hanging from the ceiling above the top landing.

A foot. A rotted, bloody foot. John moved the light up.

It was a girl, he thought, but she was too torn up and bloated for him to be absolutely sure. Knowing Bundys, it could have been a boy. Strung up by barbed wire to a girder overhang, the wire running around its waist and under the arms and tied off to the doorknob of the men's bathroom. Its back was to him and it hung there, motionless. Shreds of skin hung loosely down to her feet.

Not from rot, from cutting. She had been skinned alive. John gritted his teeth. Must have taken her hours to die. The screams must have been horrific.

God damn Bundys.

Raging, John stepped past the shit field and ran up to the first landing. Hardly procedure, but he didn't care. He hoped the giggling bastards came at him now, all thirty or forty of them, 'cause he'd kill 'em all.

He stared up at the girl and shone the light full on her. He didn't have the right angle but he could see that her lips had been carved away, leaving a perpetual death's head grin against the swollen, rotting flesh. The odor was overwhelming and he sucked it in to make a memory. When he found these bastards, it would spur him.

He walked up, keeping his light on the stairs for any tripwires, lifting the beam as he cleared the landing. He stopped, stared, then widened the light to take in the wall between the bathrooms. Someone had spray painted a purple symbol there, like an ankh, but with daggers on the points. Something familiar ...

Yeah. He'd seen that tag before. On the remaining wall of Kay Chapel.

He smiled grimly. Got your signature now, jackass.

He examined the barbed wire wrapped around the knob and contemplated untying it, but he'd get cut and the bastards had probably wiped some of their shit on it so instant blood poisoning. What a way to go, worse than the Flu, although maybe his immunity also affected that. Better not chance it. He'd have to cut the wire, but he didn't have the tools with him and the idea of the girl exploding into rotten meat when she dropped was sickening.

He turned to her and put the beam full on her torn, green blob of an almost unrecognizable face. I will find them, he thought at her fiercely, I will find them and do ten times worse ...

Wait.

He stared. Then gasped, stumbling back almost into the wire, catching himself, leaving the beam full on that one remaining blue eye shrouded by bloody lanks of red hair.

Mrs. Alexandria.

10

"You knew her?"

The old cop was laconic, unmoved. He had walked in, observed the shit field, walked up and observed Mrs. Alexandria, then walked back out, silent. His teenage partner had been vomiting in the bushes out front for a good five minutes now. John wondered at the capacity of the stomach to hold so much bile.

"Yes. Mrs. Alexandria."

"Friend?"

"Yep. She was Family."

"Role?"

"Wife."

"Hmm," the old cop gazed off, "I haven't heard of the Alexandrias."

"They're down on Jefferson Highway, centered on the Target. They don't come out here." He paused. "They've heard of you."

The old cop just glanced at him and then looked off in the distance. "You didn't hear anything?"

John didn't like the accusatory tone and he narrowed a look at the cop. "No. Didn't you?"

The cop liked that even less and they both stared at each other. "Tough guy," the cop smiled and it wasn't a challenge, so John relaxed. "What do you make of the ankh?" he asked the cop.

"Seen it around."

John waited for the explanation but none came and the cop became interested in his partner. "You done?" he asked sardonically and the punk got to his feet shakily and headed off without a word to the patrol car. "Where you guys getting gas?" John asked.

The cop turned. "Stay in touch," he said, and got in the car.

There was an urgency in the request John didn't like. Something was going on, and it wasn't good. "Give me a radio, then," John said.

The old cop started the car and shook his head. "Just do the same thing, walk out to Mass. Avenue and fire off some rounds. We'll hear it."

"I haven't got the ammo for that," John said but the old cop ignored him and drove away. A lie, but the ammo was for use against Bundys, not as distress calls. And besides, there was so much random shooting going on out here, jackass, how do you know I'm calling you?

You didn't hear Mrs. Alexandria calling.

Neither did you, John.

He sat down on Cassel's porch. God. Mrs. Alexandria. He met her when he'd gone over to Target looking for jeans after the Springfield Mall burned down. He'd been driving the Pathfinder and stopped at the long parking lot entrance that graced the front of the store like an invitation. Two guys stood there armed with rifles, eying him. He got out and opened his hands, empty. "Okay if I approach?" he called.

"Waddya want?" the one with the long blond beard responded.

"Trade?"

"Waddya got?"

"Grenades."

They both stared at him. "You got grenades?" Beard said something to beardless who hustled inside. Beard stood easy, watching John, who remained passive. The new protocol.

People poured out of the store, a lot of people. John was amazed. Two sets of riflemen came around the side and set up flanking positions to cover the approaches to the parking

61

lot. John was impressed. A tall man, also bearded, conferred with First Beard, who gestured at John. Mrs. Alexandria was standing with them. Second Beard nodded, removed a pistol, and approached with the Missus. John waited. The next few moments would determine whether he got his jeans or a shroud.

"You have grenades?" Second Beard asked as he stepped up.

"Yep."

"Can I ask where you got them?"

"Nope."

Second Beard chuckled and Mrs. Alexandria smiled and the ice broke. John immediately liked them both. "Let's see," Beard said.

He showed them. Then, with permission, threw one off to the side. They were impressed by the explosion. So were the onlookers.

He got a crate of Levis and work shirts, as well as some work gloves thrown in, for five grenades. He got an invitation to come back anytime he felt like it, trade or no.

"We're the Alexandrias," Beard had said.

John chuckled. "I mighta known."

They all laughed at that, even Missus, the lights dancing in her blue eyes as she placed a possessive hand on Beard's shoulder, a red, wavy ocean of hair dancing around her face. Lovely.

There were six in the core group, Beard and Missus, two teenagers, two kids. There were twenty cousins, ranging from the sweetest little four year old girl (Baby, they called her) to an old grumpy guy who said he fought in World War II and, by God, ain't never seen nothin' like this in all his born days, yessir. None of us have, Gramps. They all took the same name. They were Family.

"How long'd you guys stay at the Gate?" he asked her once.

"About six months," she had a voice like a harp in the

wind. She looked right at him. "You?"

"Less." They stopped talking about it. Little explanation was needed.

They were about the closest thing to friends he had. He went to a barbecue, Baby's fifth birthday, or what they had decided was her fifth birthday. No one really knew her true age and Baby kept saying, "I'm ten! I'm ten!"

Cute, but obviously not right. "Found her wandering the streets down near the Potomac," Beard told him.

Lucky a Bundy didn't find her first.

Lots of people were there. The Alexandrias had formed blocs with the Old Towners and the Huntingtons, and the Huntingtons had a particularly large core, twelve kids, five of the boys having formed Families of their own so there were grandkids, although none by birth, yet. With their cousins, they were practically a company.

"You a Vernon?" one of them, who was munching on some venison, asked John.

"No," John was surprised. "There are Vernons?"

"Yep," the guy nodded, "they've turned it into quite the farming enterprise. Even have cows."

"Really?" John licked his lips. "Are they trading milk?"

"Not yet. They're not sure it's safe. They gave some samples to the CDC but, well," and he shrugged his sauce-covered deer strip.

"Yeah," John agreed, "I'd sure like to get some fresh milk. Are you guys in touch? Can you let me know when they start?"

The Huntington shook his head. "We're not in touch. We heard about them through the Mason Necks, who are a real bunch of cowboys, by the way. The Vernons are standoffish, like they're Raiders or something. Can't blame 'em," another deer strip shrug, "they've got probably the best set up around."

"Hmm," John responded, non-committal. Yeah. Mt Vernon was ideal if you had the manpower to run it. John preferred Lonerism.

It was night and there was a bonfire; some of the cousins were playing guitars and banjos, a mixture of bluegrass and sixties rock, if that was possible. People were dancing and drinking and if you closed your eyes for just a moment, it was Before. John danced with Baby, whirling her around as she shrieked with delight, then he pleaded a sore back and sat next to Beard and Missus.

"You're good with kids," she observed.

"You should join us," Beard said and it was an invitation.

John shook his head. "I'm not much for company."

Beard and Missus nodded. Some people were Family, some weren't.

There was a weird group sitting across from them, all dressed in black and painted up like Vandals. One of the boys reached over and kissed one of the other boys.

"Jesus," John said.

Beard and Missus laughed. "You haven't met the Ballston's?" she asked.

"Ballstons? Aptly named." That got a chuckle. "They're up on the mall?"

"Um hmm," she set her Sam Adams down. "What we don't have, they have, so might be good to butter them up. Go give their dad a hug, why don't you?"

"Great," John shook his head. "Gay. How fashionable. Which one's the missus?"

They both pointed at a thin guy snuggled into the broad, butch shoulders of a real tough lookin' man. A couple of tough lookin' lesbians, next to dad and mom, eyed John balefully, no doubt reading the conversation. They looked like they could kick his ass. He said so.

"Probably could," Beard agreed, "they're real good fighters, the whole family. Took on some Raiders and just royally kicked their butts. And then probably had sex with their butts when they were done," he snorted contemptuously and that sent Missus into gales of laughter that caught Butch Shoulders' interest and he frowned, correctly surmising he was the object of that laughter.

Hard looks between the two families. John understood that. The Alexandrias, the Huntingtons, all of the traditional groups were traditional all the way and held to a philosophy that much of the deviance characterizing the pre-Event world, had a lot to do with the Event itself.

John believed pretty much the same thing. That made the Ballstons blameworthy. That meant some kind of conflict between them and the trads was inevitable. Once the Raiders were destroyed, the CDC driven off, some kind of authority established, then it would happen. For now, they all needed each other. For now.

"CDC is talking about a deal," Beard said, when the moment passed and everyone backed off their weapons.

"You're kidding. What kind of deal?"

"Give them a few people, they'll stop attacking."

"You're not seriously entertaining it."

"They said they'd give them back."

"You're not seriously believing them."

"Hell, no. Can you imagine what we'd get back? If we actually got anyone back?" Beard's eyes blazed.

For a moment, they stared at the dark beyond the bonfire, expecting to hear the sudden roar of helicopters, moonsuited troops pouring out and shooting half of them, while sealing the other half, screaming, into the tubes. Bound for Atlanta. Never to be seen again.

"Why do they want a deal?"

"Guess we're killing too many of them," Missus stretched luxuriously and John savored the form of her under the sweater. She caught it and grinned, appreciating the compliment, "Can't get good help these days."

They all chuckled at that. There couldn't be an inexhaustible supply of combat-ready biologists, could there?

He had stayed the night, sleeping with a blonde, middle-aged cousin, who was very, very horny. Sleep didn't really have that much to do with it and John was more exhausted in the morning than when he'd slipped into her futon the night before, safely hidden in a corner of Target, where lawn equipment was gathering rust. She kissed him, told him to come back often.

He did, maybe once, twice a month. Missus, appraising his trysts with cousin Barb, was amused. Proxy.

They traded ammunition, John bringing grenades each time. "Where you gettin' these?" Beard had asked. He just shrugged.

"Ft. Belvoir?"

John had not reacted. "Fort Belvoir is heavily mined," he lied.

"Yeah, right," Beard had snorted and John half feared the Alexandrias would mount their own expedition to see. That would certainly cut into his stash.

"Why d'you need so many?" John asked.

"Come see," and he'd joined them on a punitive attack on some Vandals who had crossed the bridge and tried to snatch Baby. They chased them down to the Arlington Bridge itself, and Beard lined the survivors up right under the lions and beheaded them, one by one. Except for the last one.

"All right, fucker," Missus had snarled, "let's give your buddies a good show," and she skinned the last Vandal alive, right there, his screams carrying across the water. Warning. John had watched and been very impressed.

She was tough. She was hard. She was a fighter. And she was hanging from the ceiling of Cassell, skinned alive.

They wouldn't have taken her without a fight. Beard would have burned DC to the ground to get her back. Which must mean the Alexandrias, to a man, Baby and Cousin Barb included, had lost, and were rotting in some back alley. Or were hanging skinned somewhere, just like Missus. How was that possible?

John was, suddenly, very afraid.

11

Confusion.

A lot of militias had formed on the parade field, been issued weapons by a provo commander, and marched off. In the middle of that, a regular patrol showed up and everyone thought it was a Draft Gang, so the bell sounded and the corps pulled up barricades and grabbed M1s and hit their positions, Collier taking the gap between the school and Hudgins Hall, Davis opposite him at the street. It wasn't a Draft Gang, though, and their lieutenant spoke with Captain Bock for a few minutes and then left.

"Bastards," Litton muttered and Collier silently echoed the sentiment.

"Keep the weapons," Captain Bock said grimly. "Major Rashkil, you're on CQ," and he walked away.

Davis's eyes rounded and he looked at Collier who set his jaw and told Farley to send everyone back to class and then marched down to the Ready Room, carrying the rifle.

Chief Fessen was sitting behind the high desk wearing his fatigues, usual sour expression, an M-16 laid on the counter. One of the best guys on staff and Collier would have smiled except things were tense.

"Seen this?" Chief waved a flimsy pink paper and handed it to him. It was a broadside:

ARISE!

STRIKE OFF YOUR CHAINS!

THE WARS IN ARABIA AND MEXICO ARE SLAVE WARS!

YOU ARE NOT SLAVES! YOU ARE AMERICANS!
TODAY WE STRIKE AT THE SLAVE HOLDERS!
JOIN US!

At the bottom was the logo of a clenched fist with NATIONAL LIBERATION FRONT arced below it.

"They were all over the bomb site," Fessen said.

"Where'd you get it?"

"That army patrol gave it to Captain Bock."

"Oh," Collier studied it. "What's the National Liberation Front?"

Fessen shrugged. "Who knows? Some bunch of pissants. Maybe a front for the 'Slams, I couldn't tell ya."

"Did they get the president?"

Fessen snorted. "That coward. The little bastard is hiding in some old bunker somewhere, probably in one of the missile fields. His generals are more likely to get him than these shitheads," and he pointed at the paper Collier held.

"So who'd they get?"

Fessen's lips compressed. "Little Pentagon."

"Jesus," Collier sucked in a breath, "the whole thing?"

"Pretty much."

The square of Old Town, Charlottesville, de facto center of the de facto new capital of the US. army headquarters and air force headquarters and just about everyone's headquarters, come to think of it.

"What'd they use, a nuke?" Collier asked.

"Someone said four truck bombs, timed. Pretty fuckin' sophisticated, if you ask me," Fessen started fiddling with the M-16. "Gotta be the 'Slams."

Collier stared at the broadside. "So why didn't they say so?"

Fessen blinked, chewed the ends of his straw-colored mustache. "I don't know, son. I don't know much of anything anymore." He paused. "Why'n't you go see if Captain Bock wants a fresh pot of coffee? We still got about an hour of power." He grinned at the rhyme.

Collier nodded and made the odd little cramped turn that led to the administrative offices. Collier squeezed past the lit up security console, careful not to brush any of the knobs. The cameras were on and Collier saw kids all over the place, still holding their rifles. Looked like war.

Collier could hear Captain Bock talking on the phone and he stopped, not wanting to interrupt. Phone time was precious. "They're just kids," he heard Bock say. A little bit of ice shot through his veins and he moved closer to hear.

"I know that." Pause. "I know that." An edge crept into Captain Bock's voice. "But," he said, and there was a long pause. "But," he said again, another pause and Collier wondered if he should make his presence known.

"No way. Absolutely no way," Captain Bock was animated now and Collier was glad he had remained still. "They can't just arbitrarily change things, and the militias have to go before the provos, that's the new law, that's the last decision, and congress has to reconvene before ..." his voice trailed off. "What do you mean, they've already been called?"

Collier stepped back slowly, Captain Bock's voice trailing him as it got louder and angrier, "Then let them go through the militias, dammit! Then they can come to us and negotiate," his voice more broken the farther away Collier moved, "... too damn young! Don't care ... draftees ..."

"Hey, watch it," Fessen warned as Collier backed around the corner, getting too close to the console. "Did he want coffee?"

"No," Collier turned, his breath short.

"What's wrong with you?"

"Nothing. Chief, I gotta go back to my room for a moment, okay?" and he left without acknowledgment, getting a raised eyebrow for the protocol breach. He rushed up the parapet, swinging on the balustrade, and opened his door. Davis was at the table, cleaning the disassembled rifle.

"We're in trouble," Collier said.

12

Had to be Raiders. Had to be. John stood outside on the little patch of ground that sloped away from the front entrance of Cassell, monitoring the last smoldering bits of Missus. What a gruesome job. He'd winched her onto a stretched-out tarp, only losing one of her legs in the process, but she expelled a lot of gas when he started dragging the tarp out the door and, oh, good Lord. The kerosene reek was actually a relief and he'd walked about a half block away after igniting her, taking short sniffs of the rag he'd soaked, careful to avoid intoxication. The smell of burnt body still came through.

That smell. First time with it, an aircraft accident back in 1980. The pilot had been crisped on one side, fresh on the other, sort of like a steak left on a too hot grill. Burned-body-smell coats the inside of your nose for weeks. Missus would, too.

She was just coals and smoke now and he said a prayer, a warrior's prayer, invoking Heaven and Valhalla, one a form of the other. She would rise on the smoke and sit in the company of other warriors where they would regale and toast each other and clash weapons, the sound of it thunder. And then she would rest on a cloud and strum a harp and match her voice to it, singing of lost lands and lost loves. He would have to pay her a visit, when he got there. Take Theresa. The two of them would get along very well, as long as Missus didn't mention Cousin Barb. Hell, Cousin Barb was probably there, too. Along with Beard.

Baby.

He set his lips. So, which ones, the Mall Raiders or the Independence Avenues? One or the other, and he wondered what had prompted an attack. Had they joined forces?

Not bloody likely.

Last he'd heard, they were still squared off against each other down near the White House. The Mall boys were still pretty busy with the Smithsonian, while the Avenues were still picking over the Supreme Court and Library of Congress. Supposedly, the Avenues sold the William Blake plates for around five million in gold and weapons, while the Mall boys got twice that for the Hope Diamond. That's a lot of scratch, a lot of weapons, and they were all greedy bastards so there was no way they'd join up. Accords, yes, and they'd had an uneasy truce for a while, just a little scrapping around the edges. But command such prices, there's no way to keep a peace. It's all or nothing.

So why did they reach across the bridge and destroy a Family? Linking up with some Virginia Raiders? He shook his head. Again, not bloody likely. Still just gangs in Virginia fighting over territory, too scattered, too stupid. They just didn't have the long hallowed tradition of organized criminal activity in Virginia as they did in DC. Even the Gate crooks were DC connected. The Families had the local gangs pretty much under control, and there's no way Raiders could reach out to them without the Families finding out and doing something about it.

So what happened?

And, Brother John, more importantly, how did she end up here?

He watched the last of her popping and falling apart. Lots of questions in that. For instance, how the hell whoever did this know he knew the Alexandrias? A spy in the Family? No, more likely a campus Vandal, one of the small-timers pilfering the place on a regular basis, selling off the art and valuables John hadn't managed to hide. They sometimes left his Claymore traps neatly bundled up where he'd placed them. It was a joke. They weren't even trying to kill him anymore, which was quite the insult.

But the smart aleck campus Vandals could never muster the strength to take on a Family and win. He shook his head. Better scenario, the Mall Boys or Avenues recruited one of 'em to assist. Okay, he could buy that. So, why drag Missus all the way back here for the evening's entertainment?

Warning. Threat.

But why? Really, why? Just ignore him, have a good laugh at his expense, stupid old fart cop, what's he doing here, anyway? A joke, that's what he was. "Ach!" an exasperated gasp through the kerosene rag.

No. He. Wasn't.

So what, then, revenge? Some friend or lover of some Bundy or Vandal he had done? Well, then, just shoot him. Granted, John was particularly watchful and lucky and managed to spot ambushes before they triggered, but he had to be lucky all the time and what were the odds of that? Someone wanted payback, eventually, they'd get it. Again, no need to drag a screaming, raped and ripped woman all the way back here and hang her up for him to see.

Think bigger, John.

Okay, let's see. How did he draw the Raiders' ire, but in a way they preferred to warn rather than kill? Gate. Must have something to do with the Gate. Hmm.

Last time he'd been there, three weeks ago, did anything happen? He reviewed. Uneventful drive that time, no firefights, no one trying to hijack the Pathfinder, nothing. A little odd, but sometimes all the crapheads were up on 66 going through the cars and bodies instead of loitering on 50. So, no, not the drive.

The usual routine when he got there: checked in with Bill, walked around the tents a bit seeing what was what, gave the CDC and their ever-present needles and penchant for kidnap and live autopsies a wide berth.

Not that he needed to anymore. Bill told him the CDC had pretty much given up on Gate dwellers. Apparently, living close together did something to the Flu's course. Gaters were passing the same bug back and forth, or something like that, which screwed up the trials. At least, that's what the CDC told Bill. 'Course you can't believe anything they said and maybe they'd look upon John's casual arrival as a gift. So, avoid.

He'd walked over to the Gate itself and peered through the Mylar sheets. Bank Lizards over on the far side started waving at him, like always. John helped them out by waving back as frantically as they did, but actually, he was hoping for a glimpse of Collier standing over there.

Silly, of course. It was too far away and the sheets blurred everything and the Zone Guards always came up and blocked the view, nervous about his intentions. Didn't stop John from trying.

After a few pointless minutes, he moved over to the video banks, grabbed an empty booth, and waited. After some time, the screen blinked on and there he was. "Didja see? Didja see?" Collier was excited, like always, and, like always, John lied, "Yeah, I saw ya," and then they just looked at each other.

He'd become a man. Tall and strong and handsome, puzzling genetic traits because the only thing John shared with him was the tallness. Weird combination of Asia and Scots-Irish and German that gave the kid quite an exotic look.

He had his mother's cast, the tell of her Japanese ancestry in his high cheekbones and eye slant, pale golden skin color with John's green eyes; must drive the girls wild. His mother's black-red hair, too, a color that always drove John wild, cropped short, of course. Coll's nose balanced out to something between John's honker and his mother's tiny little mound, overseeing John's very broad and merry smile, but, in Coll's case, with actual lips.

Wasp-waisted and broad shouldered in his Provo uniform ... God, he's just perfect. Must have about 30 or 40 girlfriends, especially with the army doing such a good job of keeping the bachelor pool low.

John changed the view from head shot to full body, back and forth, while Coll babbled on about the hazards of the trip, how many times they had to pull weapons or show papers to make it here. That's fine. Let him talk. John had almost unlimited time on the video because not a lot of people came to the Gate anymore. The booth was his until Bill alerted him someone else wanted it.

While Coll drew a breath, John told him about work but kept it mild. No need to depress him any further than circumstances did already. On to current events, of which John was quite knowledgeable, keeping up with Fox News Network now broadcasting out of Chicago (with none of the original anchors, of course, who never made it out of New York and DC). Then, the first of the arguments about plans, John against, and Coll for, the USAF, which John broke off before it got too heated, both of them holding uncompromising positions.

Coll backed up and then his buddies got on, always Davis of course, and a supporting cast that changed with each visit. This time it was Pearson and Reardon. They started out with how they were doing and then asked how John was doing and, always, what it was like.

John changed tactics and answered them brutally, honestly until they blanched, then he backed off. He didn't want them getting any stupid ideas about sneaking in. Davis, as always, asked him to go look for his parents. Like always, he told him no. There was disappointment in the kid's eyes, but John wouldn't budge. It was hard enough making it out to the Gate in one piece, much less Baltimore, but that wasn't John's main reason.

In the beginning, John checked the homes of Coll's buddies (those near enough, anyway), buried what he found and then came back and told them. They quit the Provos, joined the army and disappeared, maybe Saudi, maybe Mexico, who knew, because they were never heard from again. John blamed himself. He stole their hope. He wasn't going to steal Davis's.

Collier slapped in a tape, putting it in the second feed while Bill arranged picture-in-picture. Lacrosse game. Coll was a middie, an outstanding one at that, leading the Waynesboro Provo team in scoring so far this season. John watched the game while Collier and his pals provided running commentary. John loved it, watching his son's deft movements.

Where did all that athletic talent come from? About the only thing John ever did was martial arts and at a fairly mediocre level, his two black belts notwithstanding. Collier played all the rough sports, football and rugby. He brought those tapes in season and John loved them.

Easy, while watching, to let the imagination go, be in the living room with Coll while Mom got nachos together and made them rewind it so she could see the score Coll just made ...

John shook himself back to reality. The tape meandered off the game, onto other subjects like marching or some ceremony or Coll just goofing around, down at the river fishing or playing guitar. It ended and then Davis put on a few tapes because he had no one and John was the closest thing to Dad. So he watched and commented and joked just like any father would.

They got an hour and a half that time. Barely enough. He could have stood another three or four, even if it was just Coll and he staring at each other. Bill on the intercom, gentle, "Hey guys, got some others want to look."

"All right, all right," and John looked at Collier and said, "Time to go." That was the exact point, like in every previous visit, where his heart rent. "Next month on the 15th?" Coll asked, being too damn manly but John could read it. Another rent heart. "Okay."

They didn't know how to leave the first few times. There were crowds then, big ones, and they had only about ten minutes in the booths and they didn't know how very important it was to stop, just stop, so they lingered, catching a few minutes here and there as booths came open. Lingering can become your whole life. Look at the Bank Lizards, who sit there day after day watching for someone, anyone, waving and waving across those several hundred yards at the Mylar-obscured figure and hoping, just hoping, it's their own Survivor making his way, finally, to the feeds.

Collier was becoming one of them, so John ordered him back to Fishburne. "Get the hell back to school now. Come back on the 15th, next month. You hear me?" and he had stalked away, screaming in his own mind as Collier screamed in the microphone.

You have to stop.

Coll nodded and his face tightened but he didn't cry. Neither did John. That wasn't the way of things any-more. Men were men again, and they held it all in and looked stalwart and strong while dying inside because rage was for the enemy. That was Coll's big reason for the USAF. John understood but no, Coll, not you, not the last of me. Coll slid out of the seat and maybe Davis or Reardon waved a hand in the camera and they were gone.

John stumbled out of the seat and back along one of the walls, pressing against it and probably sending the alarms into shock and making the Zone Guards real nervous but he was hoping, please God, that one of those obscured moving blurs way out there on the other side was actually Coll.

Pretend. John waved and all the Lizards waved and waved and then it was just ridiculous so he stopped. It took John a few moments to recover, and a yellow-shrouded ZeeGee came up from the Outside, cocked his head in query. John nodded and backed off. The ZeeGee lowered his rifle and sauntered away. John sauntered, too.

He wandered back along the fence and then cut among the pavilions and tents and Nissan huts, keeping his head down. Everyone kept his or her head down. For reasons John had yet to figure out, everyone seemed embarrassed. Not in the beginning, of course. Then, they'd all been a crazed, frantic family running around and gripping and crying and imploring each other: "Where are you from? What street? Did you know [insert name] or [insert another name]? Have you seen name or name?"

Bill said about 20,000 people arrived during the first months. Seemed like 40,000, quite a crowd here when John first showed up, a big, scattered tent city that started at Front Royal and went all the way to Middletown before the Gate was actually sited on the bridge.

He only stayed a few days the first time because he'd already decided to live in the house but he came back a lot, a lot more after he made contact with Collier. There was always a crowd milling about, those times. But, after a while, they left, too.

Some of it was due to Raiders' attrition or recruitment. But, that was just battlefield percentage; most left because truth dawned – nothing was going to change, might as well go home. That upset the CDC initially because they thought a ready supply of test victims in the tents, a real big control group, would surely generate a cure. But it didn't, at least not so far, and probably wouldn't. That, more than anything, drove people off. Once a place drains of hope, look for it elsewhere.

Some of the first Families formed in the tents, pretty much the same way they formed in the Zone, segments drifting together. Some of them were still here, but most left as a group. John hadn't run across any of them. Odd. Must have drifted out to the country places, somewhere around Manassas or Fredericksburg, and set up shop in some old farmhouse with plenty of land. Probably formed communes. Or, maybe they all got sick of each other and divorced. Who knew?

The people still here were diehards, just sitting there stubborn, waiting for the initial promises to be fulfilled, the glaring exception being the hardy percent running the Raiders' black market. Couldn't blame any of them. They got three squares a day, the same stuff the army's eating, and medical care and movies and the latest shows. The hardy percent had the added bonus of getting filthy rich doing business with ZeeGees, virtually no overheads, occasionally stirring things up with a firefight or two.

But, they're all pathetic. Losers. Criminals. The price of staying was submission to CDC trials and a lot of that was draconian and a lot of them just died. What normal person would endure that? Bill said most of them had become so depressed they wouldn't even watch movies anymore. Bill told them to leave, go get another life, but they wouldn't listen and then the CDC got mad and threatened him with dismissal. Or worse. Like their weekly strapping of Bill to a gurney and removing half his blood supply wasn't bad enough. But they could, indeed, do worse.

John moseyed over to Bill's booth, supposed to be sealed but Bill ignored the protocols, leaving it wide open. Iconoclasm or death wish, John wasn't sure, but the rule flouting began in earnest after John, responding finally to Bill's continuous pleas, went to Bill's house in Herndon (a harrowing trip involving no less than five gun battles), found and buried his wife.

Bill had wanted to go himself. He stood outside the Gate for weeks screaming to be let in, worse than all the other Lizards. He demanded it, said he knew his wife was alive. The CDC commander became curious – what would happen to an Outsider mixing with Gaters? So they made him a deal; work at the Gate, we'll see about your wife.

They never did, of course. Bill tried to go out there several times himself, but was stopped, locked up. John had been his only hope and Bill was a good guy and no one should be this close and not have any answers. That was back in the first days, when John had noble purposes still about him. So John went.

After that, Bill started walking around the camp without a yellow suit, not even a respirator, checking on people, slapping backs, hugging, consoling, sleeping with a random woman or two. Yeah, definitely a death wish. But, he didn't get sick.

Odd. The CDC thought it was odd, too, and relented and said he could go home if he wanted, but they hadn't suddenly become altruistic. They wanted to see what would happen if he got an unadulterated dose. Bill didn't go. No need; John had already taken care of it and, while Bill might have a death wish, he wasn't crazy. Good thing, because Bill was good for the Gate. He knew what he was doing.

"How's business?" Bill asked, almost cheerily.

"Booming," John replied and Bill almost laughed.

"When you going to retire?"

"And do what?"

"You could come out here."

"And do what?"

Bill actually laughed then and flapped a hand at a chair and offered John a cigar, which he greedily accepted because it was a real Cuban. Ever since they took the island back, Cubans had been fairly available on the Outside, usually as gifts to important people. Bill had somehow convinced CDC bigwigs that he was important so they occasionally passed on a box or two.

John put it in his pocket for later and asked about satellite internet. Bill puffed and frowned and then declaimed in technical jargon about azimuths and signal ranges and connectability until John smiled and said, "Okay, I surrender."

He shrugged an apology, "Yeah, I know, I talk to myself too much. But, really, if you want to give it a whirl I can write it all up for your next visit."

"Man," John raised appreciative eyebrows, "that would be fantastic. Can I use my existing Dish system? Without changing the contract, I mean. Too expensive."

"Not a problem. I'll give you the directions on what to do and some IP addresses for free satellite I know about. You'll have to move them around a lot because someone will get wise, but if you randomize and access sub or hyper frequencies, you'll do okay."

"That sounds great, Bill, whatever you just said, it really does, but I'm not sure I've got the expertise."

He regarded John coolly, "You got here alive, didn'cha?"

John nodded. Okay.

One deal done. John asked if he needed anything from the Zone. Bill wanted any old VHS tapes or DVDs. There were, of course, plenty, Blockbuster not doing the business it used to, yuk yuk, and John said he would bring back a smorgasbord.

"Good," Bill blew a cloud into the chamber, "light stuff, you know, musicals, '50s, Doris Day, Rock Hudson silliness. But nothing dark, not *Rebel Without a Cause*, you know?" John agreed and did not ask if these were for Movie Night or just for Bill, because either answer would have been saddening.

"What's it like?" Bill asked after a pause.

John shook his head, "It's getting worse. Much worse. I'm finding butcheries all the time now and you can hear a lot more shooting going on. People seem to have disappeared, I mean, the decent people. I don't know if they're hiding or run off or dead, but all I'm seeing these days are the bad ones."

"Hmm," Bill gestured towards the tents, "it's getting like that here, too. People are stealing from each other and factions have formed and there's fights between them. That's over and above the black-market gangs, mind you. ZeeGees had to come in here a couple of times and break up some crowds. Ugly, real ugly. They leave me alone, I guess because they know the place will shut down otherwise, but they're turning on each other."

"Umm," John was sympathetic, "that's what happens. No reason to hope." John paused. "Do they?"

Bill looked at John, intense and probing, "No. CeeDees still do a lot of needle work, like always, but they're not changing their stories anymore, it's all 'wait and see' now. They don't even bother to lie. People know."

"Yeah." People did know. John had clung to the lies too, even the most transparent, a drowning man at a passing spar, because hope was ephemeral, but power-ful. John could, like anyone, make hope out of anything. But he had to be given something first.

Bill shook his head and muttered something.

"What?" John didn't quite catch it, "Did you say, 'go on'?"

"Partholon. I said, 'Partholon'," Bill replied rather absently and clenched the cigar fiercely in his teeth. John's blank look told him they didn't share the reference. Bill manhandled the cigar down to his side, "It's an old Irish legend."

"Yeah?"

"Partholon was the first human settler of Ireland. He came from the Mystic Western Islands, the Land of the Dead, with his family. He built the lakes and rivers and farmlands, fought the Formorians, which was some kind of demon race. His wife committed the first act of adultery in Ireland, establishing one helluva precedent, don'cha think?"

"I don't get it."

Bill shrugged, looking out the door, "Partholon and his entire family died of the plague. Except for his son or nephew, I forget which, who took on the form of all kinds of different animals and things until he was reborn as a baby, thousands of years later, with all the knowledge of everything that had happened before."

John blinked at him, "Why did you raise that?"

Bill pursed his lips and looked genuinely puzzled, "I don't know. It just popped into my head. I guess because we were talking about the CeeDees and I was thinking 'plague' and, well, there it was, Partholon." He took a deep, deep draw. "That's all."

"Hmm," John grunted. "That's how we're going to end up, isn't it?"

Bill didn't respond. So they sat there, saying nothing, looking off at the angles. Things were what they were. No need to console or explain, the mere act of breathing was its own consolation. Bill finished the Cohiba and offered another cigar but John refused, never having been a big smoker. Just living was risky enough. John gave him a Unix manual he'd found, which pleased Bill to no end because it was some rare upgraded version, a real treasure. John left, went home.

And now here he was. And here *she* was, scattering in the wind. And he still had no clue why.

But he knew one thing. He was going to get this bastard and his pals. He was going to duct tape them to the biggest tree on the Main Quad and then carve the Bill of Rights on their stomachs. He was going to hang their blood-drained carcasses from a telephone pole right on Ward Circle and coat them with honey and watch the bees build nests in their eyes and the birds eat their intestines. He'd invite MPD to watch while he did all this. No doubt, they'd approve.

He watched her swirling in the breeze. I promise, I promise.

13

Wasn't really much more to do. Further patrol would be anti-climactic; what, was he going to find the current president, whoever that was, staked out in a classroom? Screw it, time to end this. John watched the embers die and then crossed the street, walked up the long hill and stood in the arch, where the tunnel under Letts spilled out to the quad.

A couple of cars parked there still, one with its passenger door still open and some clothes hanging out, brushing the asphalt. He'd never closed it. Stark, that open door, communicating volumes. The students would have considered it art.

He always came here, before ending the day. Everyone needed a reminder of what they're about. Not that there weren't plenty of reminders scattered all the way between home and work. But, here, he was caretaker, and it was important to remember why.

The ghosts. Lots of ghosts. John looked at the identical Anderson and Letts main entrances, set opposite each other, the leaf-strewn steps rising to glass double security doors fronting foyers and RAs on desk duty. "Show me your card, please," and calls of "Hey Jules!" and "Yo, where you goin'?", "Anybody seen my backpack?"

John was the only one who heard it now, although it was just as active and crazy and loud as it was back then. Just on a different level.

They saw him, the ghosts. While they ran between

buildings and had fights on the stoops and threw Frisbees, they glanced at him sideways. They frowned.

"I'm sorry," John said, as he'd said a million times already.

The ghosts all stopped and stared at him. "We tried," John said, "we had meetings."

Lots of meetings. The wave of deaths in Baltimore caused great concern and all the campus wheels gathered to see if the evacuation plan, that brand new, spiffy, well written and strident document they'd put together after 9/11, applied to this situation. John was invited because, well, out of all the campus wheels, he was the only one with a military background, anti-terror at that and, well, although he really wasn't a wheel, he was known and it would look good to the parents and the students if AU's "resident expert" was present. Yeah. Some expert.

John had put on his grave face and threw in a meaningless comment or two to make his boss proud. For a university, appearance was everything, and although John thought the Baltimore deaths were really nothing, a weird uptick in pneumonia or Flu in that crappy, dirty city, he expressed proper concern. That assured a favorable impression, which assured future employment. If he looked like he knew what he was talking about, then the university looked like it was prepared.

It wasn't, but no one was and no one knew that, least of all John, so they published their innocuous, crafted-by-committee statement in the campus paper and on the intranet, slipped flyers under doors, everyone felt better and wasn't that the point? John had felt smug, even though he, of all people, knew that perception trumped reality and that reality was always something grimmer.

But it was a reality in Baltimore, not here. Placated students placated their parents and kept going to their internships at Capitol Hill and mixing with each other in

Georgetown pick-up joints and even volunteering at some Baltimore fringe hospitals, instead of fleeing to their New Jersey or Connecticut homes, going completely around Baltimore as they did so.

"Look at it this way," John whispered to the ghosts, "by staying here, you didn't spread it. Most of you didn't, anyway. You might even have contained it a bit."

The ghosts' frowns deepened.

That meeting was what, on a Monday afternoon? Next Monday, 32 students and one faculty member died on campus. John spent that entire day directing ambulances and calling hospitals and fielding phone calls from hysterical parents and random others and trying to get someone in DC FEMA to agree that his campus deaths were far more important than their Anacostia ones, or the ones at UDC, even the ones at the Smithsonian. He failed, of course.

He went home utterly exhausted and held Theresa, who was frightened, almost paralyzed, and who begged him not to go back but knew that was pointless. He was a warrior. Warriors fight. He left her crying in the living room the next morning and drove on an amazingly deserted Shirley Highway back to the campus where 375 students had died in their rooms overnight.

He could not get home that evening because 395 and the Chain Bridge and 495 and 95 were all jammed tight with the panicked.

News helicopters flew above the chaos and live-fed hundreds of traffic accidents, hundreds of vehicles smashing through guardrails, whole sections of beltway engaged in riot, overturned police cars and fires and shootings.

John called Theresa and they stayed on the phone together all night. He didn't even try to get home until three days later, making it after a five-hour ride over main and side roads, and shoulders and sidewalks, stopping every five minutes to push wrecks and pull bodies out of his way.

When he walked through the door, Theresa was in bed with the cough.

"I paid," he told the ghosts.

During those three stranded days, John walked the campus. There was no looting then, not even a lot of panic, just a determined effort to get out. John stood in the quad, pretty much where he was standing now, and watched the survivors grimly pack their cars with computers and clothes and stereos. Someone had knocked down the bollards that kept cars out of the area and a couple of students were directing traffic. Oddly, the others obeyed them.

John just watched. No one asked him to help nor did he see the need to offer. Most of them already had the cough and a few were laid out in the back seats of friends' cars, miserably hacking for air, all hoping to make their mutual hometowns and die together, he supposed.

They all knew what was going on around the highways but it didn't matter. It was better to make the effort, dying on the way, than wait here passively.

A few girls were crying in corners or looking around helplessly for someone to make it all better, but the majority just went about their business, silently. The prospect of being hanged and its wonderful ability to focus the mind. John saw numerous acts of true courtesy and quiet heroism, someone giving up a space in a car to someone else who was obviously a goner, saying they would catch a ride later, then go back inside and never come out again.

"You were heroes," he said to the ghosts, "you acted better than your parents."

The ghosts turned from him.

He held out a beseeching hand. "How do you explain? We didn't expect it. No one expected it. No one saw it coming."

All of them, the ghosts included, watched madmen turn airliners into missiles and drive innocents into the Towers, and it was senseless and unbelievable, and was never expected. Everyone watched other madmen drive another plane into the side of the Pentagon, stunned and shocked because, onboard, there was a little girl, maybe twelve years old, excited to go on a special trip with her teacher, a reward for doing so well in school.

Her last ten minutes of life were pure horror. She had to watch madmen slit a flight attendant's throat, and then yank the plane down in sickening deceleration at a building canting and looming in front. And she was terrified and screaming and it was torture for her. Pure torture for a child. That's it. That's what the madmen did. The image of a screaming, horrified little girl summed it all up.

John missed the crash into the Pentagon by ten minutes. He was late that morning and irritable as he managed to catch a last minute slug into the Pentagon hub and pick up a Yellow line from there to L'Enfant Plaza. He cleared the hub as the plane made its descent. When he got off the AU shuttle, one of the patrolmen told him what was going on and he rushed down to the lounge and watched the news reports for the next two hours. He watched the replays of the Tower attacks and watched in real time as they collapsed.

But, that little girl, what she suffered, that was his image of the day.

He'd known about those people, those murderers, those Muslim cowards so angry and self-righteous and jealous of a world that had proved, many times over, that their closed-minded religious zealotry could not advance nor feed nor edify their people but could only terrify and repress and cow.

Instead of harking back to their brilliant Andalusian forebears, who were the first lights of the Dark Ages, and concluding, through Andalusian rationality and logic, that maybe there was something wrong with a philosophy that left whole peoples undeveloped, backwards and increasingly marginalized, and that after 700 years they had barely advanced past those same Dark Ages, while the secular Western world was reaching an unheard-of affluence with little input from Islam, they reached a different conclusion – hate.

That's the way of inadequate people. They revel in their inadequacy and find fault with others' success, because it is much easier to do that than confront their own failings.

And those miserable bastards knew they would never have the ability to take on the West, the US, directly because doing so was beyond the capability of any small religion where rules were more important than thought, and severe self-righteous repression of any slight alteration of just one nuance of those many rules, was far more important than discourse. So, in their hate, in their gleeful, lustful hate, they thought it would be great to drive a twelve-year-old girl into the side of a building. What masterful warriors, what men, what true, noble soldiers of their faith.

John's lips curled in contempt, then guilt. Because he'd known all this, was very aware of it, but had filtered it through Western eyes, through Western rationality, and made the very serious mistake of believing that throwing a child into the side of a building was beyond anyone's concepts.

He screwed up. He completely screwed up. He knew hate was a relentless motivator. Hate was irrational and uncompromising; no negotiations. It cannot be changed into love or respect, all the bleeding hearts take note. You must eradicate the one who hates you. There is no other solution because you can bet the hater is trying to eradicate you. The world was far more Darwinian than anyone wanted to admit.

Funny, that. The elites, the sophisticated, the oh-so-progressive embraced Darwinism as their pet origin theory, yet refused to apply its implications. Inconsistent bastards.

But, John, you didn't apply it, either.

He shifted uncomfortably. Think of hate. It motivates incomprehensible actions, like driving children into the sides of buildings or urging your teenage son to strap on 50 pounds of dynamite and blow himself up inside a school bus. How noble. And the raging joy the haters felt. Their leering faces as they danced in the streets, firing their AK-57s in the air and screaming some barbaric ululation over the success of scattering the body parts of school children across a sidewalk.

How manly, how heroic.

They took pleasure in dragging mutilated corpses down streets and stripping veiless women naked and beating them with canes. They believed their soaring passion was a blessing from God but didn't know God long ago abandoned them because they have made a god out of their hate and mistook the subsequent raging self-righteousness as divinity's touch. They reveled in that self-righteousness and believed it a mark of God's favor.

It was not.

Their acts were used as menstrual rags thrown before God's throne, evil and worthless. John's fists tightened. All of them, every man, woman and child of them, must have their own body parts scattered on the sidewalk, food for crows.

"Do you hear me, ghosts?" John gripped his hands tighter. "It's what must happen. It's what pays back."

The ghosts turned, as they always did at this point,

and stared at him, aghast. "Okay, okay," he conceded, "I hate them as much as they hate me. I see their entire culture and history as a sewer stain, and every time I hear of some successful operation against them, I revel in their deaths. But how can you loathe me for that?" and he swept his still-clenched hands to take in the dead quad. Evidence.

They lined up and regarded him. He shook his head, "It doesn't make me the same as them." The ghosts shook their heads back at him and asked whether he could be the more civilized, the more compassionate, weep for the pain and death caused by all this hate yet, somehow, consider the possible merit of their complaint and try, just try, to meet the murdering bastards half-way. Let's put an end to all the killing and anger and misery and just learn to get along.

John stared at them. Stupid babies.

"No," he said, "no way. You see, no matter how inad-equate the culture, how inferior the people, how insig-nificant the beliefs and practices, how medieval the thinking, and how fourth rate you feel as a result, you simply don't get to run twelve-year-old girls into the sides of buildings. No matter how much your hubris is offended by the presence of a more sophisticated, wealthier, cosmopolitan society than yours, you don't get to blow up school buses to demonstrate how offended you feel. You can protest and insult and boycott and shun and denigrate and feel superior about your back-ward ways all you want, but simply, absolutely, in no way, can you run twelve-year-old girls into the sides of buildings."

John shook an adult finger at the ghosts. "You do that," he continued the lecture, "and the full weight of retaliation falls justly on your donkey-crap society and its low-class religious zealotry and all the bearded self-righteous old men who are mad because their repressive, stupid beliefs have only impoverished and brutalized their own people."

John pointed at a particularly long-haired ghost who was shaking a disapproving beard at him, "You want to call me a bigot and a racist, go ahead. If you want to think the vengeance burning in me is proof of my own backwardness, that's fine. Sit around in your coffeehouse and put that proper look of sincere horror on your face about people like me, who are reacting to what is truly a tragic event. But surely one that requires us to rise up in our humanity and reach an apologetic hand out to those honest Third World peoples who feel so frustrated by our brutish Western condescension that they have no choice but to slam girls into the sides of buildings." John put the proper sneering tone in that last comment.

"Do so. Throw back your long hair in a gesture of sympathy and sip that double latté and look deeply at the fresh faced coed across from you and deplore the violence and make sure the little muffin knows how sincere and loving you are, as you call people like me cavemen. You might get laid out of it." John saw, with great satisfaction, how that angered and embarrassed the hippie ghost.

"Call me anything you want, but step aside, little boy," John took an aggressive step towards the hippie ghost, "You see, we don't slaughter children. And whoever does, whether it's a drunk redneck throwing his daughter across the trailer or a holy mullah blessing the hijackers as the Towers burn, they are beyond compassion and understanding and possible redemption. Rabid dogs are to be killed. You don't negotiate with them or try to understand them or deplore them or issue condemnations. You put a bullet in their heads."

John was on a roll now, feeling the righteousness of it. The hippie ghost, though, stood his ground and mouthed at John, "We did that."

John frowned and stepped back. "Yeah, we did that. We found the murdering bastards' base and turned it into dust, in a matter of weeks destroying camps and homes and government and routing them until they were just shivering rags of bleeding refugees cowering in caves. And, yeah," John conceded to the hippie ghost, "innocents were killed, some of them, no doubt little girls. But these same 'innocents' allowed the murdering bastards to train and plan and come up with the means of driving planeloads of children into the sides of buildings. These 'innocents,' as you call them, wrapped their women in bags, sold them to others and caned anyone who even dared to listen to a rock and roll song. Yeah, they're 'innocents' all right," John snarled at the hippie ghost, "You support that?"

"Wasn't our business," the hippie ghost muttered and the coeds around him nodded vigorously in agreement.

"Oh yeah?" John took the aggressive step again. "Why don't you go ask the survivors what they preferred, to lose some of their 'innocent' population while getting rid of their overlords, or continue living under repression? Why don't you go do that, then? Huh? But, you better not, you better not," John waved a warning hand, "Nope, better stay here and get more lattés. You might not like the answer you get. And don't just rely on what your fellow ghosts are telling you," he swept in the suddenly angry coeds. "Go there. You can do it. You're incorporeal, you can travel through time and space with just a thought. Walk into their diseased and broken villages. Ask them, Taliban or independence? You know what they'll say, hands down, to almost a man and definitely to a woman, except, of course," John chuckled, "for the Taliban themselves."

It was a good point in the lecture, the point where John felt vindicated and superior. He had vanquished the effete ghosts who stood there leaning out from the hips, adolescent moue on their faces – well, vanquished for about a second. Because, then, they looked around, looked at the car with the open door, then back at John.

"It should have been enough," he conceded in a whisper, "We should have won. It's all we needed to do. We had them … we had them. All that was left was the final, merciless hunting, the cornering, and then shooting them dead, like dogs. That would end it, we would go home, we would celebrate, we would forget."

We were wrong. He did not say that aloud.

"We saw how they fought," this he did say aloud, "as cowards. They used their own sons as bombs. Oh sure, they fought with rifles and grenades and land mines in Afghanistan but they weren't very good. Our casualties were insignificant while theirs were catastrophic and we put them to flight. They became scattered, hunted bands that would pop up and fire wildly as our Special Forces coolly mowed them down. They had ceased to exist as a fighting force after a few weeks. We looked at each other and shrugged and wondered why the Russians had such a hard time with them. Were we that good?

"Yeah, we're that good, for what we know, what we expect. Against guns and bombs and land mines, we are unequaled. Why, look at what we did to Saudi. We're preparing the final assault on Baghdad right now while pounding the remnants of Castro's forces. We're winning, at least, that's what we're being told. Yeah, at great cost, great slaughter on both sides, but this is what we know. This is what we're good at, and we'll win." He paused. "We'll win."

The ghosts blinked at him, speechless. They looked at each other then back at John. "We'll win," he insisted and his gaze fell on the car. When he looked back up, the ghosts were gone.

And, like always, he started to cry.

14

It was getting late. John watched the sun's rays slant across the floor. 4:30ish, he figured, and confirmed it with the watch. About another half hour or so and he was outta here. Miller time.

He really should adjust his hours so he was traveling in the light, but it was hard to get eight good day-lit hours in the early spring, no matter what he did. Could work six-hour days ... what, did he wear a dress? Gonna travel in the dark. Dangerous doing that, hard to spot ambushes. Traveling in the day wasn't a picnic either, but at least you could see what was up ahead.

The cold offset the dark somewhat. Bundys and Raiders stayed mostly inside. For all their swaggering, they were kinda wimpy. On a long cold night, the commute was generally uneventful, only trigger-happy MPD patrols or skittish Loners to worry about. Unfortunately, it wasn't that cold tonight, upper 50s, so there was a good chance an unusually high number of jerks would be out celebrating. Could be eventful.

Quite a contrast with the upcoming summer months, when everybody was out all the time. Sunset became the Raider Witching Hour so John didn't travel after dark if he could help it and the long days let him help it. By the time they crawled out of their troll holes, he was safe at home. Summer was actually quieter, proof that timing trumped circumstance.

The generator had been running about an hour now and John scrutinized the Zap battery loaded in the charger. The light was red but that was okay; he'd used that battery to get here and it wouldn't be fully charged yet. It was just backup in case the return-leg battery crapped out a bit short. It shouldn't. One battery was good for about two hours of straight Zap riding, which bell curved enough to get him back and forth on a single charge.

John pulled the return battery out of the pack and went over to the Zap, which was leaning against Daria's old desk in Parking and Traffic. He loaded the battery then examined the Zap's chain and checked the tires, everything good, but he added a few drops of oil and a few pounds more pressure anyway. The Zapbike was built like a tank and was just about as heavy, able to take the pounding from all of John's carry weight and the debris on the road. But it was a royal pain in the ass to change a tire on it and if he could spot a flaw and fix it now instead of on a windblown shoulder of the Eternal Graveyard of 395, then he would. He didn't even want to think about snapping a chain, so he didn't.

He slapped the saddle affectionately. Good ole Zap. When he flipped on the motor, he could get up to 20-25 mph while pedaling, pretty easy pedaling at that, even uphill. Remarkable, considering his load. More remarkable, the Zap was holding up well. So were the batteries. He'd been using this set for about six months now and there was no sign of deterioration. Didn't matter, he had several spares and no indication in any of the literature they'd fail to take a charge, even years from now when he broke them out. That might end up being wrong, but was too far in the future to worry about. For now, he had a ride.

At least this ride. Not cars. Not that there wasn't any shortage of cars. He could have any number of Rolls or Mercedes or V-Rods scattered around rich neighborhoods like Foxhall, all just begging to be driven. He could even tool around in the university president's Infiniti G28, quite the luxuriant town car, that. But he didn't touch them. Driving a car was just asking for trouble.

For one thing, you could hear an engine starting at least a mile away. Might as well hit a bass drum in a crypt, send up a flare, tell everyone you're coming. All eyes for twenty blocks turn towards the sound, all ears strain, weapons come out of holsters and lust and murder light the mind. The zombies move, hungry.

No thanks.

It wasn't so much the engine but its undertones, the off-rhythm mechanical thrum of pistons and cams and lifters moving through the ground for miles, a sonic wave. The Magnums gave him the same trouble. And since car travel was pretty much restricted to still-passable roads (which eliminated 395, 95 South, 66 and all the other graveyards) even the most dull-witted Bundy could figure out where he was going and set up an ambush.

John found that out pretty quick. He was driving the Pathfinder, getting on and off 395 as breaks in the grave-yard allowed, bulling his way through on occasion (metal on metal screeching, that was brilliant) when someone put a round through the windshield, missing him by a half inch, at best.

That was about a month after he'd started putting the house together, about his tenth or eleventh trip to the District. He was heading towards the Mall and an ap-pointment at the CDC mobile lab set up there. Four or five other Survivors and he were in some kind of trial that the docs were pretty excited about, and he wanted to get there on time because there was a feel to it, like they were on to something. Now, he was pretty sure it was just a line, that they were actually getting ready to put the habeas grabbus on him. But, back then ... well, you trusted.

He'd actually been on 395, a trail he'd cut on previous

trips, topping the big hill past Landmark Mall when, wham, glass all over and he was careening across four lanes, smashing through cars. He ended up behind an abandoned van and jumped out, running for cover with the mini-14. He huddled under the trailer hitch between the back wheels, cold and hungry and pretty pissed off, until dark. Never saw who fired. The bastard never made a move. Some Bundy having a little fun.

John took the now windshield-free and bumper-creased Pathfinder back home and limited his driving to short trips at odd times for odd reasons, like when he needed to haul something big, and, of course, going to the Gate. That's what everyone did now. You lowered your exposure. Even Families didn't drive unless it was in heavily-armed caravans. Driving made you vulnerable.

That missed CDC appointment led John to the Zapbike. He felt guilty about not showing up. They'd told him the tests were vital, that they needed him, practically waved the flag in his face. Not that he needed a lot of prompting. He was itching to do something more than kill Bundys. He wanted to strike at the real enemy, hunt down and eviscerate the bastards but since he couldn't leave the Zone, the only thing available was helping defeat their biggest weapon. It felt like God's work, so he really wanted to get back to the Lab.

He considered a motorcycle but there was still the noise issue. He gave long thought to a regular bicycle, because he'd always loved them and had a 10-speed Bianchi in the backyard anyway. But, it was 18 miles, one way, to the District; 18 miles loaded down with rifle, ammunition, water, and whatnot. He was a tough guy, but, c'mon. He wouldn't make five miles.

He knew about Zapbikes, even thought of buying one Before. His dogsitter had one and let him ride it around the neighborhood a couple of times. It was a bit small, but fun, so he went to her townhouse in Daventry, broke in, buried her and her husband, and took the Zap home. He left a hundred dollars on the counter, should their son ever make it back from the West Coast, and only a hundred because, after all, it was used.

A week later, proud of himself, he tooled up Backlick and Edsall and George Mason Drive to 50 and across the bridge right up to the Lab. Ta da! Here I am, now let's get chemical.

You'd think they'da been happy. No, instead he got attitude about the missed appointment; the serums were experimental and they needed to check John at certain times to see what was happening and if he couldn't make it when they said then maybe he should consider moving in to the trailer encampment area with them. The little army colonel running the thing just stood there screaming. Colonel Storm, that was his name, which was certainly appropriate. John was a bit taken aback, to say the least. More so, he was suspicious. Things had an ugly whiff to them.

He still went back a few more times, but was wary. As things got uglier, he just stayed away. He felt guilty about that, too, for a while, because of the other Survivors. They just weren't taking his warnings seriously. Oh, they listened, a couple even agreed but one of them summed it up, "What else can we do?" She was right, but he stopped going, anyway. Given what the CDC devolved to, it was a good decision. Unheroic, though. Not like the ones who stayed.

In time, gasoline, more than noise, killed driving. Oh, there was still plenty of it, millions of gallons lying around unattended in gas stations and storage tanks and tanker trucks and even unused cars. Supply wasn't the problem. How to *get* the supply was.

At first, he went to the neighborhood gas station. That was okay as long as the power was on, but, when that died, so did the pumps. Eh, just siphon what you need out of the storage tanks, John old boy. Pop open the lid, drop a hose down there, and start the flow.

Yeah.

It just wasn't that easy. There was some kind of baffle system down there designed, he suspected, to prevent the casual Thomas or Richard or his buddy Harold coming along and helping themselves. Getting a hose past that was quite the chore. Then he discovered an interesting law of physics, the one that governed an attempt to start a vacuum in a hose about thirty feet long. All he got for his trouble was a lungful of vapor and a very pleasant drunk feeling. No doubt, there was some kind of backup system used to get the gas flowing when the station lost power, but he had no idea what it was and, frankly, didn't need to. He went to Plan B ...

Siphoning gas from neighborhood cars. It was about the easiest way to fill up without power and pretty convenient, too. He never had to leave the neighborhood. But, it wasn't too long before he was looking two or three blocks away. Besides, he got tired of getting a faceful of gas each time he emptied a tank.

Things became more complicated when he got the Magnums running. Trying to find diesel was a bigger problem than gas. He started siphoning from 18-wheelers, which quickly became a royal pain. He had to find the 18-wheeler to begin with, which meant searching the highways, burning up his gasoline and exposing himself to the newly awakened and very active Bundys. The Magnums used a lot of fuel and there was just no way he could keep running around looking for big trucks.

A large supply of diesel and gas right at the house, where he could access it night or day, hide it, protect it, now wouldn't that be sweet? *Ding!* Light bulb. Why not park a gas truck next door? Better, yet, why not two trucks, one gas and the other diesel, side by side? Brilliant!

There is idea, but then, there is execution. He knew where to go – the gas and oil storage center off Backlick Road in Newington, very close to where he'd taken, er, bought, the Magnums. He'd seen fuel tankers going in and out of there day and night for years. He still had the tractor-trailer from hauling in the backhoe, so he revved it up and bad clutched his way there, only smashing up one car in the process.

He pulled around the big gas storage tanks sitting beside 95 and, yes indeed, there they all were, dozens and dozens of tankers marked "Exxon" and "Sheetz" and "Mobil," you name it, lined up next to some big pumping station. Ecstasy. He picked out one likely looking tanker, backed the truck up to it, got out, and made his first discovery – the trailer hitch wasn't compatible. No problem, just go get another tractor.

Yeah.

He found the tractors, all right, about fifty of them parked in another lot across the street, but, of course, no keys. An hour of searching through some offices nearby finally located them. Cool, they were labeled and he found the right one and jumped right in and turned the key and ... nothing. Most of the batteries in the tractors were dead.

He must have tried twenty trucks before he found one that would start. Feeling quite a bit put out, John, finally, maneuvered the truck into position and, an hour or so after that, figured out how to connect the two. Perfect, great, wonderful, in business, all the gas he needed. That is, until he looked up and saw, clearly labeled on the side of the tanker, "Fuel Oil."

He cursed for at least twenty minutes. No exaggeration.

He then made another discovery, how hard it was to de-couple a fuel tanker when you had no idea how you coupled it to begin with. After about another hour and a lot more cursing, he got the two apart. So, now he's smarter, go read the damn tanker to see what it contains before you back the truck up to it, moron. He then made several more discoveries about tanker construction. Previously he thought, like every Joe Schmoe thought, a tanker was just a big empty shell filled with Mobile Techroline or Tiger Whatever sloshing around inside. Oh, no. No no no no. That would be too easy.

Turns out tankers were compartmentalized, and each compartment could have something completely different in it, gas in one, diesel in another, kerosene in another. Now how the hell was he going to know what was in each compartment? All of it smelled like gasoline, regardless of the color or consistency. He was getting a headache from smelling the fumes and his fingers were shredded from removing the compartment caps. And, it was getting dark. What to do?

What you always do when you're up against it, you go long.

He selected a tanker clearly marked "Diesel Fuel" and backed the truck up to it, slamming them together. Screw it. He was so mad he hoped the damn thing blew up. He battered his way out of the terminal and out to the house, messing up just about every turn, hitting more parked cars and median strips than a replay of "World's Most Violent Police Chases." He pulled up to the end of Hawthorne Court, which was a funny looped street below the house, hidden by the ridge line, and dropped the tanker. He whipped around the return loop and hammered his way back to the depot, hooked up the first tanker that read "Gasoline," wrecked his way back home, and dropped it behind the other one.

He drove the tractor to the last house on the street, turned it off, and walked away. Sonofabitch.

So, after a struggle of epic, Cecil B. DeMille proportions, he had supply and convenience. And it was all probably for nothing.

Viability. You can have all the gas in the world, but when it goes flat, it's just smelly water. As the Path and Magnums got harder to start, it dawned on him what was going on and that's when he'd raided Home Depot and all the auto shops for ten miles around and scooped up all the fuel stabilizer he could find and poured it into the tankers. No idea if it worked. Either reversed the deterioration, froze it in place, postponed the inevitable, or did absolutely nothing. Who knew? Bill didn't. The libraries warned about the problem, but didn't offer a solution other than what he'd already done.

If he could just tap MPD's supply ...

So far, things still ran. The Magnums started. So did the Path. He sprayed WD40 in the carburetors of both and changed the Path's plugs frequently. But, face it, one day, crank and nothing. He'd worry about that then.

Because, face it, well before the gas crapped out, the Path, itself, would crap out. Vehicle maintenance. He hadn't tuned up the truck in about two years. Changing plugs and oil and draining and refilling the radiator was not tuning and the Path had definitely lost power. It was getting harder and harder to brake, too, and it tended to stall when idling. So, shut up, tune it.

Yeah.

Since about 1982, it took an engineering degree to do that. All those damned computers inside the engine had to be tweaked. He didn't know how. No one at the Gate did, either, at least, no one was saying. CDC finds out you've got those kinds of skills and, next thing you know, shanghaied to Atlanta. So, one day, the engine will die.

More likely he'd kill the Path by doing something stupid, break an axle or flip it. The roads weren't picnics, so debris-strewn that his main worry was a blow out, not a shootout. There wasn't a Gate trip where he didn't change at least one tire, and he was worried about his tire supplies.

He had a few pre-mounted spares sitting next door but, at this rate, he'd be through them pretty quick. Like gas, supply wasn't the issue, even for weird sized tires like his – mounting them was. Without power, how do you get them on the tire rim? Sheer brute strength, he supposed and he further supposed he should go mount about fifty of them before he was too much older and deeper in debt. "You load 16 tons," he growled in his best Ernie Ford and giggled. Yeah, he should, but wasn't feeling much like it, which meant, Grim Laws of Irony invoked, he'd blow his last tire in Raider territory, moments before the engine crapped out. Double whammy.

"Get a horse," he told himself. Then he need only worry about oats.

He sat down in Daria's old chair and mused. A horse. John supposed it was inevitable, but he wasn't ready to face that yet, to abandon the sheer joy of driving, or, at least, the promise of it. As long as that remained, they hadn't really lost. Had they?

On the morning he turned 16, there he was, in line to get his learner's permit and had Mom out on the road about two hours later, screaming in terror while he careened around curves and spun around on many a shoulder. He chuckled. Sorry, Mom.

The very night of the very day he got his actual license, as Mom pulled up from work and got out, he got in and drove off. John smiled, lolling his head back. That first solo drive. Just like his first kiss (Linda Atkinson, summer of '67, Alabama), scary, daring, thrilling. In and out of big empty parking lots, cruising down the two lane farm roads of a dark south Jersey, the jury-rigged FM tuner lying on the passenger floor bringing in MMR at glass shattering decibels, ending up next to the Pemberton field at midnight, sitting on the bleachers, pitch black with a million diamond-lit stars spiraling up and out of sight. Completely alone. Completely free.

All those other drives. Don and Drew and Karen and Irene and Tom and him, don't forget Carol and Kim and, of course, Theresa, 2-300 miles a night, going from Presidential Lakes to Groveton and out to Carteret then Seaside then back to Mt. Holly before Theresa's dad found out, then back to PL. Later, Theresa and him and Forrest and Jenny, out to New York City or Trenton, and back to Willingboro. Then, just Theresa and him. Illinois, Texas, Florida, across Tennessee in the dead of winter and up the ice-shrouded Shenandoah Valley, all their belongings tied to the top of a 1967 Dodge Coronet, two years in the USAF and going home for the first time since he joined, dazzled by the Blue Ridge, vowing right then and there they'd live in the Valley one day.

Finding out Tom died of stomach cancer three months before, Forrest had disappeared, Mom's new husband didn't want him around, Theresa's family wanted his money, so they stopped going back home because it wasn't really home anymore, the frozen mountains of Virginia more inviting.

Got close, got to here, a 50-minute drive away from those mountains. Made plans that involved one house payment at a time, one move at a time, one job at a time, clear their way out, from northern Virginia frenzy to placid cabin near Lexington or Radford, all the battles fought, all the wars won, nothing more to prove, those distant blue mountains now, finally, theirs.

Close. Just not close enough. He hung his head, staring at the floor. He would, as he had done every night for the past two or three years, stand by Theresa's grave and apologize. "My fault," he whispered, "all my fault."

15

Time to go.

The sun was throwing red light across the office, sure sign it was kissing the horizon. John dashed into the third floor landing, closed off from the offices by a heavy door, and shut off the generator while covering his mouth with a hand. Yeah, like that would save him. He had a hose venting fumes out the window but it was still dangerous.

He went back inside and locked the cabinets and doors and made sure the battery-powered lamps were off. Silly. Any random Vandal could open the cabinets with a paper clip, and anything he accidentally left on could be re-charged the next day. He should just leave everything on all night. Might give some Vandal a moment's pause before burning the place down, or might even spur them on, thinking John was still there. Coming back to ashes might be reason enough to quit. He chuckled. You think a Vandal would do him a favor?

He went back to the desk and pulled a copy of the Daily off the printer and slid it into the carousel. Getting a little harder to do that so maybe he should clean out the last few months' worth, maybe stick them on the Anderson desk. Just as likely to be read there as here. He'd already put the Observation into his notebook and slid that into the desk. Tomorrow, he'd review it, paying particular attention to the very detailed report he wrote about Mrs. Alexandria. Maybe he'd pick up something.

Doubt it.

All right, reports done, cabinets locked, lights off (maybe), a heart yearning for home. Weapons check time. He reached to his right inner back and pulled the pistol out smoothly. Ruger Speed Six .357 Magnum, bought at a Texas yard sale in 1977. It was a cop's gun, six-shooter with a 4" barrel that was worn down where it rubbed against the holster the million or so times it was drawn before being sold. All the times he'd drawn it since had just smoothed the wear to a fine silver. He could blue it, but, no, it gave the pistol character. John held it to the failing light. Great weapon. The only modification he'd ever made was a set of Pacmayr grips. The trigger was still light and smooth. He'd never had to grind the sear or set the spring.

He brought it up and acquired the far wall. Iron sights, no mods, didn't need it, because there was something about the pistol that put him right on target whenever he swiveled up. It was the balance, the weight, something, if you needed a scientific explanation, but John knew it was the soul. Every weapon had one and every weapon sought its soul mate, like lovers searching the ether. He and the Magnum were one, just like he and Theresa. Very Zen.

He rolled the trigger about halfway, feeling the easy movement and watching the cylinder advance. Perfect. It was his primary weapon and together, they were deadly. He was a crack shot out to around 20 yards, which, for a combat pistol, was downright miraculous. Quite proud of that.

He eased the hammer down and popped the cylinder. Yeah, yeah, he was fully loaded, hadn't shot anything today, but you always check. The Silvertips gleamed back at him. Full magnum 138-grain hotloads, soft tipped, so effective he only needed one. Usually. He closed the cylinder and holstered, setting the butt against his right kidney where he could reach it. John had orangutan arms and the standard hip holster gave him problems.

Small of the back was just the right draw distance, something he'd shown range instructors a thousand times or so, whenever they started berating him about his rig. Sweep. Pull. Roll, hold, sight and squeeze, two rounds, center mass, 7 yards, .5 seconds. Re-holster. They just looked at him and never said another word.

He felt for the quick-release carriers on his belt and thumbed the snaps, dropping one, then the other, of the speed loaders into his hand, putting them back and testing a few more times. Eighteen shots available. If he ever had to use all 18, then he was in big trouble, the kind calling for a big gun.

Which, today, was the mini-14. It was either that or the Mossberg pump and he switched them out randomly, as the mood took him. He was more partial to the 14 so it made the trip a little more often, slung around his back. Not that it was any more effective that the .12, just a bit lighter and carried a lot more rounds, 60 altogether, two thirty-shot clips, one loaded, one in his pocket. For the .12, he carried five pumpkin balls loaded and about 20 loose ones in the backpack. Significantly fewer rounds but, hey, you really didn't need that many when just one will split a man in half. He used the .357 for quick reaction shots and only went to the heavies when he saw something in the distance. Or if he was in such deep doo-doo he needed the firepower. Shotgun, 14, at that point, it didn't matter.

He was a damn good shot with either, very fast acquiring targets and stitching them – .223, slugs, didn't matter. He could hit pretty accurately up to 50 yards with the .14. No brag, just fact. Fortunately, he didn't have to do a lot of long range sniping because most encounters were surprises and usually just a few yards apart.

His last long range fight was about a year ago, some guy he saw crouched on top of a car pile-up on the shoulder of 395, aiming a rifle up to where John would have crested the hill if he had actually been on 395 at the time. One of the benefits of paralleling on Van Dorn.

John had dropped the Zap and climbed the berm and braced the .14 across the top of a Cadillac. One shot, blew the guy right off the cars. John worked his way to him but the man was dead, shot through the back. Pretty good, pretty good. He felt no qualms. It was an ambush and John was pretty sure Mom's son John was the object. Why was immaterial. Damn Bundys.

Lots of times, John didn't take either long gun, relying just on the pistol. The long guns were a real pain on the Zap, even though he'd jury-rigged a pretty good sling system that kept them up and to his left side, out of the way of the backpack and the bike frame, while still allowing a quick draw. They were heavy, though, and they still made MPD skittish. Well, gonna have to deal, because, after Cassell, John'd be carrying the heavies for quite a while.

He pulled out the night-vision goggles, strapped them on and flipped the switch. Yep, batteries still good. The world lit up in green, somewhat tiresome on a two-hour ride home and he had green spots before his eyes for about an hour after, but it was the only way to go. You saw everything long before it saw you.

Wheeled panther, that's what he was, silent, unnoticed. Not a bad analogy. There'd been several instances when he'd ridden up on a group of idiots, probably Raiders, without being detected. Stopped, unslung the rifle, watched for a bit, then either waited them out or went around, unseen. The panther fades away, dangerous, and you got lucky. Or he got lucky.

John grinned and turned off the goggles and propped them on his head. He checked the tanto, strapped handle down to his upper inside arm for a one-motion draw and cut. The Japanese made blades to go along with their blade philosophy – penetrate and then slice out – and John's tanto could cut through iron. He practiced with it quite a bit, a miniature samurai sword, and he was confident he could do some real damage but face it, the tanto was last resort. If he was reduced to drawing it for his life, then he'd pretty much lost and was taking as many with him as he could.

Down the body now and he checked the pistol strapped to his leg, a Raven Arms MP-25, a silly looking thing, silver with smooth wooden grips. He'd bought it for Theresa in Florida in 1979 and it was fine for her but ill-suited for him. The handle barely fit halfway down his palm and it was accurate for maybe 7 yards, but he carried it, anyway.

Everyone scorned .25s but they were actually quite powerful up close and John had cut off the tops of his rounds, making them into crude hollow points. He had the Raven in a quick release Velcro holster strapped to the upper part of his calf. Strategic. Everybody looked for an ankle holster but they usually didn't check higher up. It was his someone-got-the-drop-on-me gun.

So, he's caught; slash with the tanto, roll out the .25, back in business. He patted the holster through his pants legs. You have to think of these things.

Quite a load, all this, back and forth to work every day, the hardware, water and food, other crap, while still wearing the requisite suit and tie. Made you weary. Guess old age was telling. Yeah, he was in great shape, but no amount of exercise and vitamin pills can stave off the days. He ought to give very serious thought to retiring.

He smiled grimly. Not yet, not yet. There were far too many punks running around far too many neighborhoods, all of them in desperate need of summary execution, for him to quit. Besides, geezerness was an advantage. Punks underestimated middle-aged has-beens, not knowing that treachery and experience, like a finely aged wine, overcomes youth and speed every single damn time. John was an unpleasant surprise, a sudden and very violent life lesson. The punks draped over the hedges were his cautionary tales.

All right, Mr. Fearless Middle Aged Superman, let's go home.

John stood at the door, peering out the glass and examining the area out front before pushing through with the Zap. He dodged the barrels up the ramp and then looked carefully about, using peripheral vision to detect motion.

Nothing, a few random birds, so he mounted the Zap and adjusted everything. Not quite dark enough for the NVGs so he left them on top of his head. He kicked the pedal forward and began a slow, laborious coast down the road. He wouldn't flip on the motor until he had a rhythm going somewhere down Nebraska, and, before that, he'd do a little counter surveillance. He got to the intersection and abruptly stopped, right in the middle of Newark Avenue. He turned quickly and scrutinized the area, but nothing.

Man. Cassell.

This lifestyle made one inordinately paranoid he knew, but as that old saw noted, just because you're paranoid doesn't mean they're not out to get you. Someone was out to get him. Someone used Mrs. Alexandria to announce that fact. Who could it be?

John shook his head. The list of suspects was quite large, from pre-Event students he got thrown out of school, to post-Event crapheads whose friends he wasted. Hell, it could be a pissed-off MPD officer, for all he knew. But, hey, why all the theatrics, all the effort? Just come after him.

Sure was unnecessary, doing that to Mrs. Alexandria.

Which means, of course, it was necessary, in the mind of the murderer, anyway. Vicious. Hateful. But necessary. John stroked his paranoia, nourished it, encouraged its growth. He would need it for this one.

A proper crime scene would have helped. He'd process it himself, like he used to, since it was very doubtful any of the current MPDers had his Advanced Forensics. Fingerprints, spatter, tissue and blood samples, an autopsy, send it all off to the lab, presto chango, answers.

He'd at least have the exact cause of death, what specific torturous method finally caused Mrs. Alexandria to expire. Was it the cuts, the shock of the skinning, the continuous rape, or did they just leave her hanging there to bleed to death?

Important to know that 'cause, when he found those guys, he wanted the punishment to fit the crime. Maybe he should just remove their arms and legs and leave them flopping in the road. Or maybe just a bullet to the head, short, merciless, sudden. The shock of realizing that, in the next two seconds, your worthless life ends. Have to give this some thought.

It was getting darker. John looked back at the campus, at the four quad buildings where the Lit and Math departments used to be, right behind the Fletcher Gate and the nice stone "American University" sign planted on the lawn there. The quad had closed for renovation before the Event; all the professors moved into temporary quarters, so it was ghostly even before everything happened.

That made it a good pretend point – it's those few moments of stillness between classes and shuttles. Nothing has happened. Life abounds. It was dark enough to fade the overgrowth, so the pretend actually worked.

You had to pretend every once in a while, if anything, just to remember what life could be. Day over, stuff left for tomorrow, go home. Theresa's there and they'll argue about something stupid and laugh about something stupid and eat dinner and watch TV and call Collier at 2130. Yeah, that life.

Life.

John shook himself out of it, dropped the goggles and switched them on, alert. Pretending made you inattentive and bad guys had an amazing knack of catching you right in the middle of that. The momentary shock of green light disoriented him, as usual, and he blinked to get back focus and right there, just on the edge of Gray Hall, a flicker. He went cold and stone and deadly.

Straddling the Zap in the middle of the road looking at a green world, his hand welded to the cool Pacmyers, he calculated distance and drop and wind and nearby cover. Get ready.

Ten minutes went by. He did not move, his breathing deep and rhythmic, waiting. Patient, always patient.

Nothing.

Perhaps he imagined it. Middle Aged Superman he was, but, c'mon, he was nearsighted to begin with, so maybe it was nothing but an eye artifact. Still, the movement had been peripheral, and he trusted that, and his cop senses were nudging him a bit, too, so ....

Let's wait a little more.

Were the Bundys stalking him? He frowned. That was out of character. They preferred unsuspecting or innocent targets, and he was neither. Perhaps they wanted a bigger challenge. He smiled grimly – bring it on, mofos.

Yet, no shot rang out. Maybe they didn't have night vision, a thought John immediately discarded. Always assume your enemy is better equipped than you. Besides, how else would they know he was standing here, prepared to put two in the chest of anyone betraying the slightest hint of movement?

Another ten minutes.

Nothing. Nothing at all.

Spidey sense was still tingling, though, and perhaps he should dismount, steal back under cover, and see what's behind the four quad buildings. Yeah. Perhaps he should.

But he really, really didn't want to. He wanted to go home. He wanted a beer. He had things to do. Like pretending.

So, what, look or not look? John went through a fast and calculated cost/benefits analysis. On one hand, he'd know, either way, if his suspicions were true. But, other hand, they'll be here tomorrow, a little more careless because they'll think he missed them. They'll get a little more confident. They'll get bolder. They'll get stupid. They'll die. Right now, they're ready for him, even if he made a surprise move. Tomorrow, they wouldn't be so ready.

Patience. No need to force anything. John made one last and intensive survey of the area to be sure, but nothing.

Okay.

He turned and pedaled down the street.

* * *

John was at the bottom of River Road, just past where it joined Canal for the big sweep past the hollow and echoing remains of Georgetown University. This was a good spot. The Potomac was to the right and offered a clean sweep all the way to the Key Bridge and the MPD checkpoint. He could see everything from here. And he could see that something was wrong.

It had taken him ten minutes or so to get to this point, a pretty quiet ten minutes, actually. He'd stopped at random, checked his 6, checked ahead, double-checked at the Field School when he lugged the Zap over the berm.

Hadn't seen a thing but he'd remained wary until he got to the top of Foxhall with its steep angle down to here, the most thrilling part of the ride, and goosed the Zap, big stupid grin on his face because there were no wrecks in the way and he could just whip down the road. He'd been in mid-thrill descent when he looked up, focused on the distant checkpoint and noticed how dead it was. Immediately he disengaged the Zap's drive and pulled an emergency stop with the brakes squealing a little too loud for comfort.

No movement. No white helmeted figure sauntering down the bridge out to the limit of the Kleigs, no black clad figure leaning over the bridge and peeing into the river. No signs of life.

That was really odd.

He'd watched the bridge for about five minutes with the NVGs but the Kleigs were too bright, causing the goggles to bloom, so he'd pulled them up and watched naked. And there was just nothing. Maybe they were sleeping up there, the sergeant curled up and snoring away in the booth while his two privates racked out in the car.

John shook his head. No, no way. MPD was too professional and, besides, they had roving sergeants who showed up at random times and probably shot officers caught sleeping on duty. Who'd risk it? And it was just too early. Maybe if this was mid shift.

What's going on?

Assume Raiders. They're the only ones bold and big enough to take out the bridge guys, if indeed the bridge guys had been taken out and were not sleeping or playing poker or jacking off. Further assume said Raiders were still here, idly setting up an ambush for innocent, unsuspecting passersby, such as oh, say, John.

Hmm. So the movement he saw at Gray Hall was the spotter, and he'd radioed ahead to let them know John was on the way. This is how they want to do it, huh?

Fine.

Time to see who's who, time for you Raiders to get a lesson in strategy and tactics. Like this stupid ambush. Raiders were overall antsy and one of them was going to move or sneeze and reveal their position. Then they all die.

John smiled maliciously, anticipating. No rush. Let's see what they do.

They did nothing. More than enough time passed for some idiot Raider to cough or giggle or pop his head over the bridge railing and now *he* was getting antsy. Had they developed some discipline? Not bloody likely. So, maybe there's no ambush at all. Maybe they're all gone. When you think about it, John old boy, pretty stupid to wait around for the inevitable MPD reaction. And maybe even more stupid, John old boy, to think you were the object of some elaborate ambush.

It could be, John, that you're not even a consideration.

He grinned at that. Yeah, maybe he was giving himself a central role the circumstances didn't support. Whatever was going on at the bridge, John was spectator, not participant.

So let's spectate.

John eased the brakes and re-engaged the drive, gliding silently towards M Street. He dropped the goggles and stared intently at the Georgetown Hill because it was a grand sniper position, but didn't get any vibes. Nothing from the C and O Canal on his right, either. The only sound was his wheels. Just before *The Exorcist* steps, he stopped, frowning, cocked his head and listened. He'd heard something else besides the wheels.

Yes, there, faint and fleeting and irregular, something you'd pass off as an approaching storm in normal times. A mutter, an underlying rumble.

Distant gunfire.

A mile or so up M Street, interspersed with the random, muted sounds of distant tumult.

Well, now that's disturbing. John lifted the NVGs and peered up M Street, keeping the checkpoint Kleigs out of his line of sight. Off to the left, a faint glow with a yellowish cast to it, probably fire. He squinted but couldn't make out any detail.

What the hell is going on?

John watched for a while, trying to make sense of it. Obviously, the checkpoint guys had gone up there to help out, so it must be pretty serious. It seemed far away, but if he was getting this much input, must be pretty big.

So, let's go see. John dropped the NVGs and readjusted

to the green world, examining the street as it climbed past the bridge and over the crest of the hill. The distant glow was more pronounced and he figured it was just past Wisconsin, so he'd haul the Zap up 35th Street, that god-awful steep cobblestoned throwback to horse and buggy days, right at the bridge there, and weave through the neighborhoods until he could see what was happening ...

Spidey sense went off.

There was some kind of wrong movement coming from his left rear. John turned, unsnapping the .357 and sweeping the area with it, automatically adjusting the grips deep into his hand. Gently, slowly, he got off the bike and set it down on the asphalt and then stepped away so it wouldn't trip him. He crouched, the pistol up before his green gaze, sight picture acquired, ready to go.

There was a short plain next to the road that abruptly turned into the Georgetown Hill. It was completely over-grown, from the Exxon station to the abandoned, ivy-covered dorms on top. Something was going on up there, some less-than-audible disturbance. Flanking movement, so an ambush, after all.

Okay. Not the best of positions, because he was rather exposed here, but it would have to do. Moving onto the C and O berm would get him a bullet in the back. Just stay here, just get ready. They've given themselves away, so now they'll do something stupid, fire a wild shot or come charging down the hill. Something.

And yep, there it was, scrambling sounds. Thank God for predictability. John cocked the trigger and started tracking the noise. Geez, guys, why don't you sound a couple of trumpets while you're at it? He blinked. The scrambling was frantic and loud, way too loud for an ambush. What were those idiots doing? They were either stoned or stupid and John put a hand down to a Speedloader because it sounded like quite a crowd. The scrambling became more frantic and there was movement in the underbrush and John stared, puzzled, because it sounded like escape, not attack.

It was. A deer leaped over the top underbrush, startling him and almost causing him to shoot. It was a buck, quite an impressive specimen with a rack of antlers to make the Boone and Crockett Club salivate.

It balanced itself on the decline but lost traction and started tumbling down the hill. Seven or eight dogs burst out of the same area and flew after it, overrunning the deer before it could regain control. John watched. The buck threw its rack at the first dogs, catching a couple of them and ripping one open and John started rooting for the buck. But the odds were too great and the buck was engulfed.

It fought down to the last moment, the biggest dog forcing its way through the flailing hoofs and antlers and locking onto its throat. With savage jerks, the big dog tore the buck apart, green blood spraying in John's goggles and maddening the other dogs more. The buck shuddered and lay still.

The dogs began feeding, snapping and snarling at each other for position. John watched more than he should and a couple of the dogs looked towards him. He wasn't worried because one shot would scatter them all but one shot would also reveal his position so probably best to move along. He eased the hammer forward and tracked the dogs for intent, but they stayed put.

John hoisted the Zap, did a scan, and then pedaled slowly up to the bridge turn-off, pistol ready. He turned off the NVGs because of the Kleigs and studied the approach. Nothing, so he pedaled onto the bridge and dismounted. He examined the guard shack while the generator hummed and the Kleigs popped.

No one here, all of the equipment gone, although there was a backpack thrown up against a corner, probably forgotten in the haste to get at whatever was happening up

M Street. John left it alone. The owner would probably need it before the night's out.

John walked over to the Georgetown side of the bridge and listened. The tumult faded in and out with the wind. Some kind of big battle, he figured, and he really should go over there and see. He should. Really.

He didn't move. The Kleigs bounced off the Potomac below and he watched the reflections for a bit. Be a little startling if a crew zipped by, their oars in rhythm and the guy up front calling cadence. He smiled at that and imagined Georgetown students by the dozens suddenly appearing and walking briskly along the pedestrian bridge between the Rosslyn metro and the dorms. That would be great. It would mean nothing had happened, that the past few years had been a dream. Wake up, John.

He looked over the Whitehurst towards the Georgetown Mall. All you could see were the corners lit by the Kleigs. Nothing moved and there were no sounds except for the drift from whatever was happening farther along. He really should go up there and help. He should. Really. But he just watched the dead buildings.

After a bit, he walked back to the Zap, mounted, and rode through the baffles, stopping just before mid-span. He looked back. The battle sounds had faded; whatever was going on over there was resolving.

Tomorrow, he'd ask about it. Whoever's here will give him an exaggerated version of events. He'll listen quietly and sort out what's probably true from the rest of the crap, nod gravely and exchange grim conclusions with the sergeant.

Assuming, of course, a sergeant, hell, anyone – will actually be here tomorrow.

Go look?

No. Go home.

He snapped the goggles back on and coasted down the bridge's crest towards Rosslyn.

16

The 395 had its advantages. The dead cars and trucks provided a lot of cover. Yeah, they did so for ambushers, too, but not at night. The NVGs saw to that. Besides, the LRT hill was just a delight and he loved to get a good head of steam past the Pentagon and take it at full speed, repressing the urge to scream his joy as the Zap accelerated all the way to the bottom. There were a lot of cars here but there was a clear path beside them and they became blurs as he whipped by.

His momentum carried him halfway up the Landmark Hill, where he kicked in the motor to ease the ascent. At the top he paused, slipped off the Zap, and settled behind a pickup truck, resting the 14 across the hood and zeroing in on the opposite crest. Time to surprise his tail.

He was being followed. No doubt of that. He'd seen too many odd movements during his double backs. He'd sped up and slowed down and made unexpected turnarounds to verify and, yes, definitely, being tailed. They were good, better than the usual bumbling idiots, but it was hard to stay hidden from a pro like John.

Speeding down the slope had worked double duty, giving him a good old-fashioned thrill while panicking the tail. They'd have to catch up, which meant they'd hurry and get sloppy and they'd silhouette against the night sky, just for a moment, but that's all he needed. Sure, it was too far away for an accurate shot, but, at the very least, he'd scare the bejesus out of them.

Enough stars showed through the clouds to power the goggles and he was feeling very confident. This should be fun. Idly, he glanced at the pickup's cab. Nope, no skulls grinning at him. They must have got out, frustrated with the traffic jam, and taken their chances walking, ending up in the skeleton pile at the Woodbridge rest stop. But, then again, could be Survivors. Could even be the guys following him. Laws of Irony held primacy here, so why not?

He traced the line of cars down the hill and back up the other crest. Every one of them was jammed bumper to bumper with doors thrown open at paced intervals, like an Escher drawing, pulling you to the distance.

Seen in green, it was almost aesthetic. Even the wrecks had symmetry, nine to ten cars piled together at pleasing angles, burnt down to the frames and forming a rather stark sculpture. Civilization in Death Throes #9. He grinned. Be a shame if the government came in here and cleaned up all this art.

Government. Ha.

John shook his head. Let's not dignify the thugs and idiots currently running the country with that title, shall we? The first president was, what, some third or fourth level Department of Agriculture manager, who was examining grain silos or some such nonsense in Indiana when everybody else back here died? Number 9324, or thereabouts, down the succession list, and that's all well and good for continuity of government crap but John didn't buying an agronomist as the leader of the Free World. Apparently, no one else did either, because there'd been how many presidents since?

"Who's the president this week?"

"You are!" he chuckled.

Now General Whatshisname, the Chief of Staff, some kickass NORAD guy from Cheyenne Mountain, that's a leader. Somebody ruthless enough to blow up the part of the world needing it. Somebody power-mad enough to consolidate the military under him and browbeat Sam Drucker and his myriad successors into launching a worldwide revenge-fest. Funny, he remained Chief of Staff through all the revolving door administrations.

Or, not funny, testament. A martinet with his hands on the weapons while the milksop-of-the-week gave him legal cover, not the most ideal of situations but at least things were gettin' done. And that was good.

Or not. John was ambivalent. He was all for the on-going retaliation, the beating-the-bejesus out of the towelheads, the wholesale burying of the Middle East, the slaughtering of populations, the lamentations of the women.

Good deal. But that's all supposed to happen over there. You're not supposed to use those same tactics here, General. Draft Gangs and military courts and martial law and rumors of concentration camps ... a bit overboard, don'cha think?

Granted, widespread anarchy required strong measures but, hey, General, you seem to have things under control, well at least Outside. Couldn't really say that about here, where the only government was accurate rifle fire. Still, you should count your blessings, General. And tone down the sadism.

Like the way the General abandoned DC. A month, two, After, sending in the military Hazmat teams, packing everything up, taking it all away. Had to admit, very efficient.

John happened to be at CDC's Mall lab when the teams first hit the area. He was still driving the Pathfinder up there; that's how early it was. He watched helicopters land on the White House lawn and a heavy-weapons platoon deploy. Several OD trucks roared up Pennsylvania Avenue and their crews went inside and carted out bodies.

John followed them around the rest of the day, curious. They loaded up the Archives and the files from the Federal Reserve, some bodies from the Capitol, piled up the things they didn't want, including a lot of anonymous dead clerks, and burned them. They left the Smithsonians alone. John wondered about that but figured the General had no need for treasures, just legitimacy.

Some other Survivors gathered near the Supreme Court and made moves like they wanted to get in those trucks. The platoon rifle-clubbed a few of them. They shot a few more. A helicopter came in from some other job and strafed the ones who wouldn't go away. John was aghast. That was back when things made him aghast.

Over the next three days, John, staying far out of range, watched the wholesale dismantling of the entire city. Everything that made DC, DC, they hauled off. The teams killed anyone who got in the way, even ones who didn't. They seemed to enjoy that.

John stood at the Washington Monument and watched until the last truck convoyed out, and then he went home. That was that – except for the Pentagon this morning, which was probably an afterthought.

A stake through the heart. They were already Off Limits. Even before John recovered, the army had armed patrols from Winchester to the New York border, shooting anybody attempting to cross in or out. Lead poisoning, one popular joke went, after beating the Al-Qaeda Flu!

John smirked. We Americans are a humorous people.

He figured the restrictions would, eventually, be lifted and he could go see Collier. But the Big Bugout pretty much killed that idea – if they were taking away all the symbols, then no one was planning to come back here. Or let anybody out. Ever.

Just as well. The CDC thought they were all carriers. The last thing John wanted was to hug Collier and then nurse him over the next three to five days as he drowned in his own fluids. He'd already done that with his mom.

The Gates came a little bit later, more proof of General Whoozit's sadism. John heard about them from the CDC. One of the techs told him the Army was organizing a big refugee camp somewhere out on the DMZ, the strip of land running about a mile on either side of 81 from Winchester down.

That didn't make any sense. "Why are they putting it way the hell out there? Everybody left alive is here," he said.

"Yeah," the tech agreed, carefully handling a hypodermic so he wouldn't puncture his suit, "but they're afraid of the Flu."

Really? Weren't too afraid to come in here and ransack the place, ya know. More likely, the CDC wheedled the General into it. Self-interest, of course, a huge pool of lab rats conveniently located where teams could get in and out with relative safety. So, General, build the Gates, please, pretty please. Might get a cool new bioweapon out of it.

John hunkered down so he wouldn't appear as some weird hood ornament, should the stalkers also have NVGs.

Ah, the CDC. They were nice in the beginning. John had been driving to Home Depot when one of their vans came off the Mixing Bowl and pulled up next to him, which was quite the surprise. John had just started moving around and hadn't seen anybody yet.

They were really happy to find him because they thought the Flu was 100% mortal and here was a genuine Survivor. They looked like aliens in their Hazmat suits, and John had a sense of the surreal as he submitted to their proddings and fluid-draws and question-naires. But, hey, anything to help and they seemed so good, so interested. John supposed that, initially, they were.

But didn't take long for things to get nasty, his first clue being the Colonel Storm episode. Turned out there were about 15,000 Survivors, give or take, in the immediate Metro area. Some of those never even got the sniffles, and they became of primary interest. But the Immunes didn't want to be turned into laboratory specimens and the CDC didn't react well to that. They started kidnapping Immunes and shipping them, kicking and screaming in locked plastic tubes, out of the area.

Gate rumors put the Immunes in Atlanta, slowly being dissected, alive. John didn't know if that was true, but it was a measure of how bad things were that he couldn't afford to disbelieve it. You want to stay alive, you avoid the CDC.

Which was hard to do, since they pretty much ran the Gates. When those first got organized, CDC spokesmen went on the radio and TV and urged everyone to show up. They had supplies and medicine and food and, most importantly, doctors and communication, so, please, fellow citizens of these damaged lands, come.

John went, although it was somewhat pointless since he had most of what they were promising. He and Collier had already spoken a couple of times by then and he was setting up the house so he had no real reason to go. Reason didn't have much to do with it. The nation's wounded were being called and in a very hopeful tone. Who could resist?

His Gate was on the Route 50 bridge southeast of Winchester, spanning the Shenandoah, pretty convenient for the Army, because the river formed a natural barrier between Outside and the Zone, but not so convenient for him because, man, quite the drive. Bill told him the Army had put up confinement walls pretty much along the river's whole meandering course.

John didn't go look because ZeeGees shoot on general principle, more opportunities for lead poisoning. They had remote controlled mines, too, and quick reaction forces ready to swoop down on any man-sized motion alarm anywhere along the river ... well, according to Bill, anyway. John took his word for it.

ZeeGees were ruthless. The poor bastards at Middletown found that out. The Gate's site wasn't fixed at first, could have been anywhere from Winchester to Front Royal and Middletown, appropriately enough, seemed the middle course. The townsfolk, good Americans all, opened their streets to the first wave of refugees, built shelters, housed them in parlors, provided food and medicine.

When the engineers finally settled on the route 50 bridge, everyone was driven in at the point of a ZeeGee bayonet, including the Middletowners, who were just too exposed to too many Survivors to make the General comfortable. All of them died. That's what you bastards get for being good neighbors.

That's what you other bastards get for being the victims of a terrorist attack. We, the new government, have arbitrarily decided no one's leaving and no one's coming in. You damn people are too damn infected, a bunch of pus bags. Some of you bastards got out before anyone knew what was happening and managed to kill off a lot of nice little Midwest towns, no doubt including the General's. So shut up. We'll bring you food and movies and let the Lizards wave at you from the opposite bank, but that's it. The CDC is here to help, hardy har har. Stay away from the perimeter and be grateful we don't napalm your asses.

Yeah, grateful.

John had been staring at the rise for a good ten minutes now and his eyes were starting to hurt. That was the problem with NVGs; they were really hard on you. He wondered how army patrols could wear them all night long. Strength of youth, he supposed. Bet they developed severe eye problems down the road, although he'd never heard of a study. Doubt he ever would, since there were so many more pressing issues. Point was, he couldn't stay here much longer. Ten minutes more, then go. He glanced at his watch to mark it.

Waiting in ambush. John shook his head. This was getting to be a habit. Man at his worst – ugly, murderous, craven. The pathetic stayed at the Gate and the ugly, murderous and craven drifted back, with an almost immediate effect – the looting changed from the collection of necessary supplies to wholesale smashing and burning.

That time, that period, God, it was unbelievable. John had drifted back too, in front of the murderous vanguard, with as little hope as they, but at least he had a house needing work. He'd been parked near the Springfield interchange musing over what else to collect, when a gang of Vandals suddenly burst into the Springfield Mall parking lot and started burning it down, store by store.

What the hell? John was astonished. "There's stuff we need in there, you idiots!" He'd jumped out of the truck, completely enraged. "What's wrong with you?" he'd screamed from the corner.

Seemed a pertinent question, then. There was still a modicum of reason, then. But he knew the answer even before he asked it – because. Just because. Because this wasn't life but a movie, *Escape from New York*, and there ain't no gettin' out and no rules and screw you, man. Screw everything.

That was his first real firefight, The Mall Apocalypse.

There were about fifteen of them, a pretty large group for Vandals (maybe they were a budding gang, who knew?) and they were scattered around the Target entrance. They'd turned after he screamed, startled, but then one of them started laughing at him.

Big mistake.

John whipped up the 14 and dropped six before they reacted, and dropped five more as they ran like hell. Only two of them made any show of resistance, firing wildly back with pathetic little 9 mils, but he was far out of range for those POS and John just blew them apart.

Then the rage took him.

While the mall burned and smoke blew out the daylight and turned it into Judgment Day, John strung up the bodies at various points around the parking lot.

Medieval, but it felt right. Right. So he moved across the landscape and, all day and all night, shots and screams and explosions and demonic laughter on the wind, wherever he went.

He sought Bundys and Vandals, and if they did anything, smashed one bottle, slapped one woman, he gunned them down and hoisted them up on streetlamps after pinning a handwritten warning notice – "Get out of Springfield!"– to their chests with whatever sharp instrument he could find.

It was Biblical. It was insane.

The rage was a fire, white hot and searing. John could not get his hands on Al-Qaeda but could damn sure find their offspring, the robbing, murdering Bundys and Vandals and gangs, ever-present lowlife trailer trash scum buckets, getting their kicks out of cruelty and evil.

He was Moloch and Valkyrie and the Four Horsemen, spreading death and vengeance in a swath of blood and justice and all he remembered was the white hot rage.

He came to himself at some point about three days

later. He was in Alexandria wiping out the remnants of some Mohawk-haired pieces of crap, who had dragged out some kid from a hiding place and spent a few hours raping him in the street and then cutting off various limbs for sport.

John'd shot the kid to put him out of his misery and then, one by one, caught the Mohawks and burned them alive. He just sat in the street over the ashes of the last two, not moving, not doing anything, just sitting.

He was spent, used up, the rage gone. He could die now, his three-day frenzy nothing more than another murder tally on a sheet so vast, motive and intent no longer mattered.

Or, he could do something else. The dying was very attractive but then what would happen to Collier? They hadn't met at the Gate yet because travel was still impossible for him. So, abandon your son to this New Order and just put a bullet through the skull and go look for Theresa? She would never forgive him for that. Even more, she would never forgive him for leaving a job undone.

A job undone. You are a law enforcement officer in a land of anarchy. You are commissioned to patrol a specific location and defend it.

So, let's defend it. He'd brushed off the human ashes that still clung to him and went home and finished up the last petty details of the house and the neighborhood and then got up at 0600 on a Monday and went to the campus.

He dusted off his desk, set up some generators and battery powered lights, turned on a computer, got papers and pens and folders, and started patrolling. They hadn't set up the Key Bridge checkpoint yet, he hadn't found the Alexandrias yet, it was all still pretty early, in the beginning of things. And here he was, years later, still at it.

Why?

Mission. Simply, mission.

The ratio of decent to craven seemed to be 1 to 100, taking into account the Families and Metro and the few Loners who evinced some level of civilized behavior. Given the numbers and applying the proper formula, let's see, we have 1500 decent people living here. That left 13,500 assholes (ignoring attrition and wildly inaccurate population counts).

Not good odds. So, General, you bastard, you heartless bastard, maybe you're right to keep us locked in. We are murderous in here, we are savages, and we carry the germ of total destruction in our blood. Everything you fear is here. Keep us contained. Keep the pestilence in. Let us kill and rape each other, until the last shreds of anything good turn to a rotted corpse. John set his jaw.

Not if he could help it.

"That makes me one of the decent, huh?" John whispered to himself and smiled. Here he was, hunched behind a pickup truck in ambush. How decent was that?

Pretty.

By Outside standards, he was just a vigilante, but John rejected that. First, he was a duly constituted authority. He had a badge, after all. Second, he never thought vigilantism odious. In a frontier situation, the decent sometimes had to get medieval on your ass, just to maintain some decency. Lynch mobs, while a bit uncontrolled, had good instincts. And you couldn't get much more frontier than the present situation, so he wasn't a lone wolf rabid avenger, meting out arbitrary punishment. He was just bypassing a host of middlemen, like courts and judges and appeals. Efficient.

And, thanks to the General, Outside standards didn't even apply anymore. No doubt, the hippie ghosts would tell John his actions perpetuated the state of lawlessness and that he should be spending his considerable energies reestablishing structure and the Rule of Law.

He chuckled. Love to. The crapheads seem to have different ideas, though.

"Then you must talk to them," the hippie ghost hunching next to him muttered.

"What are you doing way out here?" John asked.

"I go where needed," the hippie ghost nodded.

John snorted. "You're not needed here."

"I am more needed here than anywhere."

"How do you figure?"

The hippie ghost pointed down the road, "You are about to kill your fellow man."

"My fellow man is about to kill me."

"You do not know that."

"It's a pretty good guess."

"But you still don't know." HG made a dramatic gesture at his chest, "It may be their intentions are pure. Maybe they seek your wisdom, your companionship, a return of the human community. You will not know until you talk to them!" HG pointed skyward.

John shook his head and adjusted the rifle. "That's why you're now extinct."

"No." Dramatic head shake. "If you thugs had spoken to Al-Qaeda, listened to their grievances, made adjustments, were truly remorseful ..." dramatic sweep of the hand across the ghost landscape. Sheesh. What was it with this guy and dramatic gestures? "... none of this would have happened."

John chuckled. "Let me ask you a question. Do you believe in God?"

HG said nothing.

"Thought not. Okay, so you believe in evolution."

"It seems the more plausible explanation."

"Well, how progressive and open-minded of you. Tell me, then, hippie, why you won't apply it."

"I apply it all the time. I see the advance of man from

brute to sophisticate, across the sweep of history."

John shook his head, "No, you don't. First of all, sophisticate?" and he made his own dramatic gesture over the wrecked landscape.

"That's because of people like you," HG said smugly.

"We'll leave that argument for later, but, stay with me. Your evolution theory is pretty convenient, right? It means there's no God so there's no one you have to be responsible to, right?"

"We have to be responsible to society. It is the evolved method of our collective survival."

"Really? Yet you advocated unbridled drug use, sex with everyone, defiance of authority, do what makes you feel good, right? Doesn't sound very responsible."

HG shook his head. "You don't understand. The secure society allows self-actualization."

John laughed. "Yeah, that. But, what you don't get, your irresponsibility is the direct ancestor of your evolution."

HG just blinked at him, so John continued. "Whose genes got passed along? The rapists, that's who, the ones who stole their neighbor's eggs and replaced it with their own, and the ones who murdered and ate the passive lizards and subjugated the neighborhood. That's who we are."

"Those were in ancient times."

"Don't say? As ancient as, oh, what? Fifty years ago? World War II? Did you hear about that?"

HG stared at him. "And from those ashes, a greater world community arose."

"Yeah," John nodded towards the highway, "I can see that."

There was no answer and John looked around. HG was gone. He smirked. Figures. They always ran when the argument got too much.

The argument, though, had distracted and John

133

frowned, studying the opposite ridge. Still nothing, and that was wrong. Were they flanking along Van Dorn? John glanced nervously over there, suddenly feeling exposed. Damn HG, trying to get me killed? Well, enough of this. John no longer felt confident, and that meant a change of position was needed. Slowly, he crouched over the Zap and righted it. He checked the area and then made a run below the line of cars, using them as shields until he suddenly popped out on the shoulder and began pedaling fast, engaging the motor at the same time. He half expected a shot to ring out, but nothing. Had he evaded them?

He didn't think so.

17

Home. Late. Too late. No, wrong adjective. *Very* late. Yeah, that was better. Let's hope it wasn't *too* late. John shook his head then froze. Idiot! Don't give yourself away!

He was at the edge of his property, where the east corner touched the sidewalk. The honeysuckle bush here had gone native and draped and rolled and pushed its away along the fence and ground, giving him perfect cover. That is, if he didn't do stupid things like shake his head ruefully while peering out between some breaks he'd made in the brush. Good spot to examine the street from, or to take a bullet between the eyes, if you keep making stupid moves like that.

He was off rhythm, out of his routine, and John didn't like it. Paranoia was screwing things up. Instead of turning on the power, checking the pool, feeding the dogs and talking to Theresa, he'd put the Zap in the backyard shed and immediately come out here. It was already a couple of hours past his normal schedule – setting an ambush every mile or so had greatly extended the commute. Frustrating, because he hadn't seen any hint of his followers since talking to HG. That didn't mean they weren't still following.

There was a wrongness in the air. John didn't believe in any of that psychic, precognitive crap, but something was certainly tugging at his pants cuffs, and it wasn't just Lupus or Hairbag, either.

Both dogs were pressed against him, highly unusual,

especially for Hairbag, who was stand-offish from the beginning and never really warmed up. Now, here she was, giving off little growls and whines every time Snuffy barked from inside the house.

Damn Snuffy. That dog was too verbal, which was why he remained the Inside Dog. Hairbag and Lupus were more street savvy and only bayed at the proper times, like when that pack came out of the woods, or when they had a deer in full flight. They did respond to Snuffy on occasion, just to let the Inside Dog know he wasn't 'all that.'

But, not now. They felt the tension. John wondered if it was pheromones, something they picked up from him, or borne on the wind from something that approached.

Whatever, everybody was uneasy. John stared down the street, listening more than looking. He wasn't sure how much of a charge was left in the NVGs so he had turned them off. Would be just great to see the greenish outline of some Raiders emerging from the woods and then have the things crap out. Better to listen. If he heard some thrashing, he could drop the NVGs then drop whoever approached.

A good plan, but John wondered if he should go somewhere else. Engaging from here would reveal his base.

So maybe he should move to one of the blockhouses, like the one down on the corner of Harwood. It backed to the woods and would be a great place to counter-ambush.

John considered. He had an M-60 with 400 rounds, one M-16 with 1200 rounds, one 12 gauge with 100 shells, 25 hand grenades, 5 LAW rockets, and one Beretta M9 pistol with 500 rounds sitting in there. Thank God for Ft. Belvoir. He had sandbagged the four corner windows into fighting positions and had three cases of water and MREs, a Coleman, flashlights and batteries, other survival stuff like matches and blankets and even stacks of Daily Wear contacts and eyeglasses in there, too. He was geared for a siege.

If, somehow, the jerk-o's coming through the woods survived his onslaught and counterattacked, he could retreat through his pre-planned escape route to one of the other blockhouses, like the one on Kenmont or down on Heather Court or across the street on the Harwood extension, all similarly equipped, and fight on.

Sounded like a plan and John made some half motions towards Harwood, but stopped himself. If he went to Harwood, he'd sit there all night, and he was irritated enough with his now-broken routine. He'd be too tired to go to work in the morning and he really needed to go. How else would he find out what happened up M Street? John frowned.

"Boy, you really can't stand one thing out of place, can you?" Theresa chortled from behind him.

"Don't start," John warned, "I gotta concentrate."

As usual, she ignored him. "I mean, really, you used to get so upset if you left the house at 8:01 instead of 8 on the dot. And, oh geez, don't let me suggest a spur-of-the-moment night out if you didn't have your clothes ready for the next day yet."

"Okay, I'm a putz. One of my endearing qualities."

She giggled and faded away and John smiled. She was right. A slave to routine, which was why he would blow off Harwood and start his nightly ritual, late or no. Things felt better in their proper places and, these days, anything that made you feel better was holy. But he should give this a few more minutes. John shifted the .14 below the hedge breaks and peered over it.

A golden glow on the eastern horizon announced moonrise, and, judging by the strength of it, a full one. Hmm. That wasn't good. In about two hours, the whole place would be lit up like a stadium. Made an attack easier and maybe that's what they're waiting for, hunched down in the woods, calculating. John'd lose the dark's advantage, so, really, he should go over to Harwood.

But, really, why? Other than the feeling of wrongness, he had no evidence someone was out there. He hadn't heard anything. It's impossible to make an absolutely silent approach. You're going to stumble across something, some bit of debris or uneven ground or a can or a stick, and any sound in this silence was like a gunshot and John would know and John would move and flank and hit and fade into the night and circle and hit again.

But there'd been nothing like that, not even the usual scurrying of chipmunks and foxes and owls. So, what? Was there someone out there or not?

Trust your gut, his gut said.

Trust your mind, his mind countered.

Damn. He ought to reconsider cameras down Old Keene Mill. For that matter, a couple of them in the woods would be pretty smart, too. That way, he wouldn't have to stand out here straining his ears and having existential arguments with his body parts. But, oh good Lord, what a bitch of a job. That's why he'd rejected the idea in the first place.

Besides, you can get way too dependent on technology. Like right now, John had a suicidal urge to say "Fuck it," stalk off, turn on the Magnum and spend the evening in modern bliss, relying on the motion alarms and low light cameras next door for warning, itchy trigger finger hovering over the Claymore switches, hoping everything works the way he expected.

Sheesh. Imagine if he added more cameras. What a great way to get complacent. What a great way to get killed.

But John, face it, you're gonna get killed anyway. Every day since the Event has been borrowed. That note's coming due. He'd rather it be on his own terms, but the odds weren't too good for that. So, maybe he shouldn't worry so much.

After all, he didn't set up the neighbor's house as early warning but as decoy, last ditch, actually. Hairbag and Lupus were early warning. He glanced down at the dogs. They were damn good early warning, too, well, good enough. They often ran the neighborhood far from the house, and odds were they'd be gone when someone blundered up from Daventry, but so what? Would cameras do any better?

John doubted it. They lacked the personal touch that sound and peripheral vision and Spidey sense provided. How 'bout a motion detector instead, maybe two, with a trip-wired Claymore down towards St. Bernadette's? Yeah, and then he'd know when every deer or dog for ten miles around strolled by. He'd be up fifty times a night and, count on it, each time, it would be Lupus or his partner. No thanks.

Overkill, and meaningless. He was already on alert, without cameras. He'd always be alerted, somehow, if someone approached. The issue was his response more than the knowledge and it was now time to respond. "Guys," John whispered to the dogs, "let's go take a look."

John stepped out of cover, crouching. If someone was out there, they'll shoot, but over John's head because they'd assume he was standing straight up. He'd bead on their position and shoot low, assuming they were prone and, at the very least, throw dirt in their eyes, which would give him a few seconds to race over to the Staley's place and through their back fence onto Old Keene Mill, flanking the ambush. But no one fired. After a minute, John straightened and moved to the front of the fence. He held his breath. Nothing.

The glow in the east intensified, the patch of gold

pointing down to itself, herald of the moon. Dangerous, but man, beautiful, just beautiful.

Flashback. He was fourteen and antsy and trembling with a constant flood of hormones and excitement because he could swear, just swear, peering through the scratched lens of his crappy 60x telescope, last month's birthday gift, that glint he saw on the moon's horizon was the orbiting Command Module and that brightness in the Sea of Tranquility, the Eagle. He waved frantically at the eyepiece. Hey Neal! Hey Buzz! Using the Alabama greetings he'd picked up easily since moving from Oklahoma, hey all y'all! They had to know he saw them.

What a sense of the universe he had that night. Frantic, squinting through crude optics, all the possibilities opened because, sure, no doubt, he was going to walk on the moon, too. And they would be exploring Mars by the time he graduated from college, and nosing around the asteroid belt by the time he entered astronaut training. Cancer would be cured and so would war and poverty and drugs and crime and the human race would stand as one and look knowingly towards the horizon, chin tilted with purpose and hope.

Hope.

John held at the word because he didn't need a derisive snort about now. Dead giveaway. As if moving down the sidewalk cautiously, Lupus pressed against him to the point of impediment and Hairbag a few paces off, wasn't giveaway enough. He moved slowly, listening and looking but distracted by moon glow, taking about ten minutes to reach the front of the Whiting's house, where the road started a descent to the woods. If he moved farther, he'd cut off his view behind, which wasn't good, so he stopped. The trees were still spring-thin and he could see Old Keene Mill down to Daventry. He studied the street. Nothing. *Nada*. Not a twitch, not a strange bulge, no odd flickering. He was beginning to feel somewhat stupid.

Feeling stupid, of course, eased the tension. John relaxed, took in a deep breath and patted Lupus, who wagged his tail. Hairbag ambled up and sniffed the air but didn't react. John looked towards Daventry and then watched the top of the moon break the horizon, huge and golden.

A breeze picked up, moving through the houses and the woods. Details were starting to form in the moon's glow. John looked back. No movement, no sound, no lights, dead, some of the crosses he made poking out of the ivy, white and contrasting with the overgrowth.

Ghost world.

It could be a photograph of a peacefully slumbering neighborhood, caught by some pretentious AU art student who thought the contrast between stillness and architecture a comment on futility. Except a picture conveys some sense of living, at least the potential of it, with a porch light or streetlight on somewhere. Not here. This was ruins – an ancient Greek hillside, once great, no longer.

The only life here was peripheral, just out of sight, a hint of something flitting away, crying and lost in the dark and always out of reach. Alone, dead, a tale of its own tragedy, because it shouldn't be dead. There should be an assurance of life. Everyone just sleeping now but if you wait, you'll see stirrings as the night wears away and people wake and emerge and smile; gather their papers and light cigarettes and wave to each other; children slouch towards school; cars back in and out and service trucks meander while dogs are walked, joggers exercised and sheer, simple movement takes over.

That's what's out of sight, that's what the peripheral ghosts cry over, and there's no use trying to see it anymore, no use remembering and imagining and peopling the dark with shades because they're all gone, and even their traces will vanish in a few years.

Damn, he was depressed.

The moon had cleared the horizon and John turned to it. Still lovely, the warming light of spring, even if it surveyed a silent one. Maybe later John would set up the telescope, the nice 6-inch Meade he got from Featherstone in the mall before the Apocalypse (yes, paid for with a credit card slip) and see if he could locate a bright spot on the Sea of Tranquility. Look for a reminder of old hope. Or maybe he'd turn it to Orion and scrutinize the star factory in the Belt for any new births. Or, straight up, zenith, looking for God.

He was out there somewhere. On the surface of the moon, in the planets' ellipses, the rings, the galaxies, somewhere. Father.

John was no atheist and he couldn't understand why some people proudly were. Look up there, naked eye or optics, and you're watching the entire universe wheel in rhythms and movements that just screamed "Design!"

Astronomers as atheists: incomprehensible. They look up every night, trying to glimpse the borders and beyond but failing because it's just too vast, applying arcane math to powers and actions that leave only a slight hint of themselves, while formulating mind-bending theories about time-bending and light-bending and fractals and speeds and distances. All that overwhelming evidence, God's own signature, and they deny Him. Proof that higher education doesn't necessarily make you smart.

But then, look down the street, pick out a few crosses, dull white against black, and you may have far more proof of randomness, that a few half atoms banging in just the right sequence created all this. Pure chance. Design was nothing more than our subjective ordering of the data while the real world, Plato's world of Forms, was nothing but chaos. We simply choose to see it differently so things remain in sequence and order only because of perception, not God's grace. The world itself doesn't end up collapsing into a massive black hole simply because of the distances involved. Plenty of evidence for that view, and everyone, most everyone, except for the Utah Crazies and the Flailers, seemed to believe that these days. They weren't without argument.

Because God, John's God, powerful and benevolent and caring, could make the universe on reflex, so why couldn't John's God, maybe in a moment of pique or amusement, move a little finger and alter the course of a human's life? Why would it be so hard to nudge a few things at the right time, have a biplane crash into a field and spores be discovered, or make a slight change in blood chemistry so pre-cursers don't pre-curse?

Why? Or why not? A reason. Please.

John deliberately shut off the standard argument of free will and the laws of nature and how God made no exceptions, even if the result led to small crosses poking through weeds. No rationality tonight. No logic. Fathers do not stand idly by and watch their children drown in their own mucus, not if that Father could wave a hand and relieve it.

Well, exception for John's father, who would have stood, arms crossed, next to the bed as John lay in coma, slapping him repeatedly while screaming it was John's own fault, richly deserved because of constant inadequacy. But not The Father. He was better than that.

John hoped.

The moon cleared the horizon and it was a bad moon, Fogarty. It was grinning at him, the eyebrows down, too much in the way of teeth, the evil moon in cartoons. John peered at the woods and the street and still, there was nothing, but the feeling would not go away, the feeling that he had only, for the last few years, delayed the inevitable, lingered too long alive while things leisurely moved in place to put an end to him. A frustrating and painful end, more so because it would be anonymous.

No, not true. You will be remembered.

Collier is the future, Collier is the future, the chant in his mind, mantra, his ward against despair, the reason he would not go into the house and eat the end of the .357.

John's end, whenever and whatever the method, would be in defiance, because, if you can glimpse a possible future, then you cannot give up; on the contrary, you are required to strive. Collier was his glimpse, and he was Collier's. John was the voice out of death, the stirring from annihilation, proof that decay does not win.

If there was no glimmer in the dark then everyone lies down, everyone dies and is buried by the dust and becomes nothing but vague shapes on the landscape; an uninteresting hint that, once, there was something else.

Collier needed the glimmer so John had to stay, had to fight, resist the coming death because Collier must have something to fight for or he will be swallowed whole. And John could not have that.

The moon was three degrees up now, the illusion of bigness dissipating, as was the gold color. Everything settled back to its normal position. Normal.

The hell with this. John turned, no longer taking precautions and headed towards the neighbor's, the dogs trotting with him. Time to fire up the Magnum, do a light check, test everything, settle in, distract himself, forget.

Pretend to, anyway.

* * *

"Hey, baby," John said.

He stood beside Theresa's grave, overgrown like the others down the street, but he had cut a small path through the weeds for access. It wasn't a tell; intruders

144

would focus on the neighbor's house, with its trim lawn and orderly yard. Bait.

"Been a weird day. I'm off schedule, as you know." He told her about Mrs. Alexandria and the bridge and the dogs attacking the deer and M Street. He described his raging paranoia all the way home, something that still gripped him. For the millionth time tonight, he checked the .357, the .25, and the tanto.

He'd already flipped on the Magnum and done a light check, but not the cables or pool yet. Instead he went inside, to Snuffy's great joy, and lost a lot of time watching the monitors, expecting any moment to see someone crashing through the neighbor's door. Nothing.

He stepped quietly outside again, listened for a while, strolled back out to the street and examined the woods now silvered by moon. Still nothing. Hairbag and Lupus were gone, probably running the neighborhood. No barking in the distance, so God knows what they were up to.

It was pretty close to 8:00 p.m. by then, which was the time he normally ended the chores and stood here, so he'd decided to interrupt the flow. You can futz with the chore schedule; you can't futz with seeing her.

He looked back at the neighbor's house. "'Due for its first trim," he commented. Pain in the ass job that, using a push mower and clippers and moving Theresa's car a few feet in the driveway to simulate movement. It was getting harder to start her car, probably because of gas breakdown. Not good. That meant the stabilizer was reaching the end of its life, which meant the gas and diesel tankers were reaching the end of theirs, too. Year or so and he'd have those large containers of smelly water. "Eighteenth century in no time at all," he told her.

She never responded during these nightly talks. She

only showed up at odd moments, when he needed a bit of berating, like earlier tonight. Kept him straight, and he appreciated it. She was silent the rest of the time, he guessed because she didn't really have anything new to say. There wasn't a lot of action around the mound and she wasn't allowed to discuss Heaven, so, she listened.

He appreciated that, too. He missed her talk, though, how she used to get so wound up about some innocuous event at the school or something Collier had done, until he'd get so tickled he'd start laughing and then she'd punch him and they'd wrestle and God knows what it would turn into.

"You were a fun ole gal," he chuckled.

Test. He was hoping the use of "ole' gal" would get a rise out of her, but, no. It would have before, and there'd be more punching and wrestling and God knows what. He stirred a bit uneasily, recalling his brief interludes with some of the Gate and Family women these past few years. Legally, not cheating, but in his heart it was, even if all he was doing was resurrecting their moments together, eyes closed, seeing her, holding her, remembering her the right way.

Instead of the nightmare way.

When John woke from his coma, she was next to him in bed. Not a pretty sight. It took John three days to actually make it out of bed, three days with her slowly putrefying corpse. He could not move at all the first day so he spent it staring at her sightless eyes and her opened mouth, the discoloration advancing as he watched.

A corpse's open mouth had always given John the willies. He'd had an inordinate share of gruesome crime scenes over his career, like the girl up in Plattsburgh who was dealing drugs and one of her competitors used an axe on her head. That girl's mouth and, he could swear, every other mouth of every other body he'd processed, had been wide open. He'd looked at that silent rictus scream and knew, just knew, all the corruption inside was stealing out and towards his nose, trying to find another home in which to root.

So, there he was, helpless with the Flu, staring directly into Theresa's crusted, decaying mouth. He couldn't sleep until he mustered the strength, a day later, to turn away from her. No relief, that, because he crossed into Nightmare Lands, where her dead arms reached out and pulled him to her for a corpse's kiss, over and over.

Twelve hours and 900,000 iterations of that lovely scene later, he suddenly woke, spontaneously rolled over while gasping in terror, and found himself inches away from the dead face of his slobbering dreams. Must have screamed for five minutes.

John was sure that heart-stopping shock had a lot do with his very rapid recovery. CDC told him the average was a month to a month and a half and there he was running around after only two weeks.

That's why he didn't see anyone, why he thought "I Am Legend" and was able to get a lot of stuff, like the weapons and hardware and Magnums, before anyone else showed up. It also explained why CDC was very, very interested in him. They thought he was a cure, and, with all their blood and other fluid harvests, they almost finished what the Event started.

He tried to tell them about the shock awakening, but they ignored it ... there, there, you little peasant, shut up while we take another five gallons of your blood. At least the psychologist listened; seemed genuinely aghast. He gave John the sleeping pills, hoarded in the medicine cabinet now, in case blowing off the back of his head seemed a bit too messy.

"I'm not going to do that," he assured her.

She'd have gotten a big kick out of scaring him three-quarters to death. John smiled, remembering the pranks

147

they loved to play on each other, from the stupid little whoopee cushions to elaborate phone scams where one tried to make the other think they'd won the lottery or inherited millions. Got so they'd both walk into the house like SWAT, trying to figure out where the next gag was planted.

"You win," he said. Waking up had been one of the best scares in his life. He could almost hear her chuckling.

And she *was* chuckling, across whatever these distances were. The soul survives. It just does and hers was still intact. Somewhere. Maybe that was just a plea, but John could not accept the dissipation of so much energy, so much thought, simply because the heart stops. Conservation of Energy, moving on to a different form, whatever, but the soul is the house of everything, and hers remained, and it remained interested.

There were many years in their 26 together when they didn't get along, mostly due to his self-centeredness. "I am a man, after all," he told her. But, they were always interested in what the other was doing and they always talked.

Married people get bored with each other when they run out of things to say, but Theresa and he never did. About once a week, one or the other would stumble across something, like land in the Shenandoah Valley, and they'd be on it for a while until something else caught their attention. And they always made each other laugh.

That's the other big marriage secret, ya gotta tickle each other, real drop dead falling all over yourself peeing kind of helpless laughter, not the fake snickering of those pre-Event Washington power couples over some poor schlub's office faux pas. That's not real humor, that's viciousness, and a mutual viciousness won't keep a couple together, unless they're Bonnie and Clyde.

Funny about that Shenandoah land; if he'd had followed up, she'd be alive today. "My fault," he said.

Snuffy barked a couple of times at that point and John looked back at the house, irritated. Shut up, dog. God, just no sense at all. Shoulda shot him years ago. Well, no – John was way too fond of the little bastard. Funny looking, about the size of a Spitz with a Labrador's head, white with horribly patterned brown spots and a plume of a tail, like ostrich feathers, curling up over his back. But he was the smartest dog John'd ever had, and he'd had plenty.

He'd taught Snuffy how to crawl on his belly for a treat. Theresa, in one session, had taught Snuffy to shake, roll over and bow. Just smart. He, also, was strong as a bull, had extremely sharp teeth and was incredibly loyal. That's why he was the inside dog.

They'd left him outside. Didn't mean to, they just fell so quickly no thought was given. Snuffy survived on squirrels and rainwater. He couldn't get at the pool because the cover was already in place. When John finally shuffled over to the door and opened it, fully expecting to find the dog's carcass, Snuffy came racing over from the back of the yard, falling all over himself in greeting. He was starving and filthy and half-mad with thirst and one of John's first acts was to feed him a healthy post-starvation doggie dinner of Snausages and Cheweez, interspersed with water bowl filling, three times in as many minutes.

John realized how fortunate it was that no thought had been given. If Snuffy'd been inside, he'd have fed on Theresa's corpse. Imagine waking up to that.

"I'da run screaming from the house and never come back," he chuckled to Theresa. Well, eventually, he'da come back. It was, after all, their house, the second one they'd owned in their lives, the one they'd lived in the longest. It wasn't a bad place, split level brick with a carport and a weird triangular lot larger than most. The backyard, secluded with a privacy fence, had been his sanctuary. He used to sit in the back patio after dark, watching the Summer Triangle, sipping a beer and periodically jumping in the pool to chase away mosquitoes. Heaven.

Theresa had complained about the place, wasn't big enough, wasn't modern enough, but that seemed the way of her, some prod for him to do better, not get complacent. Like he was ever that.

"Could move," he told her. There was quite an inventory of big sprawling mansions on the market right now. Why, if he was willing to disable all the clever little booby traps left behind by the Secret Service and then spend every day fighting off MPD and Raiders, he could move right into the White House. Less trouble would be one of those toney Clifton or Great Falls mansions. "Waddya think?" he asked. Stoney silence and he chuckled. Leave her behind? Forget it.

Besides, Collier could only find them here. Well, not Collier but the anticipated grandson, kicking down the door and beholding John's bleached bones wrapped in a blanket before a long cold fire. More likely before a long cold TV, but finding him was the point.

Follow my wishes, unknown grandchild, and bury me beside her.

'Course, by that time, the government or whatever will have confiscated the place, bulldozed it, paved it over, burned it to the ground, who knows. They'd have a legal right because John hadn't paid the mortgage in almost a year and a half. He no longer felt the obligation since the government federalized the Zone. No resale value and no interest exemption so what was the benefit?

The mortgage company still had the nerve, though, to send a foreclosure notice, three of them, to be exact. John got them all at the same time, during some trip to

150

the Gate. Bill gave him a packet of envelopes and the first notice was right on top.

"Can you believe this?" John waved it at him, a big piece of yellow paper with "Warning" in caps and red letters, all kinds of boilerplate threatening all kinds of dire actions and seizures by dates that had long passed.

Bill read it. "What are they going to do? Come in here and throw you out?"

John laughed, "Yeah, if they've got those kinds of balls, they can have the place. I'm sure I could find another one." They both chuckled at that. But, then John had a thought, "Hey, Bill, can they garnish me?"

He pursed his lips and shook his head slowly, "I don't think so. The Soldier/Sailor Relief Act has been updated and I think you're immune. Don't know for sure if it applies to retirees, but, since you're subject to recall, it might."

That may or may not be true but John decided to leave well enough alone and not call complaining about the mortgage company. Best to lay low. He hadn't received any more notices and his pay remained the same, so he guessed the mortgage company decided to lay low, too.

With a rapacious government seeking new and innovative sources of income, it didn't pay to advertise. Besides, insurance and moneys attached to the Emergency Proclamations reimbursed the company somewhat, so they really didn't have anything to complain about. They didn't lose two-thirds of their income, like John did.

Which, of course, was the real reason, moral dudgeon aside, he didn't pay the mortgage anymore – he simply couldn't afford it. Pre-Event, John's military retirement covered the house payment and maybe a part of one utility. His AU salary covered everything else with enough left over to play. Theresa's salary paid for

151

Fishburne. Now, his retirement was his only income and he needed that to pay for Dish and the cell phone and Fishburne and American Express. There just wasn't enough left over to pay for the mortgage.

He'd like to upgrade Verizon to get internet, but there was just no way. That his Verizon cell phone worked at all was miraculous, since the microwave towers should all be dead. Further proof of God, but more likely of shadowy government involvement, and he was smart enough not to ask questions and just be grateful for watcha got, especially since Verizon was now charging $400 to $500 a month for 100 minutes without long distance and their cost for internet access was in the thousands. John couldn't afford it, so he had to leave his contract alone.

Freezing all pre-existing contracts with Zoners was one of the two or three things the post-Event government did right and it kept John solvent. Must chap Verizon's ass, him paying a little over $60.00 a month for 400 anytime minutes and unlimited nights and weekends, no roaming and long distance. Nothing they could do about it, though.

He still had to pay for Theresa's line, which was an irritant, but canceling that would change the contract and then they'd have him. "Besides," he chuckled, "maybe you'll give me a call."

Internet would be great. All the hard lines were down and he never got around to hooking up through Dish before everything happened, so his only chance was Bill's instructions. Hope that worked because it would certainly make life easier – he could manage his bank accounts better, for one thing.

John had left Theresa's insurance payout in the savings and, once Collier graduated (and changed his mind about the air force), John was giving him the password. It was a little over $100,000, not much, but Collier could pick up a fairly decent secondhand car with that and maybe even get about two years of college. Hell, with the colleges now offering every incentive to get students back, he might even make a whole four years, even with a wife and kids. If he'd just freakin' do it.

"He's still not listening to me," John told Theresa. "You should probably start in on him." She should. She was relentless and could get Collier's head out of his ass and off joining the USAF. "Better than the army, Dad."

True, but not much better. Collier was sure his Fishburne background guaranteed a sergeant's rank and choice of specialty, crew chief, which would put him on the flightline or in the air, far away from the 'Slams' murderous human wave attacks, and so drop his mortality from the average of 75% to only 50. "That's good odds, Dad."

John knew better. He'd lost enough pilot friends who were riding a mile or more over battlefields. So he'd waved the Surviving Son exemption and urged Collier to invoke it, avoid military service, take engineering or agriculture or computers or something that made him valuable to the rapidly changing government so he could be ensconced, safe, in some Byzantine officialdom, keeping his head low, avoiding the politics and subsequent firing squads. Just work on cables or systems or roads. Just do that, Collier. Freakin' do that.

"No," Collier said and John could almost see the set of jaw and hooding of eyes, marks of intransigence. "It's payback time."

Which John had to admire. Everyone wanted payback. "After all," he said to Theresa, "we are Americans." But not at the cost of Collier's life. Whether the kid accepted it or not, he carried everything that preceded him – John, John's father and grandfather and beyond, ad infinitum.

Not that the Rashkil's were so noble they should be

preserved. On the contrary, if a bloodline were due for expiration, it would be this bunch of car thieving, cousin marrying, rapist druggie crapheads. But, so many families were now lost, names erased, posterity vanished, that it was sinful even for the lowlifes to go.

"Speak to him," John urged Theresa, "or, at least, make something work out." She was in a good position to elbow God a bit, get Him to get Collier married in a year, take advantage of the government bonuses and have a million kids, stay in the Provos, linger in college, make himself valuable to some government toady, avoid the service. He might come to his senses or the wars might end.

"And pigs might fly," John said. "So, Theresa, get a little face time with the Almighty. Make this happen. And, while you're at it, Theresa, how 'bout elbowing a bit of explanation out of Him?" John stood quietly and dared her to call him blasphemous. She didn't, and she wouldn't, because his questions were legitimate and God always allowed good questions, even if He chose not to answer, even if John was on the outs with Him right now.

Not for the first time in his life, of course, but he hadn't been feeling this rebellious in a while, probably since being cashiered unfairly out of the air force nine or ten years ago. See, God allowed some self-indulgent president, who wanted to look like he was cutting government waste, to shuffle out all those war-mongering officers running around wasting tax payers' money, especially all those prior enlisted 20-year guys who were just a tad bit too rightist.

Presto, instant civilian. John was given six months, just like that, no notice, no warning, and there he was, having to find a job and a place to live in competition with 20,000 or so other unceremoniously dumped officers. After 20 years of good service, to be thrown out like that, just because some boy president wanted to be well thought of at Hollywood parties. Thanks. Thanks a lot.

That was bad enough, but this? John turned and looked at the crosses down the street. This? "You've definitely got some 'splainin' to do," he said, not to Theresa, but to her new Boss.

A loving God? Do tell. Unless that was the error and He's really a roaring, uncompromising God who visits the most severe repression for even the tiniest of deviations from His millions of rules, the kind of God the Baptists seemed to like. Maybe the Baptists weren't so kooky. Maybe John skulked in ruins, a hissing and a curse, because they were the Nineveh and Tyre the Falwells and Robertsons had so gleefully warned about.

But so harsh a God does not deserve love, only fear, and how long could so harsh a God have tolerated the Assyrias or Egypts or Attilas and Hitlers before collectively crushing the entire species, separating chaff from wheat, and burning them forever? The Baptist God would have incinerated men centuries ago, so He can't be the Avenger. He must, indeed, be the loving God Episcopalians and Unitarians worship. That God would weep over the insanities and mourn the pain and be consoling and would never, ever have allowed this tragedy.

Yeah, but, there's the Holocaust, slavery, Vlad the Impaler, the Twin Towers, and now the Event, so, which is it? Loving, roaring, compassionate, vengeful, which God should John address?

Yeah, yeah, free will. He got that. God is a gentleman and a respecter of boundaries and does not go where not wanted. He allows the full extent of desire and urge, even if it means six million people shoved into ovens. He makes quite a point by doing that. Proof, over and over, of the species' sin, depravity, evil and hopelessness, and

155

how lost they are without Him.

Point more than made.

"How much more evidence do you need, Lord?" John asked the ascending Dipper. "The species was in desperate need of Your Intervention. It was well past the time that Christ should ride out of the sky on His white horse, the clouds of believers accompanying Him, the sword issuing from his mouth and slaying Satan's legions on the plains of Megiddo, or the Plain of Jars or the Great Plains, for that matter. Just pick a place. Just come. What the hell is the hold up?"

John stood on the windblown carcass of his dead street, watching the rot slowly claim all evidence, Theresa's mound sinking ever lower, Collier growing more distant, the moon casting silver shadows of burning crosses and mushroom clouds and killing fields across abandoned lawns and cars and moldering roofs and he just had to say, just had to mention again, that the point seemed made. "While You and Your buddy Lucifer were making legal arguments in some golden throne room, a lot of bystanders were getting killed. How 'bout you both ease up?"

"Not being irreverent," he told Theresa. "God is God, there is no Other and He is the Father of all, period, over and out. No argument there. God exists. Slam-dunk. No thinking person can conclude otherwise. The only possible controversies are the form of God and at what level He involves himself, the Deist-Theist continuum."

John watched the moon and stars fight each other for lighting privileges. Look at that. How much more evidence do you atheist assholes need? Pre-adolescents, puerile, creating complex series of half-rationalizations and pretext to avoid any sense of responsibility. Didn't want the boundaries of morality or authority or ethics; wanted power and libertinism and lust and guiltlessness, and so intellectualized God's non-existence. Bunch of babies.

And so were the Holy Joes. Simpering bunch of hypocrites, Falwell-worshiping, fake smiling, sugar sweet judgmental jerks; they didn't know God any more than the athees. Dulcet toned, hypersensitive and easily shocked, willing to attribute the most mundane things to God's Own Will, so that crossing the street became a special Act.

"You make me sick," John said. "You make God sick, too." Self-righteous pricks all over TV, talking about perdition and the rightful justice of an offended God and implying the athees and sinners brought this all about. No, they didn't. If anyone caused an offended God to raise His hand in anger, it was you bunch of arrogant wimps.

"Screw you guys," John said, pointing an aimless middle finger in some aimless direction. Useless bastards. John needed to find the three or four reasonable believers left in the world, the ones who really knew God. Explain, please, 2000 years or so later, why we await the Messiah.

"Just give me your best thinking on this, okay?"

Here he was, sexton to this national ossuary, attending the forgotten bones and kicking the shards off his feet, and he needed to know why.

It cannot simply be punishment, no more than the night trains into Treblinka were God's Judgment of His Chosen. There was more to it, having to do with the nature of Evil, the nature of man, the nature of life itself and he could not accept that God, for some simplistic, superficial reason of necessary Justice, made John the solitary pallbearer at thirty or more funerals, eulogies lost in the wind, names already forgotten.

God is not vindictive.

He can't be.

John stood for a moment and felt the silence from Theresa's mound. The universe whirled above him.

He went off to check cables.

18

John stood on the edge of the pool, the NVGs down so he could see it. The cover was still on, but he was clumsy by nature and knew his toes would find some way to hook the canvas and send him sprawling. Supposedly, an elephant could walk across the cover without breaking it, but, knowing his luck, John would hit the right angle with the right speed at the weakest point and plunge through. Death by drowning, in his own pool. Embarrassing.

Snuffy was standing next to him and giving off a pleasure growl every moment or so. No doubt remembering when the pool was actually a pool and he ran around it barking his head off because John was in the middle, tilted back in a floating chair, unconcerned, beer half submerged to keep it cool. Snuffy had a pathological hatred of water and figured John should, too, so what the hell are you doing out there, man? Bark bark bark.

He reserved even more hatred for the Polaris automatic pool cleaner and howled his rage during its cleaning cycle. John chuckled, remembering how the Polaris periodically surfaced and sprayed the dog in the middle of his stalking. Once, Snuffy actually got his teeth on the cleaner and dragged it out, ready to eviscerate. John had, fortunately, been nearby and rescued it.

No longer a problem. John ran the Polaris only once a week, at midnight on Fridays for an hour, standing by while it cleaned. Noisy as hell, that thing, so he stayed outside and kept a wary eye, while Snuffy stayed inside so he wouldn't go nuts. An hour was enough – since the cover stayed on year round, the Polaris didn't have that much to do, just pick up some sediment.

And that might be overkill because John didn't have to keep the water squeaky clean anymore, just potable. He ran the pump every night for about 8-10 hours, which wasn't enough, needed 12, so he compensated with heavy chlorination. Forget the Ph.; there's no way he could keep that balanced and scale would eventually force replacement of the lines and pumps. No problem. He had extras next door.

Worth it. Very worth it. Water was an issue now, somewhat scarce unless you lived on the Potomac. There were only so many reservoirs and creeks, and Bundys and Vandals and Raiders staked those places, waiting for victims. Yeah, bottled water was available by the truck-load, but try filling a bathtub or sink with that. Besides, the bottled stuff was for drinking. Everything else required a big water source and getting to those meant running a gauntlet.

MPD patrolled the few District spots, like the McArthur reservoir located near AU, but there were far more Raiders than cops and John heard gunfire from that direction all during the workday. On the Virginia side, you were on your own and to get water, you went heavy. The Alexandrias drew from the Potomac in armed convoys, at least, they used to. John frowned. Sometime this weekend, he had to go look for them. Wouldn't be pretty.

Theresa had never liked the pool. She wasn't a pool or beach person and saw it as a waste, especially when she'd come out and find John and Collier spending valuable weekend chore time splashing each other. She complained it dropped the house value, too, because no one wanted to buy a pool.

"Yeah?" John had snorted, "Why'd we?" She had no

answer for that. Now, houses with pools were prime real estate, the object of Bundy desire, a built-in cistern eliminating one more vulnerability in this State of Nature.

John jealously guarded his. It was hidden behind a six-foot wooden fence, itself hidden with creeper and a few years' worth of leaves. Be a job just to hack through all that and find the fence alone, never mind the pool. John had a motion detector camera trained on the pool that sounded every time he let Snuffy out, a nightly test of the system that he didn't mind because the pool was too important.

John reached down and patted the cover affectionately. No one's getting close to you, baby.

John unhooked one edge of the cover and peered at the water level. A couple of inches below the tile. Eh, no big deal. John had by-passed the internal lines and attached intake and outtake hoses directly to the pump, draping them over the side into the water. It wasn't pretty, hoses splayed along the deck and lay at the bottom, but John depended on rain and snow melt and couldn't keep the constant half-tile-from-the-top level the internal lines required. Besides, the pool was no longer decorative.

He reattached the cover, picked his way across the lines and stood by the pump. Pressure was up, hmm. Have to backsplash this week, which was a pain because he had to move the concrete blocks and mattresses he used to muffle the pump's noise. Which meant resetting those blocks and mattresses afterwards so the noise would drift down the back hill, just like the secondary Magnum did. Pain in the ass Saturday job. Do it before searching out the Alexandrias.

Eh, might as well do a Claymore check on Saturday, too. John grimaced. He hated doing that. Dangerous, real dangerous.

John had a lot of Claymores. A lot. Not even sure how many anymore. He found them when he liberated the grenades, the LAWs, the M60s, the M-16s, and the ammunition from that Ft. Belvoir ammunition bunker. They were all piled up in a corner and John immediately knew what they were – he'd seen a few while fooling around with the army on some joint missions. The air force didn't use them because, after all, they were the dignified service and didn't trifle with such vulgarities, but John always thought they were cool.

He'd loaded up a few, along with the other stuff, but came back after the Mall Apocalypse and got the rest. Figured they'd come in handy.

The army designated them the M18 because the army's just gotta call everything by a number but everyone knew them as Claymores. They were the dumb man's high explosive defense. They came in individual bags with all the trimmings for a do-it-yourself killing field: a blasting cap, an infinite amount of wire on a spool, a triggering device, a circuit tester, instructions, and even little legs which stood the mine up. Claymores looked like curved olive-drab bricks and weighed about the same. The bricks had sights on them and were further idiot-proofed with the words "Front Toward Enemy" on the murder side.

They were destructive little buggers, 700 steel balls wrapped in C4, one gigantic shotgun blast. John played with a couple of them in the big soccer field on Route 1 across from the Belvoir main gate. He put one on its little legs, aiming it at a set of bleachers, unspooled the wire to about 100 yards away (just in case it wasn't completely idiot proof), then pressed the lever on the M57 firing device (there's the army again). *Wham!* Ball bearings, heat and shock shredded the bleachers, throwing parts of it all over the field. John was astonished. "Hoo wah," he said, and loaded up the back of the

Pathfinder.

He placed the first group of Claymores inside the neighbor's house – three directly underneath the Magnum facing out, three in the ceiling and one in each corner of the room, all facing in. He set two Claymores apiece in the other rooms, one in the opposite corner facing the door and the other in the ceiling right over the door. He wired them back to a control panel next to the camera panel and labeled each to correspond with its closest camera view, then folded all the wire extensions into a master M57 which would blow all the Claymores at once.

Pretty satisfactory set up. He could take out one room at a time, or take out the entire house, depending on what he saw in the cameras. One or two intruders, and he'd just wait for them outside. Five or six in a room, *bloowie*. Ten or fifteen in the house, *ka-bloowie*. Setting everything back up would be a bitch, but that's the price you pay for security.

John planted the rest of them along the back hill, triggered with plain old trip wires. No cameras; not necessary, given the unlikelihood of an approach from that direction. People always take the path of least resistance – why kill yourself fighting up a bramble-laden slope when there are so many easier ways to get at him? Besides, he had enough cables to sort out.

The trip wires worked fine in test and were low maintenance; he periodically checked them to make sure they remained taut and the blasting caps didn't get too rusty. That, in itself, was somewhat hair-raising. The wires were hard to see and John was sure, every time he went out there, he'd forget quite where they were.

He'd cut a small path through the field to help him get through without blowing himself up but even that was hard to see because, well, he'd made it hard to see. Why show someone else the way? So he stood a good

chance of being shredded while doing routine maintenance, which fit in well with the Grim Laws of Irony and
spurred him to a caution of almost ridiculous proportions – taking a good five minutes between steps, peering
intently at the brush.

Pain in the rear, but you don't tempt the Universe.
Dogs or deer setting them off was a problem initially, but
John sprayed wolf scent, which he found in a gun shop,
around the area and that seemed to work. Reminder, do
that this weekend, too.

No Claymores around the pool. That was just asking
for trouble and he had enough of that with the pool
itself, like the constant worry of frozen lines. John bent
down and fiddled with the intake. Seemed okay. It was
chilly tonight, but not so bad. Spring was here and the
danger of frozen lines was pretty much over, although,
this being DC, there could be a surprise mid-April
freeze. Sacrilege to keep the pump going in winter, but
he needed water all year so the pumps had to run, even
in the snow.

John had double wrapped the lines with insulation,
even where they hit the water, and threaded in some
pipe heaters. Seemed to work, at least, he never had
such a freezing problem that the water wouldn't flow or
the pump busted. Of course, there hadn't been a really
hard winter since the Event. Due. Push came to shove,
he could always draw water through the ice and replace
the pump and lines when it got warmer.

"C'mon, dog," he said to Snuffy and walked over to
the side gate. He pointed and Snuffy did his snuffling
thing, which had earned him the name. John watched
him for any signs of alarm but Snuffy's tail wagged, and
he looked up at John with a big green grin.

"Good boy," John patted the dog and cautiously
cracked the gate, a hand on the .357. Satisfied no one or
thing lurked there, he stepped out and quietly closed the

gate behind him.

The garden was tucked at the corner of the house, so well hidden John didn't bother with monitors. If someone got close enough to find it, John had bigger problems than someone stealing his harvest. He'd already turned the soil and dumped the compost he'd cooked all winter so, this weekend, he had to turn the soil again and then lay out the plastic to keep the weeds down. Geez, going to be busy.

He had lettuce and spinach started inside the house and, in a week or so, could go ahead and put them out. By early June, he'd be back on fresh greens. He was about a month behind, but he purposely erred on the side of warm weather. He'd rather the crops were a little late than risk their loss through a surprise freeze. It's not like he could go to the store and replace his mistakes.

He examined the irrigation system, a rigged up series of soaker hoses coming out of a huge tin washtub with a hole in the bottom of it. The washtub was up high, between the bucket shelves of a couple of stepladders facing each other, so gravity could power it. It was quite the workout to fetch a few buckets from the pool and dump them in the washtub and he really should set something up, like a small electric pump, to make the job easier. Later, later. He had to let the pool water stand for a day or two to evaporate the chlorine before he released it through the hoses, otherwise he'd burn everything up, but the garden got a good soaking this way. Especially during dry seasons.

John was a good gardener, one of his few natural talents. He'd grown corn and watermelons on a small patch of ground at the family house in Alabama when he was a kid. He'd been in 4H and knew the Extension agent and entered the contests and seriously considered studying agriculture, before the world pushed him in other directions.

Theresa was a bit amused by his hobby, "Big tough guy like you, gardening?" she'd chuckle.

"That assassin in *Three Days of the Condor* painted little tin soldiers, you know," he pointed out.

"That was a movie," she countered. True. But she never complained about the fresh cucumbers or Chinese beans or eggplant. A hobby that served them both Before. Now, just him.

He did mostly greens through the summer, string beans and kale and turnips, highly nutritious and very dense for the small area he used. They also canned very well, a talent he picked up from his grandmother and supplemental reading at the library. He actually had a root cellar, the area in front of the crawl space in the basement, where he stored his cannings. He didn't really eat them because cannings weren't exactly the tastiest of foods and he still had a huge stock of store-stolen goods (not stolen, paid for, dammit). Should all that Libby's stuff go bad, he could get through the winter on the cannings, high vinegar content and all. And on deer.

He thought about a greenhouse. The Whitings had one in their backyard, but John wasn't big on greenhouse vegetables. Too grainy and thin. Greenhouses were better for flowers, and those seemed frippery now. Pass. Stick with the cannings. Besides, a greenhouse presented power and water problems. He just didn't need any more problems to overcome.

So many problems to overcome.

Like, right after waking, right after gaining the strength to actually step outside and shuffle weakly down the street knocking on doors, opening doors, breaking down doors as he got stronger, finding everybody dead, at least one body per house, realizing he was alone.

The average was about one Survivor per block, taking into account all the square mileage and spreading it over

166

the typical size of a city. Of course, random distribution wasn't so neat, and there were several city blocks where no one survived, like in Springfield, and then several more where three to four did.

Chaos theory could better explain the pattern. Bill told him some mathematicians at the Geological Survey actually mapped it but the then-government shut them down. Too morbid.

John buried everybody, after the Magnum project. He had the backhoe anyway, so what the hell. Took him a week and a half. It was winter, so the bodies stayed pretty preserved, except in those houses with automatic thermostats and electric heat, one drawback of the power staying on so long. Not that bodies bothered him, except for their damn open mouths. Crime scene bodies, though, were anonymous and these were people he knew or at least recognized and, in one case, loved. The Zone was one massive crime scene, but it wasn't faceless.

He buried Theresa first, of course, within a day or two of his getting up. The silence of the world convinced him there were no hearses to call, and he damn sure wasn't going to leave her to rot in bed. That was a few weeks before he got the backhoe, so he used a shovel.

He was still pretty weak and it took him all day just to dig the requisite six feet. He trimmed and squared the hole and made sure it was as perfect as possible. He laid her in gently, using some rope. It was cold and there was a steady wet wind blowing. He had shed his coat and shirt while digging because it was sweaty work, but the sweat dried and froze over his dirt-layered skin and he didn't want to put his clothes on over that, so he shivered and quavered his way through an off-key rendition of "Amazing Grace," everybody's favorite hymn, just the first verse, the only one he could remember, over and over. He was too exhausted to cry. Afterward, he slept for another three days. That wasn't recovery; that was grief.

He held a similar ceremony for each grave he later dug with the backhoe, putting the neighborhood to a decent rest. He did economize, digging just one hole for everyone he found in a house. If they weren't family, oh well, they at least knew each other. Imagine the surprise of some window salesman who wakes on Judgment Day beside the husband and wife he was hustling when the Flu got them all. Funny.

John varied the hymns, using "Nearer my God to Thee," "The Old Rugged Cross," and even the Doxology, all the Baptist standbys. He hummed over the parts he forgot, but at least made the effort.

He didn't sing for the Jewish family, or the Buddhists, or Muslims, who were all very well represented on this very diverse street. He didn't know their music and didn't want to insult them with Christian themes, so he just prayed, asking that their souls be consigned to whatever Paradise their teachings described. The God he used to know wouldn't begrudge that.

Their graves were pretty much invisible now, except for the telltale crosses, which he put on everyone, regardless of faith. C'mon, how do you make a Star of David? Or a moon and crescent? The mounds dissolved in the rain and wind and melted into the undergrowth. Only some trained archeologist could spot them. That was actually good because the neighborhood now looked just like every other dead neighborhood around here. Dead street, dead town.

"Look upon my works and despair ... tremble?" John stood beside the garden and frowned, trying to remember exactly how that went. The sentiment remained, either way. The Hittites, the Assyrians, the Romans, wild and thriving and swollen with strength and power, Ajax tall and arrogant before Troy ... reduced to overgrown mounds dissolved by rain and wind.

168

Hundreds of years from now, some bespectacled geek with a doctorate and a bush hat will squat beside John's graves and brush at the dirt, trying to figure out what the dickens happened. It'll probably drive him nuts – why did graves show up on the front lawns of these dwellings and not others? Geek'd write dissertations on post-Event ritualistic internments associated with street names or sun orientations or magnetic displacements or whatever cockeyed idea someone can cook up just to get published.

He'd never consider it was just John being decent. Maybe that's all any ancient ruin was, some local being decent.

Springfield as ancient ruins. John shook his head. You'd never, in your wildest dreams, ever consider that. Even a hundred years from now, it should be bedroom, playground, rest from the hard world. Walk down the streets or ride the sidewalk escalators, whatever they had by then, go to stores, eat at restaurants, see friends and strangers and know it was all safe.

Safe.

Just to be safe. To take safety as a given, to feel so safe you think nothing of leaving a door unlocked or a car unattended or a child playing alone ... well, okay, that was more of a '50s-'60s model, but John was a child then and remembered it and grieved that Collier didn't grow up that way, safety dissolving into dread and caution sometime in the '70s. Now, John'd kill, give up a major limb, just to have the dread and caution days back. Beats the hell out its state-of-nature replacement.

For the thousandth time tonight, he checked the .357, the .25, and the tanto. For the ten thousandth time, he stared off to the woods and felt the sense of wrongness. No, foreboding. And not confined to this specific place or time, but over everything. No matter what he did, no matter how hard he fought, he'd end up a calcium

169

deposit in some odd area of these tumbled ruins, or a piled up set of bones lying next to a rusted Zap bike on the collapsed pavement of 395.

Enough of this crap. It's about what, 8:30, 45? John glanced at the moon and headed inside.

19

"You know, Snuff," John said as he dialed through the cameras, the dog's lazy tail waving beside him, "one day, I might have to take this stuff back." He just might. You never knew, AU could reconstitute, form a student body, start holding classes again.

Not in his lifetime of course, but he didn't want some future administrators labeling him a thief. Yes, he did take the control panel, and video processor, and monitor, from the dispatch office, as well as the cameras, but without power, they were just going to waste. Since their purpose was university security, and he was a university employee, they were now fulfilling their mission. Think of John's home as a satellite campus, you future deans.

They were pretty good cameras, motion activated. Back Before, Gary, the Grants Administrator, and he had spent a couple of weeks setting them up to catch whoever was stealing projectors out of the classrooms in Ward. They worked great, kicking on when the thieves walked in one morning and ripped the projectors out of the ceilings, stuffed them inside giant backpacks and casually strolled past first-arriving students who, of course, didn't remember a thing.

Great video. If they'd ever identified the bastards, woulda put 'em away. That was one problem with photos – you had to have a name to go with the face. No doubt, the bastards had dissolved down to bone now. Or they'd became Raiders and John had already shot them. Either way, he could take comfort.

The control panel had audibles, a really annoying bell, which John activated to coincide with any motion detection. Necessary, because Snuffy hated buzzers and bells and any kind of technological noise – crawled under the bed when the cell phone beeped – and John needed to spur the dog into a frenzy of barking so he'd wake from his nightly coma.

The plan was to stumble over and take a look, see how many, how armed, their distribution throughout the house, which Claymore to trigger, all that stuff. John did a daily inadvertent test when he went next door to start the Magnum, walking out and hearing Snuffy going crazy until he ran back inside and cleared the alarm. "Silly dog," he said and patted him good-naturedly. Snuffy wagged at him and John was grateful he hated bells that much. Otherwise, John'd probably sleep right through an invasion.

There had been a real-world test about a year ago. A raccoon got into the Magnum house about 3:00 a.m. and set off a camera. Snuffy freaked and then John freaked, falling out of bed and just about somersaulting down the stairs, dragging the Mossberg and shoes with him, heart pounding, oh shit, this is it, this is it. He flipped through the cameras with one hand while keeping the other nervously over the Claymore switches until he spotted the little bastard playing around some chairs. John went over and herded him out the door. Why kill him? It's his world now.

He should site the processor in the bedroom, but there was still the power issue. So, yeah, then he should sleep in the living room next to the panel or, at the very least, in the basement just one room away, but he loved Big Iron, his monster four-posted queen size bed, the only one he ever had where his big flappy feet didn't hang over. These days, you take your few comforts seriously.

Besides, the bedroom formed an excellent defensive position. The only way to come at John was through the easily covered lower doors and stairs. Only one or two Raiders at a time could approach, funneled into a shooting gallery. Little chance it would come to that, though. Even with the Laws of Unfortunate Timing guaranteeing a Bundy busting in next door at 1:00 a.m., when John was unconscious, there was enough buffer between the alarm sounding, John waking up, arming up, seeing what was going on and taking care of it before the Bundy figured out it was a trap.

He switched through the various cameras again. Okay.

John grabbed three pails and went back outside, Snuffy following and giving off a couple of warning barks to whoever was out there, watch your ass. John shushed him. No response from Hairbag and Lupus, hmm, where'd they get off to?

He cocked his head and listened for distant baying, a deer chase, but, nothing. Odd. It was getting close to doggie dinner time and those boys loved their Kibbles and Bits. Dogs supposedly couldn't sense time but those two were always waiting at the gate when he brought out the dishes about fifteen minutes from now. Maybe they were around and had decided to ignore Snuffy. Dogs were like that. John listened a bit more, but nothing. Hmm. Check again in a bit.

He filled the buckets and grunted them back inside, hoisting them up on the counter. One for the toilet, one for the dishes, one for the shower. Thank God for the low tech of toilets; they pretty much ran on gravity and stayed pretty clear with a periodic snaking of the pipes. He'd hate to go the outhouse route as many were now doing – seemed the end of all true civilization. If you couldn't luxuriate with a book and a cigar while downloading into your porcelain convenience, then the barbarians already owned the gates.

Yeah, eventually, roots and broken pipes would render the toilets unusable, but not yet, not yet. Dish water bucket, stationed and ready for use, the heavy chlorine making it almost sterile. John did the dishes every night, not only for the hygiene, but Theresa's love of her plates. She considered them art and not utensil, often begrudging their use, so he took care of them. They were pretty valuable, a set they'd picked up in Okinawa. Little chance you could go pick up a set there anymore, what with the Japanese and the Chinese using it as their DMZ. Too bad, was a pretty place. Once.

So were they all, John, so were they all.

The last bucket was for the shower and would stay out all night evaporating chlorine. Hot chlorine-laced water tended to leave marks. Boiling the water before pouring it clumsily into the camp shower also left marks, but there was no other way to do it. The microwave wasn't big enough and the gas stove didn't work so he used a Hot Pot, trying to be careful when he filled the bag but, always, burning his hand. Think he'd be used to it by now, but skin reacts to boiling water the first or five hundredth time. Helped wake him up, he'd give it that. It was one of the first things he did in the morning so that by the time he finished breakfast, the water'd be cool enough. Well, not fatal, at least, and he always yelped when he released the stream and the first bit of superhot water smacked into his back.

But now it was spring, soon summer, so he wouldn't need that hot a shower anymore. No longer the need to feel warm. Winter did that to you, created a craving for warmth, and about the only way to satisfy it was risking third degree burns from the near-boiling water. And it seemed the cold bothered him more these recent years. Gettin' old, gettin' old. Maybe should get a condo in Florida. Yeah.

Spring, soon summer, meant his fruitless efforts to heat the house would end, too. Cooling the house was easier than heating it. Without central anything both were problematic, but heating, well, that was downright impossible, at least to the pre-Event levels of toasty warm. Above freezing was about the best he could hope for; during the worst of winter days, barely that.

And, geez, these past winters hadn't really been that bad so what was going to happen when a true ball-buster showed up? Freeze to death, probably, despite the space heaters arranged around his lounger in a circle while he shivered under 20 blankets in front of a frozen TV. He wondered why getting warm was much more work than getting cool; they were just opposite dynamics.

Maybe because the house itself had to get warm before he could get warm, while cooling was personal. Well, there was just no way the house would get warm. There weren't that many space heaters left in the world. Forget core heaters, they're just too damn noisy, and absolutely forget the two fireplaces. You can smell fire a mile away.

In winter then, shiver, curse it, and do what he was doing now, wish spring would get here. He grinned. Now you know how spring fertility rites got started.

Ah, April, with its cool winds and comfortable days and all night open windows – bliss. Still needed a blanket or two to stave off chill but, overall, very comfortable. Sleepin' weather, as they used to call it. Bundy weather, as he called it now, the seasonal increase of risk. But risk was worth not shivering.

Of course, when the brutal DC summer roared down and booted spring to the corner, he'd yearn for a little shivering. John hated hot, the sweat streaming down his armpits, flowing into his eyes and chafing his neck, that horrible, uncomfortable wetness underneath his T-shirt, which was exactly how he arrived at work even during winter.

It was so bad in summer he immediately dumped a bucket of water on his head and sat in Dispatch, naked, fanning himself before even thinking about patrol. That'd be a sight if someone walked in, wouldn't it? No need to shoot them; they'd laugh themselves to death.

Could centrally cool the house. There was enough power to do so and his unit still ran great, even though it was about 35 years old (American craftsmanship at its finest), but it sounded like a Space Shuttle launch, so no way. Should have replaced it for something more modern, far more quiet, when he had the chance but, really, why spend unnecessary money?

Besides, he always got a kick out of the mechanic standing there staring at the antique, shaking his head in admiration as the unit roared and shook and put out great gobs of cold air, "Man, they just don't make 'em like that anymore." No, they didn't. Back then, people were proud of their work and John had been proud of his rusty, bent, airplane-loud unit. It was like owning a Model T in a world of Ferraris, different, hopelessly out of date, but workable.

Didn't really need to cool the whole house, though. The floor air conditioners, a couple of Delonghi PAC210 Pinguino Portables he raided (bought) from Fisher's Hardware, worked just great. He left one running in the bedroom and tooled the other around the house as he moved, balancing a little fan on top and turning both on wherever he happened to park, the hose out the window, and the vents pointed right at him. Plenty cool, especially after a bucket of water over the head. Bedtime, haul it up to the room, set it next to the other one, and self-created sleepin' weather. John was looking forward to it.

An eighteenth century life, eased by the comforts of the twenty-first. If you're going to live through Armageddon, then you deserve it. Electricity and satellite TV and movies and music and refrigerated food. Booby-trapped houses and Claymores and M16s.

Man.

Trade it for just an hour of Before.

He stilled. Yeah, an hour, just that, cars going by on Old Keene Mill with those damned big bass radios blasting that stupid rap crap for ten blocks around, speed demon bikes roaring past at about 90, Snuffy and the neighborhood dogs chorusing, a helicopter flying too low, a 727 flying too high, Collier and his buddies screaming and splashing in the pool ... God, give me an hour. Then take me.

Take me.

The cloud descended, the black oily one that seeped through his pores and rolled around his heart, muddying it. Oh, man, just leave me alone, will ya?

But no, no, it urged him to forget dinner and chores and calling Collier and plod up the stairs and sit on the bed and draw the .357 and stare at it, glint some light off the bluing, look at the bright, white Silvertips gleaming from the cylinder. Now, cock it, place it against your temple.

Hold, and let the debate begin. Go ahead, pull it. What's the point of all this struggle? What's the friggin' point? It'll be two or three generations before anyone gets back inside here, and you'll be dust. So will the country, some bastardized socialist state or a series of confederations or maybe just one big medieval fiefdom. The casualties outnumbered the untouched, so who would know, who would blame you, if you just became another? Go. Go find Theresa. Go find God. And with just a little pressure on the trigger ...

Stop. Because Collier is the future, Collier is the future.

That stayed his hand. Every time. One bit of positive

evidence trumped the preponderance of negative. Besides, what would Coll think of him, if he succumbed, if he put a little pressure on the trigger? Not much, of course.

John didn't think much of people who just gave up, unless they're swallowing a cyanide tablet as the enemy breaks into their last stronghold, something like that. Giving up, no matter the odds, is weakness. And if it's your dad? God, imagine that. Imagine what a crater that would drill in your soul.

Collier had plenty of soul holes to fill without John making another one. Besides, he didn't want to establish a precedent for Coll's own future date with a heavy caliber exit. So he always eased back the hammer and, gently, laid the revolver on his lap.

Didn't mean he wouldn't, eventually, do it.

Despair was insidious, can't be forestalled forever. Maybe when John had a sense that Collier was okay, that, no matter what happens, he could handle himself and this Brave New World, then, yeah, okay, eat the barrel. Especially if, by that point, John'd stopped wondering what would happen next.

Experiencing more than his share of disasters growing up had imbued John with a real morbid curiosity about how things played out. Like, when his high school girlfriend (the one before Theresa, June, yeah, that was her name) told John she was pregnant, instead of freaking out and jumping off a bridge, he got curious about what came next. In her case, an abortion, with all the attendant mortification and embarrassments for both of them.

He got through that, and even got through her standing in the middle of a crowded school hallway screaming and slapping his face over and over. "Let's see what happens next," he kept thinking between slaps. His pariah status for the rest of the school year, of course, but he was even curious how that would go, so he stuck around.

Several disasters later, he was still curious. Life had a geometric capacity to get worse; only a linear ability to get better. Watching it do so, though, had a certain appeal, like standing on a beach as the tsunami looms. Right now it's anarchy, but how much lower can we go? John didn't have an inkling. But he would stick around and see.

He shook himself and shook off the cloud. Not tonight, bub. Time for dinner.

* * *

John was in the basement eating a bowl of chili, courtesy of Hormel, and watching the news. He felt relaxed. He shouldn't, because Hairbag and Lupus were missing. He'd placed the bowls in the carport and even encouraged Snuffy to give off a bark or two, but nothing. He'd dropped the NVGs and walked out to the street and peered around and then turned them off because it was bright outside, moon bright. Didn't see anything, didn't hear anything, either, after he gave a low whistle. Where are those damned dogs?

No idea.

Maybe they'd tangled with a pack. He frowned. Unlikely. They always came back to the house whenever they found one. They weren't stupid. So, maybe they got cut off, but he still should have heard it, even if they were way down Greeley. You can hear everything now. Snuffy should have heard it, too, dogs being attuned to each other on some subsonic level. But, no.

They might just be taking him for granted, gallivanting down some side street off towards the golf course, and weren't worried about dinner 'cause it'd be there when they returned. Or they'd fed on a deer carcass and weren't particularly hungry right now. Maybe. But it was just one more odd occurrence in an evening of them,

179

and John wondered if he should move to one of his blockhouses and wait out the night.

Nah.

Really, why? Whatever's going to happen, will. Most likely, this was just a series of false warnings, innocuous things that he was constructing into a threat because Mrs. Alexandria had so rattled him.

The surveillance, now the missing dogs, all had reasonable and unreasonable explanations. Trying to handle either would drive him crazy, so just let things play out. In the morning, you can laugh at yourself. Absolutely the wrong reaction, he knew, but sudden violent death eventually becomes a friend. And it wasn't like he couldn't meet it well. He went back inside.

Dinner was always cans and supplements. Might as well use the bounty of the grocery stores as long as the bounty lasts, which would probably be well past his demise. The cans might even be the cause of his demise, what with spoilage or botulism or whatever happens to canned food over time.

He figured that a bad can would telegraph itself with weird colors or odors but, you never knew, so he stayed away from raw stuff, like sardines and oysters. Not Spam, though, which had a shelf life measured in centuries. Processed food, filled with salts and preservatives and microbe killing chemicals, yes sir. And spicy, too.

His homegrown vegetables offset the poisons. Whether that was true or not, eh, 'twas the thought that counted. Wash it all down with a bottle of something cold, well, quasi cold. The refrigerator pretty much held temperature all day and John always looked forward to that cool bottle of Sam Adams. The several cases in the basement had already skunked but the flavor came through, especially when you followed up with a shot of Laphroaig.

Sometimes John got ambitious and cooked something

from scratch, like a very thick spaghetti sauce out of the summer tomatoes, mixing in canned meat he figured was still good or leaving it all vegetarian, depending on the mood. He had bread, too, homemade, courtesy of the bread machine and the never-ending supply of flour he had locked up in a couple of freezers he'd lugged inside the neighbor's and which ran when the Magnum ran. Ice-cold flour seemed to keep the mold away. He'd stored several hundred bags of flour as backup inside one of Giant's now useless meat lockers and that kept the rats away, but not the mold. Still, the number of bags outstripped the mold's progress, and he figured he had about ten years' worth. That is, until all the flour went rancid.

He microwaved and crock potted, saving the crock for the weekends when he had more power. Theresa had loved crocking, the working couple's best dinner strategy. She used it more than him but, every once in a while, John would throw in a pork roast smothered in apples, sauerkraut, onions, potatoes and carrots, and crock it for about 12-18 hours until the meat just fell off the bone. Man, could eat the whole thing himself. John smacked his lips thinking about it.

He should go hunting, pick up a pork roast, or an equivalent. There were wild pigs about, feral farm animals, not the javelina type. They'd formed packs like the dogs and moved into the suburbs because that's where all the food was. Pigs broke into the houses and feasted on the mummified bodies and whatever else was lying around.

They got into it with the wild dogs but held their own and prospered because they avoided live people. Not all the time, though. Pigs were actually pretty bold and there was a group of them in the parklands down Foxhall that, every once in a while, John had to warn off with a shot or two. Pigs hunt. They'd go after an unwary target, which John wasn't.

So maybe he should go after them, prove that he was still man and master, you little bastards. But he didn't want to butcher the meat. John never liked doing that. Dad was quite the avid hunter and always had a deer or two strung up from a tree during the season and John had done his share of bloodletting and evisceration and skinning, but hated it. Messy, stinky, pointless work when there were cans and trays of prepared meats of all type and grade available in the shining rows of the commissary. "Wotjewdo if there weren't no more com-missaries?" Dad asked.

Geez, those Depression era types and John wouldn't say anything because, c'mon, that wasn't going to happen. And it hadn't. "Commissary's still there, Dad," John pointed out, "still lots of cans. Difference is, no lines." John grinned. Humor.

John did shoot deer, but not to eat. Damn things, tearing up the bushes and having a go at the garden whenever they could. John had put up deer fence and used the wolf spray liberally, but they were persistent bastards. John left them where they fell, except if they were too close to the house; those he dragged off to the woods. If he thought putting their little deer skulls up on pikes would warn the others off, he would. Lupus and Hairbag had at the carcasses, which was fine, be-cause that bound them to him even more and gave them a taste for deer meat.

Deer may have lost their fear of man, but a couple of crazy dogs chasing them through the woods helped keep them at bay.

John was maintaining his weight, which was surpris-ing, given how much he burned getting back and forth to work. The advantages of empty calories.

There was a distinct shift, though, from the portly belly of Before to an After six-pack. He was stronger, he knew, and felt good, having regained just about all his youthful speed and endurance. He could go *mano a mano* with any number of punks and prevail. He seemed as fast and hard as in his younger days. Bring it on, mofos. Hmm, maybe the CDC started the Flu to combat the national epidemic of obesity, get everyone back in shape.

Kidding.

John took vitamins and his Before prescriptions, blood pressure and cholesterol medicine, the inevitable result of a Type A personality. "You'll be dead by 55," Dr. Kim had warned as he handed John three or four continuing scripts. "Stroke or cardiac arrest." Ha, now, he would *hope* to die from that, or anything natural, for that matter. Given his fat loss and very active lifestyle, he probably didn't need the daily dosage anymore, but, hey, maintain. You never knew. He had a couple of years supply of the medicine stored in the back bedroom and he'd keep popping the pills until gone or some doctor told him he could stop, which meant he'd end up finishing them because the only doctors left were CDC and there was no way they were getting hold of him. Didn't really need a doc, anyway. He hadn't been sick since the Event, not even a cold. The upside of depopulation. He did get hurt, pulled muscles and cuts and sprains because he was a clumsy oaf, but those were easily fixed, especially with his restored youthful healing powers.

The benefits of catastrophe.

John spooned another mouthful of chili and idly watched the anchor. News, what a joke. No one was fooled. The government took over the networks almost faster than they declared the Zone off limits, and even though the talking heads went to great lengths to declare how independent they were, c'mon. The biggest giveaway was the other programming, '60s sitcoms and

'50s movies, all the bright and cheerfully brainless crap that passed for TV back then. John loved *The Partridge Family* when he was 12, had a thing for Susan Dey, but now?

Independent networks, ha ha ha. The anchors looked too nervous and their phraseology was too neutral. So, you listened to what they said and figured out why the government let them say it, deducing what was really going on. An art form.

Like, right now, Nervous Nellie, the little pasty-faced white boy reading the news ("Live from Chicago!") was trying to sound stern about some new registration effort, our beloved junta requiring all US citizens to prove they were so by gathering at designated locations with their documents in hand. Nellie was failing.

John wondered how many people were stupid enough to actually comply. Draft Gangs would be there with little regard for the exemptions allowed married men or men with families or men not quite 18. John'd tell Collier to ignore this decree, like he ignored all the previous ones.

Pasty-face switched to some fighting in Arizona and New Mexico, isolated, arising from the Chiapas Revolution, easily contained by US forces and probably over by tomorrow so don't worry about it.

John frowned. That was odd. Supposedly, we'd kicked the crap out of Castro a few weeks after he got on his high horse and sent an army to Chiapas, causing Mexico to implode. Supposedly, we had Havana and Castro himself and, supposedly, we stopped the Chiapans somewhere in the Sonoran desert just south of the Rio Grande. Yet, fighting continued. Hmm.

Maybe we weren't as successful as previously portrayed. Maybe we didn't actually have Castro and maybe there's some real serious crap going on down there. Castro in Mexico? Double hmmm. That would explain the increased Draft Gang activity, although the Middle East meat grinder seemed motive enough. Better warn Collier to watch his ass.

And, like clockwork, Pasty turned to the Zone. You always got some commentary about it, usually some encouraging word or the other. Irritating. Tonight, the usual CDC hogwash about cleaning up the Zone soon and vaccine advances and the encouraging results of "trials" (read "experiments") on the poor bastards still in CDC labs. A little twist this time, though: the CDC was predicting a clear Zone in two years.

Now, that's different. Either the crapheads were expecting everyone to be dead by then or they just might be on to something. John blinked, his little core of perpetual hope twitching, but he shook that off pretty quick. More likely the CDC will nuke the Zone in two years and burn out the virus, when they were sure doing so wouldn't turn it Andromeda Strain or something.

John glanced at his watch. 9:00 p.m. Half hour to go. Good. He really needed to talk to Collier. Settle down, ease the day's concerns, find out what was happening at Fishburne.

Best decision he and Theresa ever made, sending Collier there, about a month before Sep 11, some four to six months before the Event. That's why he's still alive. John wasn't prescient or anything; he'd just had it with Fairfax County Public Schools. Collier was floundering and the school wanted to stick him in Basic Skills and label him Learning Disabled and drug him up. They encouraged his loser skateboard social life because he wasn't going to make it in college anyway so he might as well have some fun.

John got a little upset with that so, off to Fishburne, kicking and screaming, of course. In as little as two months, complete turnaround. Collier made honor roll. Honor roll! Take THAT up your Ritalin-prescribing asses, Fairfax County! He made cadet company first sergeant. Even more amazing, Collier loved it. Instead of being a loser, he was somebody.

Fishburne saved his life After, too. Collier came up with some harebrained idea of going home in the middle of everything. He tried to sneak out by going down a sheet rope, but the knots came apart and he broke his heel in the fall. They put him in the infirmary and literally handcuffed him to the bed. John was so grateful. A few cadets did sneak out and were never heard from again. No doubt their rotted corpses now decorate a few side roads just inside the Zone.

"What if you had gotten away?" John breathed in the phone the first time he recovered enough to call. "What if you had? You'd be dead now! You get it? Dead!" He'd been so upset.

All Collier could do was cry, upset himself, his mother gone, his world gone but here, from the grave, Dad's voice. "You'd have missed this call, Collier. I'd have missed this call." His only son, John's only link to a future, gone. "Don't ever do anything like that again!" Because you just don't know what's going to happen.

You just don't know.

Like planes that come from a clear summer sky and incinerate buildings, death unlooked for, unnecessary, cruel, fanatical death. A bolt from the blue, unanticipated, Pearl Harbor, Nagasaki, Hue.

The letters.

Those first deaths, in that newspaper office down in Florida. Odd. John and everyone else furrowed a collective brow and wondered what the heck was going on. Then five or six died in New Jersey and DC and New York, and everybody looked at each other with the still-furrowed brows. What the hell? It looked like someone was going after Senators, but clumsily, killing bystanders instead. Collateral damage. Eh, no big deal. Unfurrow the brow, shuffle off to work, shovel out Ground Zero.

Oh, of course, some panicked. Some always do, the superficial, the self-centered who somehow believe everything is about them, but, overall, there was more puzzlement than fear. It was too personal, too small, too weird. A single madman, a Ted Koscinski catalyzed by the Towers and the Pentagon, lashing out from some twisted revenge epic and sending anthrax through the mail, imagining, somehow, he was bringing about some needed apocalypse.

Small and weird and personal. Just that. Nothing bigger.

A couple of odd news stories about crop dusters showing up at odd times and letting loose some kind of aerosol the farmers or housewives or field hands being interviewed had not ordered, "Colsarnit, 'cause hit wuz waaaay past tahme fer dustin'," spit. Was that true? Were the farmers and housewives and field hands reporting Bigfoot? John thought so, even when he watched some climatologist telling a barely credulous fluffy-headed morning news anchor that the release points described by the farmers and housewives and field hands coincided with prevailing winds that wafted over very big population centers. Yeah. Right. Time for work.

When the first few people got sick, no big deal. Winter cold and flu season. Take your AlkaSeltzer and cough your way onto the Metro and the buses and off to the job. Gather at the lunch counters and McDonald's and cough some more, your leavings on trays and cups and doorknobs and paper towel dispensers. No one minded.

They watched, instead, for more airplanes falling out of the sky or gasoline trucks exploding on bridges or maybe that fabled dirty bomb, not a few more letters leaking powder or a couple more apocryphal crop dusting operations.

They smugly watched Al-Qaeda being ground to hamburger in Afghanistan and it was victory, victory, sweet Pyrrhic victory.

The first actual deaths from the Al-Qaeda Flu happened so sporadically no one really noticed. Old people, the kind of disheveled society-fringed derelicts you expect to die from something easy, like a cold or pneumonia. Because they went to the fringe emergency rooms dedicated to disposing of such wastes of human space, they didn't get the best of medical observation and were, in fact, written off as nothing more than the pneumonia victims they appeared to be.

Bill told John that one or two apparently halfway competent doctors at those meat shops actually raised some concerns because the morphology did not quite follow pneumonia. They were ignored.

John thought it would make a good Movie of the Week – heroic young iconoclastic doctors defying a system that, ultimately, lets them down.

"Hmm," Bill considered, "you're right. Good drama. Maybe I'll write it."

"Okay," John said, "but give this one a happier ending."

Neither of them laughed.

And then there was Baltimore.

Talk about caught with your pants down. In one week, almost a thousand people dead. Stunning. It seemed to radiate from downtown Baltimore to the Loops, jumping randomly from neighborhood to neighborhood. Given the origin, most doctors assumed it was some kind of new venereal disease, some virulent AIDS-type virus that the VD Capital of America had managed to incubate.

Sexual politics then interfered. The always-complaining gay organizations started screaming that this was a completely unjustified scapegoating of their lifestyle. People were keeling over right and left, no one had any idea what was going on, and the gay guys were crying about their rights. Unbelievable.

And tragic, because the ever-sensitive CDC slowed to a snail-like response. Not that any immediate quarantine would have stopped the inevitable, but maybe, just maybe, a few more would have lived.

They had their meeting at the campus and John was smug and then came the next wave, or waves, and all politics and social justice and progressive thought and attempts to be cooler-than-thou went right out the window in favor of mere survival.

A hammer-like series of sudden outbreaks quickly overwhelmed whole towns while John spent his three days walking the campus. It seemed like everyone between Baltimore and DC got sick and died, hundreds of thousands.

Hundreds of thousands of others outside the Beltway fled, packing kids and dogs and spouses and all they thought important into vans and Beetles and Amtrak cars and rushing out to New York and Delaware and New England. Going home, back to the parents and grandparents and hometowns they had left, starry eyed, years before to make their political or corporate or legal fortunes at the center of American power, leaving a cloud of death behind them and trailing an even bigger cloud of it along.

And still, no one knew what was going on.

The Al-Qaeda Flu started out small, barely noticeable, a cough that usually became a full blown wheeze, then the eventual drowning in one's own mucus. All of this in three days, max. Some people went in just hours, others lasted a few weeks, but the average was three days.

What it did to the medical community. Hospitals took in the first victims on the first day of their local wave and, by the end of the week, everyone in the hospital and the surrounding neighborhood was dead. What it did to the whole Northeast. The fleeing families piled gratefully into grandma's front room and clucked at each other and started hacking and, by the end of the week, everyone in grandma's neighborhood was dead. Except, of course, for the two or three who, coughing a bit, packed up their own vans or Beetles and headed out towards Maine and upper New York and Ohio or wherever they could get to, the cloud trailing behind them.

The CDC stood around looking helpless. They had lots of press conferences on just about every channel at just about every hour of the day and the sum total of all their words: we don't know.

They played the game perfectly, of course, showing white-coated white-haired grave-eyed experts, weary and disheveled, outside some medical facility droning on about tests and epidemiologies and progressions and then wisely speculating in their best deathbed manners.

Thousands more died. More press conferences, with more speculations and the reporters, those self-appointed intrepid protectors of the public weal, shouted stupid questions and tried to outsell each other's airtime by stoking whatever rumors they could find about whatever this was. Everyone would have done better to keep their mouths shut. All the despair they created.

They figured it out by sheer accident. A lab technician was working late down in Atlanta and had a sample from the Brentwood Post Office letters on a side table while he was checking blood from a Flu victim. Something clicked when he looked through the microscope so he grabbed the anthrax sample and started doing some comparisons. He smelled a rat, called a few of the scientists over and, after twelve heroic hours, the team unraveled it.

Set up.

It was a well-crafted attack, quite sophisticated, quite marvelous, really, coming as it did from a bunch of towel-headed fanatics.

The anthrax was a precursor, a conditioner, that was the word most used. Camouflage, distracting the immune system and, therefore, weakening it. It made people more receptive to the real attack, a virus. Brilliant. The best experts were about 80% sure it was developed in Saudi and transported by the same Al-Qaeda group that ended up driving the planes. Which, of course, was the reason Mecca was now a glass parking lot.

The anthrax letters were far more pervasive than anyone realized. They went everywhere throughout the Great Northeast, from Albany to Charlotte. The attacks on the Senate and the newspaper office were a clever distraction, offering up a particular MO to make everyone look for crudely written envelopes leaking lots of anthrax powder.

The real anthrax letters only contained a whiff and were in professional mass mailings offering credit cards and vacations and rebates, the kind of stuff most people tossed but some would open. They banked on the openers, and those people released enough of a cloud of the anthrax to make most immune systems respond properly. The four or five who died from anthrax kept everyone from seeing the hundreds of thousands of others who caught a mild cold for a few days about the same time. Very smart.

The crop dusting stories were true. The virus was on the wind, carried from Ohio and Kentucky over an area bound north from Albany to Fredericksburg and west from Winchester to the New York border. Because the ragheads were not sure exactly where the aerosol would fall, they had blanketed a much larger area with the precursor anthrax, from southern New York through southern Florida. It found everyone primed and ready. John found Theresa on the third day, in bed, coughing the hard cough, obviously engulfed in the stage of the Flu that paralyzed you with the effort to get air. John had seen enough of the symptoms by then to know what was going on so he wrapped her in blankets, felt the raging fever on her brow, and forced brandy down her throat, all in an effort to raise her temperature even more.

Fever was a friend because it burned viruses and he figured getting her up to 106 or 107 just might do what the CDC couldn't. She didn't fight him. She knew what he was trying to do, even though she was completely delirious. Two days of this before John felt the first tickle in the back of his own throat. John and Theresa were outside the various bell curves. He contracted the virus late, and she suffered longer than most.

Three days later, John crawled into the same bed, racked with the cough and choking for air and feeling the burning behind his temples. She was already in coma and John was glad she would go peacefully and he would, eventually, go at her side. At some point, John was in coma. At some other point, he woke up. And screamed.

John watched the news shift to weather and the big topic of jet streams and currents, which was more important now than local thunderstorms or tornados. You just never knew what else the towelheads had.

He turned it off. Enough. Enough.

20

Mood change. Needed one. The few times he'd called Collier in the middle of a black despair, he'd almost driven the poor kid to joining the army right then. He pushed out of the chair and walked over to the stereo. Music, the best mood changer short of a pill.

He thumbed through the albums. Yeah, albums, the pop of dust in vinyl tracks and the hum of the needle in the background. Screw those CDs. Overproduced, artificial and computer enhanced bastardizations of real music, which had to have flaws and fades and even a skip or two or it was just a lab experiment. Some rocker, drunk in the studio, missing a chord and the producer frowns but cocks a head and, after a moment, says, "We'll go with that."

Before, John used to crank the speakers to earthquake level, driving Snuffy outside, Theresa to the Mall, and the neighbors to move. Now he used headphones because even volume level '3' traveled well in this morgue-ish atmosphere. Dangerous, because the Laws of Unfortunate Timing guaranteed his alarms would sound at the very moment he was air-guitaring "Won't Get Fooled Again," so he had to keep an eye on Snuffy or pop one 'phone off and listen which, of course, ruined it. Damn towelheads.

He flipped through AC/DC, Floyd, Clash, and His Royal Majesty and God of All Music, Springsteen. He stopped. "Boss" didn't quite express his importance. Springsteen had managed to capture, in one song or another, every single moment of teenager John's rampage through New Jersey. Bruce was more than music; he was chronicle. John wondered if he Survived. If so, he's probably putting together the best material of his life. Not that it'd ever get airplay, unless he managed to hook up with a pirate somewhere and blast it out for a couple of hours before Sam zeroed in and missiled the transmitter.

The junta didn't like competition. Their radio stations were horrible, a continuous Public Service Announcement interspersed with the Archies or Perry Como, and their DJs were the smarmiest bunch of self-righteous goody-goody's ever collected under a broadcast tower, worse than a Christian station.

That's what happens when generals run the government, they play only what they like and this particular group had either forgotten the power of rock and roll or were suspicious of it, probably listening to Brahms back in the '70s while John was Lou Reed-ing it. Buncha nerds.

Rock and roll was America reduced to three or four electrified chords, the individual, the person, the rage against the machine. Didn't force Noriega out of that embassy by blasting Dean Martin at him, did we?

John really missed radio, good radio. Before, there was 94.7, the DC Classic Rock station, and John would tune in there for about twenty minutes of nostalgia. But how many times can you hear "My Best Friend's Girlfriend" before it drives you crazy? So he'd switch over to Baltimore's 98 Rock, the best station in America, bar none. They knew how to mix it up, a classic or two and then segue into the new stuff and John had to admit a lot of that was better than a lot of the old. Purists would have a stroke but, hey, things move, and rock moved. You have to move, too. You don't prefer Milton Berle over Eddie Murphy, unless you're stuck.

Granted, after the '70s, it looked like rock was dead and the purists were justified. The '80s were dreadful, with a few exceptions like the Cure and, of course, Springsteen. The early '90's was a rock graveyard and John only listened to his albums, putting on Traffic and early Genesis (never that late Phil Collins junk). But, about 1995, rock took off. Aerosmith returned, Metallica was going crazy, Limp Bizkit, and that utterly amazing Creed ... rock was back, man. Then the Event. Then everything died.

John turned Collier on to rock. After the kid got over his *Raffi/Sesame Street* stage, John sat him down in front of the turntable and put on some Hendrix, looked at him and said, "Any questions?"

Collier never went back. John took him to see Alice Cooper, J. Geils, the Scorpions and the Offspring. He even let Collier go with a group of friends to the last OzFest. That was Collier's coming-out party. He fell in love with the guitar and John was more than happy to pay for all the lessons.

Collier, and John, thought music would be his life. He would go to school for a while then roam the country doing back-ups, living off waiter tips and whatever gigs he could manage. Become a rich and famous rock star? Nah, that rarely happened. But live the life, surround himself with music and musical people and the attendant creativity and instability and craziness, sure.

What, was he nuts? What kind of trailer trash parents encouraged such a gypsy lifestyle? Well, trailer trash parents like John and Theresa, who both grew up hard, under cruel and violent circumstances. Life was not opportunity. It was struggle.

Early '70's, they were both nineteen. John was painting roads and she was working at a sewing factory. He was living in the back of a gas station with a buddy and she was sharing an apartment with a junkie friend of hers. They met at Gino's Hamburgers on 38 and fell in love and moved in together, two against the world. Their families hated them and their friends said they were crazy and they had no money, no prospects, no future.

So John did the only thing a low-class white boy living at

the time could do, married her and joined the USAF, a real loser move in the '70's, proof you had reached bottom. But he had, so what else was there? Turned out a good move, because he made a career and a life for both of them out of it. It wasn't his dream, but John hadn't really defined that. The need to survive trumps dreams.

But Collier could have dreams, so they taught him the premises. First and most important, money isn't everything. You can always get money. There's always a job out there and even the most unskilled of workers can make money, if they're willing to put themselves out. It depends on what's important to you.

If your reason for living centers around a big house and a big car and vaulted ceilings and dinner parties for the coworkers, so they can look at your Bang and Olufsen stereo, your collection of original opera recordings, your Van Gogh pencils and gush about your elevated tastes, with a slight tone of envy in their voices, then, welcome to DC, where the majority of your type live, and more power to you, Coll.

Second, gain control of your life, never beholden to but beholden by, create something for yourself that depends solely on you, not on boards or partners or corporate cultures. Stand on your own. Don't be like us, Coll, spending too much of life at the whims of others, from horribly abusive parents to capricious bosses; wage peasants, always fearful, never sure when the axe would fall.

An apartment over a garage is a palace if your guitar or paintbrush or typewriter pays for it, if *you're* deciding what your daily schedule will be, if *you* take or leave a job based on your own standards. That's freedom, that's what you want, and that's a real dream.

So find it, Coll.

Yeah. Find it ...

Ah, crap.

John was holding *Darkness at the Edge of Town*. How

appropriate. He put it back. No, no music. Let's read, instead. He walked over to the lounger and fingered the books loosely piled there. Frazer's *Golden Bough*, a compilation of all of Shakespeare's works, a compilation of all of Milton's works, the *Inferno*, T.S. Eliot, the *Decameron*, and, believe it or not, *War and Peace*. Those were his. Next to them were ones from the library, some Heinlein and C.S. Forester and some pre-Event popular things like *Snow Falling on Cedars*.

John was reading all those books at the same time, two or three pages each, switching around until he got tired. He wasn't a genius; he was just interested in too many things and wanted to keep the library books circulating as much as possible. In a separate pile were the how-to's, covering things like home wiring or fixing a foundation. John did whole chapters at a time in those. Not pleasure, study.

John stared at the books a moment and then sighed and shook his head. Nope, didn't want to read, either. Maybe he should watch a movie; one of his own or whatever he'd gotten from Blockbuster. It was about time to return those, anyway. Some other Loner appeared to be going in and out, treating the store the same way he did – return a movie, then take a movie. Didn't want to deprive a fellow traveler.

John had watched action movies at first but then turned to the classics and character studies, like *Dark Victory* and *Barry Lyndon*. He was getting all the real live action he could stand but little personal contact, so movies became his people simulator. He watched *It's a Wonderful Life* quite a bit, even after Christmas, tearing up at "the richest man in town," line until it dawned on him that George Bailey was a chump. His principled stand only got incremental improvements. Had he joined Potter, he could have taken over the old man's operations within six months and made everyone's lives an epoch better. And that premise, the you've-never-been-born angel thing, please. Were that true, none of those people would have mattered, none of those events would have registered, so who cared? Chump.

No, no movies, either. Felt like artifice. Game, then? John looked over at the card table. He had Squad Leader set up over there, the "Hedgehog of Piepsk" scenario. John had always liked board games, especially the complicated Avalon Hill ones, before Hasbro swallowed them up. He had just about every decent AH title, collected long before the Event. He'd played quite a bit Before, but rarely against an opponent. Theresa hated those games and his coworkers barely could handle Monopoly, so he ended up being his own opponent.

A thousand years or so ago, he and an Immigration agent up at Champlain, NY had played but the agent always kicked John's ass, no matter the game, and started calling him the French. You can take just so many insults, so it was kinda relieving when John got orders and had to leave Patton behind.

Playing solo now, it was like the French versus the Italians, but there was no one to criticize, so hey. Sending cardboard soldiers and tanks to their doom. War as hobby was so much more relaxing than war as a lifestyle.

But not tonight.

John stood still, trying to suppress the restlessness. Wouldn't go away, that maddening little itch at the base of the stomach driving him from one distraction to another. What did he want? He didn't know. For things not to be the way they were, of course, but, really, they'd always been so, in one form or another, as a capricious and cruel Fate repeatedly targeted him.

Born into an imploding family that, finally and mercifully, split up when he was thirteen, followed by poverty and hopelessness then escape, Theresa beside him, then the 25-year struggle to get some level of control and there, within sight, mastery of his life and, poof, the end of the world.

He thought he'd be used to it by now, would chuckle at

his role in the Universe. God's hacky sack. But he still had those damned expectations, a feeling that everything would turn out great. He must be, at heart, an optimist. More likely, at heart, delusional.

He looked at his watch. Five more minutes. No calling early; Fishburne was death on time. He had to wait the whole five minutes. He could fidget and fuss and get exasperated or he could simply watch it pass, five minutes where nothing was happening, no conflict, no guardedness, no fear. Time travel. John held his breath and slid down the moment, disappearing.

It was now five years ago. But the silence, unearthly. What explains that? One of those rare nights, yeah, that's all, where the whole neighborhood has gone out, be back later, and a trick of atmosphere has masked traffic noise. Theresa's just made a run to Giant.

Five minutes is five years is forever.

He closed his eyes and savored it, repopulating the world and reinvigorating the culture. Everything's fine, everything's okay. He was not armed and bunkered and crouching at war. It's a quiet moment, that's all, and nothing has happened. The moment extended, though, well past the few seconds of stillness only an odd combination of traffic interruption and a shopping neighborhood would explain. John opened his eyes. Back to the future. Back to the emptiness.

Was he lonely? Nah, not really. He didn't miss the great blob of people all that much, never having been big on them. His contacts had been few and selective and never permanent. Theresa and Collier were the exceptions, all the companionship he ever really needed and he still had one of them, so ...

The Event was just something that happened and he was spared and was now responding appropriately, going through requisite routines and vengeances. He didn't seem to be as upset as he should be. He was probably numb, but he'd felt like that his whole life so maybe, just maybe, a history of personal tragedy gave you tools. You could deal. And you could still maintain an optimistic sense that, even after all this, everything would be okay.

Okay? That made him laugh aloud and he shook his head and saw only two more minutes to go so, good, worthwhile exercise. But nothing was going to be okay, come on already. This was not a good life. Sheer existence, just being alive, was now the point of it all and wasn't supposed to be. Only in Fourth World hellholes was that true.

Fourth World hellholes.

John stood quietly, watching the second hand sweep around his watch. Face it. Accept it. The Shining City on the Hill was now a mudflat. The life of richness and detail and possibility had given way to fear and danger and ugliness with absolutely no prospect of becoming anything else, indeed, of becoming worse. Chad. Abandon all hope. This is the way things are. You are defeated. You lost.

Like. Hell.

John flipped open the cell as the second hand hit twelve. Not him. The country, yes, Western civilization, okay, but not him. He would never be beaten. Send more of your anthrax, spray more of your viruses, loose your radiation. Dance in your shit-strewn streets and ululate your weird-ass desert yowls and fire off those AKs until the barrels melt and smirk at each other and hug each other and screw each other up the ass. Bring it on, motherfuckers, you, your wives, your children, your whole shitrag culture. And bring it on, Bundys and Vandals and Raiders and soldiers and Draft Gangs and Cubans and everyone. Fuck you. Fuck you all. John would dance on top of their shattered bones, even if it takes forever.

Yeah. Absolutely fucking yeah.

He grinned. He hit "send."

21

Collier stood impatiently by the pay phone mounted in the breezeway, Davis dancing next to him and a few others dancing behind him. C'mon already, Dad, it's 2131, you're a minute over and we only get thirty, now twenty nine, and there's things, Dad, things, and I need some advice. He looked at his watch for the ten thousandth time. Yeah, could be a matter of unsynchronized timepieces although he and Dad calibrated at the end of each call but please, Timex. Could be a matter of the last functioning pay phone in a three mile area finally crapping out and he looked suspiciously at it. Work, damn you. Don't fail tonight ...

Brrrriing.

Like a cartoon character, Collier ripped the receiver off the hook and juggled it to his ear. "Hello?" he said. A ripple of anticipation flowed through the spectators and Collier saw Sergeant Zell, the night guy, standing outside the CQ office, pointedly look at his watch. Collier gestured at his own and frowned. Zell nodded and walked inside. Rules is rules, but damn, man.

"Coll?" Dad's voice, tinny, distant.

"Hey, Dad," his relief was evident.

"Hey, Coll, how ya doing? It's good to hear you."

"Yeah, good to hear you, too, Dad. How are you?"

"I'm good. There was some weirdness coming home tonight that's got me a bit edgy, but I'm okay."

"What kind of weirdness?"

"Well, when I left, I felt like I was being followed.

When I got to the Key Bridge, there was no one there and it sounded like some kind of fighting going on up the street."

"Really? Did you go look?"

"No. I'm not stupid."

Collier frowned. Wasn't stupid to check something out. "I would have," he said.

"Difference between us," Dad's voice had that underlying ridicule that so grated. "I'm partial to seeing the next day."

Collier held his snort. Piss Dad off and he'd just hang up and Collier had other things to discuss. "What do you think it was?" he asked.

"I dunno. Raiders, probably, but they had to be complete morons to strike so close to an MPD checkpoint."

"So you don't think it's Raiders?"

"No," Dad paused. "Something else. Someone challenging MPD's authority. Not a smart move."

"Yeah, MPD probably kicked their ass."

"No doubt. I'm going to go look tomorrow."

Tomorrow? A little late to help, don'cha think, Dad? Collier kept that to himself, "Be careful, Dad."

"You know me, the epitome of caution." Epitome, what a Dad word. Collier rolled his eyes as Dad continued, "Besides, I'll know MPD won if the checkpoint is manned again."

"Yeah, that's true." All right, enough of this Zone talk, Dad, there's some real issues out here.

"You sound down, Coll."

Collier blinked. Dad's ESP again. The guy could smell trouble miles away, a talent severely cramping Collier's style growing up. "Yeah, yeah, guess I am."

"Something happen?"

He hesitated. You had to be careful. Saying right things in a wrong way could get you a midnight disappearance. "This and that," he glanced at Davis. "You gonna tell him?" Davis whispered in his ear, and Collier frowned him off.

"Is Davis with you?"

Geez. Dad also had radar ears. "Yeah, he's bugging me about a DVD we're going to watch on the computer." Davis tapped him on the shoulder and Collier brushed him back. Play along, dude.

"Don't get caught. What's the DVD?"

"*Braveheart.*"

Dad chuckled, "Well, that's about perfect."

"That's what we thought."

"So you're willing to risk a week's stockade for a little inspiration, huh?"

"Of course. Wouldn't you?"

"Coll, I'm willing to lose a limb for some hope these days."

Despite himself, Collier chuckled. "Dunno if I'd go that far."

"Eh, what's a leg? Can always get a wooden one."

"Yeah, patch and a parrot, you'd be set."

"Arr, matey," Dad was quick and they both laughed.

"Wadesay wadesay?" the hangers-on pestered Collier and he turned, irritated, "C'mon guys, small joke."

"Coll," Dad said, "tell it to them."

Coll sighed. Dad insisted he share their private conversations. Makes the hangers-on part of something, he said. Right, right, but geez, Dad, there's things and we're running out of time! "Look, he just made a pirate joke," and Coll explained and Davis grinned bigger than he should and the hangers all guffawed and slapped each other's backs way out of proportion to the humor. Collier stared at them like they were idiots.

The small memory of good, Dad said, is far more powerful than the large memory of evil. These days, the small memories sustain. Coll supposed Dad was right, but, guys, come on, it wasn't that funny.

"So," Dad said, "you still haven't explained why you're down."

Okay, good, but beeeee careful. "Oh, I don't know, the usual crap."

"Yeah, but I'd think you'd be used to the usual crap by now."

"Hmm." Signal, Dad.

He got it. "What's going on?" Dad was suitably alarmed

"Just some rumors." Danger. This made the conversation interesting to eavesdroppers.

"What kind?"

"There's some talk about activating us."

"There's always talk about that."

"I suppose," Collier let that hang for a long moment, knowing that Dad's dismissal eased the monitors and they had now fallen asleep. "But it's coming from inside this time."

"How do you know?"

"I heard it. Myself." There.

A long, long pause. "Damn," was all Dad said.

"Yeah," was all he said.

They sat in silence for a long time. Dad was probably trying to figure out a way to tell him it was just a rumor, there was nothing to be concerned about, nothing is going to happen, you'll be all right. Stay out of the army. Forget the air force. Go to school. Get a girl pregnant, get a lot of girls pregnant. As much as he enthusiastically agreed with that last one, he was no longer sure he could avoid the first one.

"I've been watching the news and they haven't mentioned anything like that." There it was, Dad's pathetic try and Collier gave it the appropriate snort, "Didja think they would?"

"Jesus, such a cynic."

"Come on, Dad." Davis was restless next to him and

the others were restless beyond and he waved all of them
down. They'd picked up his mood and yeah, what a
buzzkill, but we have things to face, fellas, things.

"They'd have to say something." Dad was still trying.

"They don't have to say anything, Dad." Collier was
still snorting.

"Yeah they would, they'd need to prepare us."

"Why?"

"Because history tells them to. We lost Vietnam because they wouldn't."

"*Phw!*" Collier let Dad know his thoughts on that.

"It's true. I happened to be there, you know."

"I thought you joined the air force *after* Vietnam."

"Well, yeah, six days before it ended, actually, but I
grew up back then. We won all the battles, but we didn't
pursue victory. It was like fighting a weekend war, so no
one wanted to go."

"Did you want to go?"

"Well, no! I wasn't crazy. Getting killed for no reason?"

"So what's the reason now, Dad?"

"Survival." One word. One indisputable word and
Dad was, as usual, as maddeningly usual, right.

"We lost Vietnam because we lacked the will to win,"
Dad was still on it. "The idiots running things right now
know that. If they're going to pull something major like
activating the Provos, then they have to prepare us,
otherwise they'll lose this one, too."

"Dad!" Collier winced. That probably regained the
wiretapper's attention.

"All right, all right." Dad was getting wound up and
he always got political and said scary things and Capt.
Bock always warned Collier to avoid those conversations,
saying guys in black fatigues would come by and demand assurances of Collier's loyalty. They'd never
showed up, as far as he knew, but why take the risk?

"So," Dad was finally getting to his convoluted point, "until you actually see something on the news, I wouldn't sweat it."

"Really," the perfect pitch of disbelief.

"Yes, really," the perfect pitch of don't-be-a-smartass.

"Did you watch the news tonight, Dad?"

"Yeah, and there was nothing like that."

"Was there anything about the car bomb in Charlottesville?"

A collective gasp from Davis and the others. Collier had just guaranteed a black fatigue visit and Captain Bock exploding and probably some confinement time and, worse, loss of phone privileges. But, so what? Collier's footing had lost purchase, his grip slipping. He needed a lifeline. Dad, throw me one.

Dad was appropriately stunned. "What?"

"Didn't mention that little incident, did they?" Big surprise.

"No. What are you talking about?"

Collier told him.

"Who did it? The towelheads?" Dad asked after some moments.

"No. Somebody else."

"Somebody else? Who else is there?"

"The National Liberation Front?"

"What?"

"National Liberation Front. NLF. You're not seeing anything on the news about them, either, are you?" Not a question. Dad's resulting silence was definitely an answer.

"We've seen some flyers," Collier pulled away from Davis' frantic sleeve-tugging. "They're against the government, this new government, anyways, declaring them tyrants and saying they're here to free everybody from oppression."

"And they're not the towelheads?"

"No, Dad. More like Communists."

"Communists?"

"Yeah, Dad, geez!" He rolled his eyes. Would you catch up already? "Something like that, anyway. The flyers talk about oppression and striking off the chains and the people shall rise, you know, that kind of stuff."

"You're right. Communists. How sixties."

Collier let out a long sigh. Dammit, Dad, tell me what to do. "This isn't funny. It's not funny at all."

But Dad said nothing.

Something big and ugly was moving out there. Collier's lost footing became vertigo, the floor beneath cracking, the supports giving way. The earth became Jell-O. No anchor, no reference point, no bearing. He didn't know which way was up and he was out of control, the wing dipping too far and dumping the air and the controls unresponsive and the spiral starting, loose and long and slow, but picking up speed, growing tighter, loading him up and he was paralyzed, unable to grasp the stick, push down and try to regain the craft.

"Dad?" he breathed. Save me.

"Coll ..." a pause, "did you ever study the Dark Ages?"

What the hell? "I don't know, maybe."

"Well, I guess if you had to pick the worst time in human history, that was it, after the fall of the Roman Empire, when the hordes swept Europe."

"Okay." Is this really the time for a history lesson, Dad?

"I mean, you can't imagine it."

"Yes, I can."

Dad ignored his flat tone, "Not only was there no organized society, but all of the learning disappeared, everything people had known about science and medicine and civilization just, *poof,* gone. I don't know if you know this or not, but the Arabs actually collected all the

Western knowledge, Aristotle's writings and things like that, and took it to Baghdad."

"I think you told me that before."

"Yeah, well, it's important. Hadn't been for them, there'd be no Western civilization. Anyway, things were bleak, people died in their twenties, plague and superstition and war was just everyday life. The Catholic Church had an iron grip and was more interested in power and wealth than salvation. Most people were slaves of their governments, which were nothing more than ignorant strong men bashing everybody with swords."

"Dad. Point?" Collier looked at his watch.

"You want a point?" Dad was irritated, but come on already. "Here's your point – things were bad, and we came out of it."

"*Phffft*," Collier let him know what he thought of that. "So, I should just wait around for, oh, say, a thousand years and everything will be okay again?"

"Oy," Dad always said that when he was really mad and wanted to control his temper, but Collier didn't care. "Would you let me finish? No, you're not going to wait around. You're going to do what good men of the time did."

"What's that?"

"Find an island."

"Huh?" An island? Had Dad, finally, gone crazy? "What island? Like in the middle of the Shenandoah? Little too shallow, I'm thinking."

"No. Listen," Dad's voice was tight and controlled, the here's-why-you-don't-do-drugs tone. "Not what I mean. Islands of sanity. Sanctuary. The monasteries in Ireland and England that preserved what learning they could, the Andalusians who brought the Greek and Latin masters back to Europe, a few brave men, here and there."

Last time we checked, Dad, your son was basically a

prisoner and the world was a giant concentration camp. "Now how am I going to find those?"

"They're there," Dad's voice was grim. "You have to find them. Or, make your own."

He was at the end of the spiral, the ground rushing up, but a thermal, a slight rise, and he made for it, hope like a wolf in him. Make his own. He looked at Davis and the hangers and, yes, these were good men, not boys anymore, and they would form an island. But, details, Dad. "How am I going to do that?"

Instead of an answer, Collier got Dad's sharp intake of breath. Collier blinked. There was an odd sound in the background. "Dad? What's that? What's wrong?"

"Coll," Dad's voice was quiet but Collier could read the underlying panic. His own rose. "Coll," Dad repeated, "that's the alarms." Collier gasped. He could hear Snuffy barking now. "Dad!" he shouted.

"Coll," the same quiet voice, but now steel underneath, "I'm going to have to call you back."

"Dad!"

"It's probably just another raccoon, but I gotta go see, and I gotta go right now."

"Dad!" Collier was shrieking by now. Davis had him by the shoulders and the hangers-on were shouting "What's wrong?" and Zell was out the door "What's going on?" and doors were opening all over the decks but Collier kept an iron grip on the receiver and screamed for Dad over and over. But the phone was dead.

22

You can prepare and drill and practice for the anticipated emergency, considering all possible responses, practicing them until they're rote memory, but, when it actually happens, there is still that first moment of surprise and panic.

No amount of planning, no matter how finely honed, ever erases the conviction that the emergency, however conceived, just won't happen. The river won't rise, the hurricane goes elsewhere, the earth never shakes. Never.

John was in that moment, paralyzed, unable to breathe, gripping the cell phone, while from upstairs came the insistent *whee whee whee*. Snuffy wasn't paralyzed; he'd jumped to the bottom of the stairs, ears up and hair bristling, barking at the alarm and glaring back at John, asking "what the hell is going on?" Good question, Snuff, but John was still frozen and that was damnable because he'd been through this before, when the raccoon got in, so you'd think he'd just spring up, ready for action. You'd think.

"No way." That was his first thought; that was why he couldn't move. Just no way.

The people in the Tower, standing at the window sipping a coffee, looking out and, surprise, isn't that airplane coming right at us? No way. So they stood and stared, puzzled, realizing too late, just a few moments too late, what was about to happen. Like they could have sidestepped it or something, but, maybe a faster reaction would have given them a few extra seconds to go "Oh, shit" and dive under a desk and whip out their cell phones and call home and tell someone they haven't told in months that they love them.

Oh, shit.

That broke the spell. "Snuffy! Shut up!" and the dog went to a growlwhine as John stood while the battle song roared in his ears and he was back in control and flowed, just flowed, to the landing, inventorying the .357 and tanto and .25 and let's get the mini-14 ...

The lights went out.

Utter surprise, that, and he gasped, standing in pitch blackness, one foot on the stairs, his mind whirling. Getting caught by the alarm was one thing, this was another. The dark was like gauze pressed to his face, stifling, and he threw out his free hand against the wall, misjudging the distance and stoving a finger. Dammit! Complete disorientation.

What the hell did he do now?

Snuffy was pressing and whining against his supporting leg, threatening to topple him, and all he could do was stand there, unplanned. Light! Light! his mind screamed. Where in the hell did he put those candles and did he leave some matches next to them and when was the last time he checked and Jesus it's so freakin' dark, fuckin' absolutely dark and he was completely unprepared.

Wasn't supposed to happen this way. Lupus and Hairbag would start barking and the alarms would sound and he would move to the panel and look at the cameras and see what's going on and relax because it's another raccoon. Or arm up because it's Vandals and engage the Claymores or slip out the back and engage by rifle but there was always going to be lights and power and the advantage of surprise.

Now who's surprised?

His heart pounded and his eyes craved something so they started making dots and waves and that was distracting so John shut them tight. Didn't help. All right, all right, get control. John gritted his teeth. Think, you idiot. The only noise was Snuffy's whining but it's nervous, not alarmed, so okay, whatever it is, it's still distant so you've got time. Time. You know the house and the area so you've got advantage and, c'mon, face it, this may, very well, be nothing more than some water in the lines, yeah, maybe that's it, that's all, caused the alarms to go and the power to cut and all he had ahead of him was one bitch of a job replacing cables.

He took a breath, a sense of relief washing through him. Things might be all right. You may have scared Collier to death for no reason. Good, good, getting that grip, heart slowing down, hyperventilation over.

Now, see to this. Hell, see, period. A dungeon in here and he didn't want to break a shin stumbling around. Reflexively, John squeezed the cell phone and suddenly there was a pool of green light illuminating the steps.

He laughed. Dumbass, had a flashlight in your hand the whole time. He waved the corpse light around, a corpse's view, and oriented himself. So, where were those damn candles ... hey, wait, why bother with candles? The NVGs were on the dining room table.

Perfect.

John walked upstairs, guided by the phone light, while Snuffy, big coward, pressed from behind. He grabbed the goggles and put them over his glasses and turned them on. Vision, blessed vision, even if it was still corpse light green.

No use looking at the panel. He had to go outside. Better do a little recon first – while this was likely a mechanical problem, you never knew, and he shouldn't just stroll out of the house whistling, as if he was going to replace the porch light or something. He moved toward the kitchen door, telling himself to take it easy, open it gently, just a crack, nothing fast, nothing betraying, you'll be all right. You're safe in here ...

John froze, because a line from a movie suddenly jumped into his head. "Fortifications are a monument to man's stupidity." Something like that, from *Patton*, George C. Scott in character, expressing his contempt for the Siegfried line. He'd need to see it again to get the quote just right, but the sense of it, oh, yes, he grasped that, and chills shook him.

He'd built his own Siegfried, hadn't he, with redundant generators and power sources and fighting positions and cameras and alarms, feeling rather smug while doing so. Monumental stupidity. Nineveh, Tyre, they fell, as did Constantinople and the Alamo and the Western Wall and, yes, the Siegfried. So did the US.

And so will he.

His confidence, well maintained to this point, cracked and shuddered and crashed around his feet. Hubris. In this anarchic nightmare post 9/11 world, there he was, smarter than the average bear and no one's going to get the best of him, nosireebob. Nobody out there among the 15-20,000 immediate Survivors could outthink him, could they? Oh no, not at all, as the war grew closer and the shooting around the campus more continuous and a savaged body was left for his amusement and someone launched a full scale attack on MPD.

Nope, don' mean nothin', and he just blithely biked back and forth, five days a week from the Siegfried to the heart of the beast, setting a pattern, arrogantly thinking he wasn't, pointing a big red neon light right back at the house.

You moron, you brought them down on you.

John stood for a moment, blinking in the green world. Okay, your fault. Now, let's take care of this, shall we?

Snuffy had worked his way between John's legs and

was standing at the jamb with his tail down, looking defensive, hearing something John wasn't. John kneed him out the way and cocked his ear to the door window. Yep, there it was, a thumping sound, like something falling or, more likely, some*one* falling. John held his breath. A crash, loud now, the sound of glass and wood breaking so no doubt about it, this was an attack.

All right, take a moment, get control, don't panic, above all, don't panic. Consider the situation. It's all next door. They've taken the bait and are looking for him there. Advantage, but power's out so no panels so he didn't know how many so advantage diminished. To get it back, he needed information, and quickly.

He fished the keys out of his pocket and, brushing the handle of the .357 for luck, unlocked the door, thanking God he regularly oiled the hinges. Slowly, he pulled it open and peered out.

The world was green and bright, the moonlight fueling the NVGs. A group of people, about 20, leather clad and long-haired and dreadlocked, spiked chains around their necks, weapons, so many weapons, strapped across backs or hanging from hips or clutched in hands, maces and knives and guns and clubs and rifles, definitely rifles, assault types, were scattered between the driveway and the neighbor's side yard. Another 20 or so were running to and fro around the back of the neighbor's house. Certainly were a lot of them. And a lot of them were wearing night vision.

Oh, shit.

Hastily, John shut the door, stood back, and told himself, again, not to panic. Yeah, right. Pretty quick, they're going to see the cables leading out the neighbor's and into the ground and pointing oh so clearly at his door. If you're going to do something, John ole boy, you better do it now.

Faster than he should, especially with Snuffy hugging

214

his legs, he crossed to the living room, grabbed the panel off the table, and quickly checked the wires while matching them to the proper numbers. He uncapped the plunger and, for just a second, hesitated. Oh man, has it come to this? Yep. He pulled it up, switching the connection to the master control, twisted and pushed down hard.

All self-contained, this, it generated its own spark and, even though the wire was about 20 yards long, no problem. Not much of a spark was needed, just a hint, actually.

John felt the shaking of the house at the same time as he heard the sharp roar of an explosion. That was satisfying. At least this part of his defenses was working. He could imagine it, the Claymores spraying the inside of the neighbor's with grapeshot, a gigantic shotgun blasting huge lead balls every which way faster than the speed of sound, blowing out windows and doors with the overpressure alone, wreaking death on everyone inside and havoc on everyone outside.

He would have a lot of cleaning up to do.

No time to gloat, though. He slapped the .357, the tanto, and the .25 in sequence as he raced up the stairs, depth perception be damned, and grabbed the mini-14 from the pegs over the bed, ensured a full clip in it and grabbed the additional clip he kept on the nightstand. He ran down the stairs but stopped on the landing because the NVGs suddenly bloomed. Too much light and he ripped the goggles over his head and blinked away the green flowers, readjusted his skewed glasses, and peered hard at the door.

It was glowing, red and yellow light pouring through the curtained window, illuminating everything, making the NVGs superfluous. Must be the fireball from the explosion. Wow, big one. John heard screams and curses and running and, couldn't help it, smiled. That's for

Lupus and Hairbag, you fucks. Killed the dogs, did you? Well, I am going to kill all of you.

Battle blood raged in John's ears and heart and eyes and he was Mars and Kali and the gods of all death and he will tear out their hearts and sate himself on their meat. Snuffy was entwined about his feet and howling and he kicked the dog away. No time to attend to you, pup. War is on us.

There was a loud crash to his left and John instinctively ducked, turning towards the French doors. Frantic movement there and then another crash and the butt end of some kind of rifle broke through the panes. A lot of jostling around that smashed point meant a lot of people, and John brought up the 14 and let loose. Screams and jerky movement told John he was hitting those people. He emptied about half the clip and the movement from the door was clearing and he was winning, by God ...

The whole world lit up.

John smacked back hard against the stairwell, the concussion from the flash grenade hitting him before the sound, double whammy. His brain scrambled, which is what flash grenades were designed to do. Snuffy began howling somewhere in the living room and John looked for him but was too dazzled and thought maybe if he just used the NVGs he'd regain his sight and his balance and clarity and he pawed at his head before it occurred to him the last thing he needed right now was more light. There was plenty of that. Get a grip, get a grip, do something, anything, gotta come out of this.

He swayed towards the French doors and, just on instinct, fired a few rounds that way. That should make them cautious.

All right, okay, settle down, settle down, you're not hurt, you're not. Come on, man, pull it together. John took a breath and felt his mind falling back to its normal position.

Good, but you've lost time and, damn, now someone was smashing at the front door. John looked over. The neighbor's burning house was lighting up everything rather well, to the point he could see the front door starting to buckle from whatever was being used on it.

Well, they're going to have a hard time getting in that way because John had two huge plastic trashcans filled with old Christmas stuff blocking the foyer. All the lights and ornaments and even the plastic tree he'd bought in Florida in 1979 and subsequently, lugged around the world were in there. He set it all up every year, minus the outside lights since the Event, of course. This past season, he'd convinced himself it was pointless to put everything back into the attic so he packed everything into the trashcans, instead. He never used the front door anyway. Now wasn't he glad he'd succumbed to laziness?

A fusillade of shots sprayed from the French doors, a real firestorm and John ducked into the stairwell. Snuffy screamed and howled, twisting on the living room floor. Sonofabitch, they've hit him. John cursed as he watched the dog writhing in pain and blood. There was nothing he could do. Bastards, you bastards.

He turned the 14 towards the French doors and let off about ten rounds. "Fuckers!" he cried. They fired back in fury, screaming some kind of inarticulate battle cry. Well, two can play that, and John roared, some long drawn syllable of defiance. Kill my dog, huh?

He raked the French doors with about six more shots and they redoubled their return fire, bullets flying past John's stairwell haven and into the front door and wall, shattering the picture window. More light from the burning neighbor's house poured in, as did a volley from the cretins at the front, zipping past John and out the French doors.

John watched in amazement. These idiots were killing each other!

Bullets flew back and forth ripping up the living room, blasting furniture apart, gouging out the walls and tearing up the carpet and there were screams and curses and fire and shrapnel. The display case against the far wall evaporated and all those beautiful Andrea bird and flower figurines and cool Norman Rockwell statues Theresa picked up in Okinawa fragmented and went flying, scything the air with deadly shards.

He couldn't see Snuffy – must be down out of view. His house and memories were being shredded but John almost burst out laughing because these guys were doing his job for him. They had John flanked, but so what?

The least he could do was exacerbate the situation so he fired the rest of the clip at the French doors and was rewarded with a redoubling of fire back into the house and out the front. He dropped the clip and slapped in a fresh one as the guys in the front raged and cut loose back out the French doors and this time he couldn't help it, he laughed out loud. This was too damned easy! John busted off about ten rounds both front and back, thoroughly enjoying himself.

Suddenly, a loud voice roared out some kind of order, the exact words lost but the tone of it clear and commanding. The shots from out front stopped and the ones from the back stopped a few moments later. The voice bellowed some more, rich and deep and sonorous and John knew who it was, the chief of these maggots, who had realized what was happening. So, possibly not an idiot.

Which probably meant the fun was over.

John heard the clink of broken glass, hesitant movement from the French doors. There was movement at the picture window, too, and someone started pounding on the front door again and then someone was turning the kitchen doorknob, opposite John on his line of sight. Flashlights lanced in from front and back. Well, we can't have that, can we? John fired five quick shots in both directions and a couple out the kitchen door.

All hell broke loose. Two more flash grenades blew up in the dining room, dazzling John, although the stairwell protected him from most of the effects. Bullets again poured from the back and front and somebody began blasting through the kitchen door, which was most unfortunate, those rounds splintering the stairwell wall and whizzing past John's head. The step he was sitting on shattered into wood pulp as the guy from the kitchen stitched it.

Why John hadn't been cut in half he didn't know, but, obviously he couldn't stay here. He fired toward the kitchen and then crabbed up the stairs, trying to blink away the white spots swimming in his vision while Kitchen Boy's shots followed him up. Man, could they see him or were they just guessing?

John let off several more rounds as he reached the top and ducked around the wall, hugging the linen closet next to the hallway bathroom, safe for the moment. He took in a deep breath.

Jesus.

Kitchen Boy started firing again and John watched as rounds ripped up the landing wall opposite him. More fire poured in from the back and front but that stopped after a few moments and he heard, again, the sounds of hesitant movement. They're coming in, that is, if they can get Kitchen Boy to stop shooting. John was out of harm's way here, so he could afford a few minutes break.

A few minutes. That was about all the time he had left. Face it, you're screwed. His only option was retreat into the bedroom, and he had only one bad option after that, jumping out the window, but it was a second story so he would most likely break a leg. What's that old poem? The best laid plans ... yeah, yeah.

He couldn't help chuckling. If this was an old war

movie, he'd light a cigarette right now. Hell, a cigar would be better. Maybe he should go down in the living room and get one. John chuckled some more. Resignation has quite the calming effect. Take a few moments, catch the breath, relax a bit, quickly review the last forty years or so and have a regret or two, and then go into the bedroom and get ready.

There were fifty more .223 rounds under the bed in a backpack, not in a clip, dammit, and he doubted he had enough time to load them. But, the shotgun was in there, fully loaded, and there was another 50 shells of pumpkin ball and buckshot in the same backpack as the .223s, along with five grenades, and yes, the .357, the tanto, and the .25. He was going to take some maggots with him. But not enough.

John no longer felt like chuckling. No way he was going to win this. Even if he barricaded the bedroom door with the bed and chest, he'd only manage a few grenades and a few shots before they stormed him. They don't even have to do that. They could wait him out, let him starve, or, better yet, set the place on fire. Houses burn pretty good 'round here, as he'd just shown them.

John blew out a long breath in the universal sound of exasperation. Idiot. Idiot, idiot, idiot. He was hosed. He'd been partially successful – the Claymores worked, he got a goodly number of the punks while they only got Snuffy, but, ultimately, he'd lost. He was going to die. In a blaze of glory, naturally, but die, all the same.

Collier would never know what happened, the house would be ransacked and John and Theresa and their particular history would blur into the general tragedy of the times. Inevitable. Ever since the Event, he'd been moving toward this moment. John rubbed the back of his neck. He'd been on borrowed time all along and wasn't sure he'd made the best of it. Find out when he and the Lord had that long overdue face-to-face. Get ready, Jesus.

John grinned, working his neck around to loosen the kinks. Wouldn't do to get a cramp in the last few seconds of life, might mess up his aim. He tilted his head back as far as he could, feeling the tension cracks in the base of his neck, and stared straight up at the attic trap door.

He blinked just once.

Instantly he was through the bedroom door, doing a slide-for-home-base, desperately clawing under the bed until he found the backpack and yanked it out. He dropped the .14 and groped for the shotgun, locating it next to the nightstand, and ran back, snagging a bedroom chair with one arm and throwing it under the trap door. Flashlights were converging in the living room so he had, at best, seconds.

He scrambled up the chair, punched the trap door, threw in the shotgun and knapsack and grasped the attic edge. He pulled himself up, stomach braced on the inside lip, and prayed his natural clumsiness didn't take this opportunity to assert itself as he swung his legs hard against the chair. It careened away, clattering back into the bedroom.

Shots raked the landing and, motivated by that, John levered up, momentarily catching the .357 on the lip. He canted to one side, rolling over as he grabbed the trap door and slapped it into the attic opening. He took one gigantic breath and held it.

No way he just pulled this off.

The attic was cold as hell and too damned dark, only a little bit of the fire from next door managing to bleed in from the vent at the far end. John could hear a lot of running and yelling and a few shots from outside, but he was safe for now. Not only safe, sonofabitch, look at this, he had the high ground, he had the advantage.

You bastards are going to pay.

John pulled the NVGs down. All the boxes and suitcases and other crap Theresa and he put up here since moving in jumped out in sharp green relief. He crawled over to the knapsack and sat up, careful not to bang his head on the roof trusses. He was covered in spray insulation and felt itchy and had to suppress a cough. Least of his worries right now, in fact, was actually a good thing because the insulation deadened the sounds he made. He reached into the knapsack and felt the grenades and pulled out several shotgun shells and stuffed them in his pockets. All right, check, .357, .25, tanto, shotgun.

Bring it on, motherfuckers.

The shooting stopped and John heard movement in the living room. There was some muttering, the maggots down there having a conversation. Probably about him. The noise suddenly picked up as someone began stomping around and yelling nonsense and then someone else yelled, "Shut up, man!" and it was pretty still.

Creaking. Okay, they're on the stairs.

Let's review. They don't know he's in the attic. They're coming up the stairs very carefully, figuring he was in one of the bedrooms, the doors of which they could see from the bottom landing. They're going to be cautious, probing, trying to figure out exactly which bedroom. That's going to take at least five minutes, and maybe another two to three beyond that before it dawned on even the dimmest of them that John wasn't there.

They'll check the bathrooms, the closets, getting more and more frantic. Someone will then figure out where he'd gone and they'll start shooting up the ceiling. So, John had ten minutes, at most, to get to the other side of the attic and to the opening located in the car port, drop down on top of the Pathfinder and scoot across the street to another fighting position or back down the fence to the woods and away.

That is, if none of the maggots notice the drifting insulation as they're going up the stairs, if he could make it completely across a crap-filled attic without bumping anything and giving himself away, and if no one happened to be standing next to the Pathfinder when he dropped down. Given how everything's gone tonight, what were the chances?

He didn't want to think about it.

There was jostling right below him. They were crowding the stairs and would reach the bedrooms any moment. Damn. He didn't have ten minutes anymore, maybe two. Got to get out of here. He peered down the attic towards the carport side, the fire from next door bleeding through the vent and causing the goggles to bloom somewhat but illuminating the wooden walkway.

All right, a mad dash down that way, fast enough to stay ahead of the bullets, crash through the carport, run like hell. Stupid plan, but what else was there? He braced himself, gathered up the shotgun and the pack, then waved a hand in front of the NVGs to refresh them. His fingers brushed against a leather bag of some kind.

John looked. Why, yes, his old bowling ball, from that short-lived summer Theresa and he played in a JC Penny league. Was a lot of fun, but work got in the way. He patted the bag affectionately. Gonna miss this. Probably should put it to one last good use, toss it through the ceiling and conk a couple of them on the head ... the whole thing suddenly came clear to him, the proverbial bolt of lightning. John pulled the bag onto his lap, turning back towards the bedroom. Gotta time this just right.

Shots erupted from below and he jumped, figuring they'd had an epiphany and were probing the ceiling, but no bullets zipped past him. Ah, they're hosing down the master bedroom because they think he's there and they want his head down while they assault the place. There goes the rock maple bedroom set Theresa picked up in Vermont. Bastards. John really liked that set.

Some sudden yelling, war cries and a lot of stomping so they must be rushing the place. Shots went crazy and a few even found their way into the attic, holes appearing and letting in streaks of flashlight. John tensed. They're all standing in the bedroom, confused and firing wildly, and wondering where in the hell he was.

Now.

John heaved the bowling ball in the direction of the bedroom and heard more than saw it crash through because he was just too busy pulling out a couple of grenades. Sudden yelps of surprise, followed quickly by sudden blasts from a couple of rifles back through the hole. At least a few of the maggots had good reactions. John pulled the pins, plunged the grenades and tossed them after the bag.

Haul ass. John grabbed the knapsack and shotgun, hunched over, and flew down the wooden walkway, well, as much as a stooped-over run allowed flying. Had to get as far away as possible. Yells of "He's in the attic!" from below.

No kidding. He must sound like a herd of elephants charging overhead and bullets came ripping up from the living room, dryboard and roof trusses splintering all around him. John ducked his head and leaned forward, using his weight to get distance because in the next few seconds ...

Whoom!

A gigantic fiery hand slapped him hard in the back, knocking him off his feet. He gasped for breath in the suddenly superheated air as he landed hard, almost missing the walkway, breaking his fall rather rudely with the shotgun and knapsack. Now, wouldn't that be great, plunge through the ceiling and end up right at the feet of these assholes? John hung on to the walkway's edge for dear life while hot air roared past him and blistered his back. Oh, Lord that hurt! He looked back.

A column of flame and whirling debris shot up from the bedroom and coiled down the attic, reaching for him.

Most of the floor, almost up to his feet, was gone, so the bedroom, the landing and probably half the living room must be, too. There were screams and curses from below, which meant a group of pretty messed up people down there.

It was very bright and hot and the goggles bloomed like crazy. He tore them from around his neck, losing a few precious seconds readjusting his glasses, and blinked back into focus. A damn good flame enveloped the trusses and the attic crap. His house was on fire.

Must have been phosphorus grenades.

A shot ripped through the drywall next to his face and another two or three blasted holes ahead. Someone down there was mightily pissed. Command Voice began calling from somewhere near the front of the house, "What the fuck was that?" Nice timbre, distinct. Someone yelled back, not distinct, and a couple more shots went through the ceiling, too close for comfort.

Well, what worked once ...

John reached into the bag and pulled out another grenade and hoped it wasn't phosphorus because, geez, we've got enough fire, pulled himself up to a crouch (God, his back), grabbed the shotgun, pointed it towards the floor and let loose. The roar deafened him, the hot air was choking him but he didn't care, kept cycling the pump and pouring rounds into the living room. Jerks in his house were trying to kill him and everything he owned was going to burn because of those very same jerks so all of them, every damn one of them, had to die.

Kali roared in his veins and the battle song wailed in his ears as he wreaked havoc, the sudden screams from below a tonic. He stopped, slung the shotgun, charged the grenade, dropped it through one of the shotgun holes, grabbed the pack and ran.

He almost made the carport. The attic floor volcanoed and the pressure wave slammed John into the far wall, hammering the breath out of him.

Definitely not phosphorus.

The floor canted at a crazy angle and John looked back in time to see the shattered walkway plunging down into the dark smoky hole of what was once the living room. A few people down there were screaming in pain.

Man, grenades sure do a lot of damage, don't they?

Out towards the front of the house, Command Voice was roaring something and there were a lot of answering yells, a whole lot, from the same area. Just how many of these cretins were there? John forced in a deep breath, exchanging air for smoke and was suddenly dizzy and choking. Wouldn't do to have a coughing fit right now and he slapped a hand around his mouth, spluttering into it.

Really need to get out of here.

He dropped down to all fours and crawled the short distance to the trap door and pulled it up a bit, peering out through the crack. The top of the Pathfinder was illuminated by fire. He could hear people running but didn't see anyone. It sounded like they were all gravitating towards Command Voice. There was still some screaming from the living room and John supposed a rescue was underway. Excellent.

Slowly, he lifted the door out of its place, watching the whole time. People notice sudden movements better than gradual ones and he willed patience, take your time, John old boy, pull the door out easy and set it gently to the side. He eased his head through the hole and looked around. No one there. The yelling and cursing from the front of the house got louder, sounded like 20 or 30 people.

Jesus, what the hell was this, an entire freakin' army? Just for him? What an honor.

John grabbed the backpack and dropped it on top of the truck. He levered into the opening, wincing, hot pain racing up and down his back. Really going to feel that tomorrow. John probed for the truck, placing his feet on top. The shotgun got caught and he fiddled with it before it finally came free. He crouched, looking around but no one was there, then crawled down the front windshield and dropped in front of the Pathfinder, shotgun ready.

No way he'd pulled this off. No freakin' way.

He sent a quick "Thank you" heavenwards, reminding himself to be mad at God again later, and did a quick inventory. Shotgun with shells, backpack with two grenades, .357, tanto and .25. Also some pretty good burns and bruises and his left knee felt weak but overall, in good shape. Fighting trim.

He peered around the front of the truck. The neighbor's house was a full-blown bonfire, lighting up the whole area with garish yellow flame. Nobody in sight, but there was a lot of commotion from the front of the house.

All right, take another deep, deep breath. Flush out the lungs and pump oxygen through because you're going to need it. John was about ten feet away from the corner of the fence that led around to the back of the house. Go that way, take the zigzag path through the Claymores (hope he can remember it) and be down on Kenmont exactly two houses away from a well-stocked fighting position. He could re-arm, reset, get some rest, get some Amoxicillin, then spend the rest of the week hunting these bastards down, one by one. That's what he ought to do. That's the common sense thing to do.

But they're all here now, right around the corner, in one place. And he had two grenades, a lot of shotgun shells, the .357, the .25, the tanto, and a really bad attitude. And, most important of all, total surprise.

No contest.

John eased back around the Pathfinder and peered down the garage wall towards the front of the house. It might as well be daylight, the fire was so bright. He

227

crouch-ran to the corner, shotgun ready but no one moved into his line of sight. He edged a bespectacled eye over the corner and looked.

They were all over the front yard, ranging from the street to the big pin oak, but about 15 of them had bunched up on the porch, with maybe ten others scattered around the periphery. Big mistake. Lots of milling and pushing and scrambling around a locus dead in front of the door. John couldn't see the person standing there but would bet a dollar it was Command Voice. They should have stormed the living room by now, but were probably worried John was still in there laying for them, even though the bedroom side of the house was fully engulfed. Right instincts, fellows, wrong location. Too bad for you.

A strange bunch, neo-punks who had taken extraordinary care with their costumes – black leather vests laced with chains, bizarre haircuts, lots of Mohawks and dreadlocks and strategically cut patches to reveal scalp in the most ugly of ways. John shook a disgusted head. Intimidation, of course, a signal to the straights that here is a dangerous person and you better watch out because I'm going to hurt you and rob you and do anything I want to you. Freaks, piss ants, pieces of crap. "Oh they're just expressing themselves, it's just a form of social protest, it's free speech …" what a load.

These Mohawked chain-laced metal-pierced unwashed cretins were arrogant and evil and drugged and sexed. And you bunch of damn cowards, you hand-wringing fearful muffins wanting to be well thought of and considered progressive and cutting edge with great wells of tolerance, accommodated these things, these scabs; you too afraid to call them what they were – scum, just infected pieces of green, rotting scum.

No wonder Al-Qaeda loathed us.

John had never been intimidated by these types. When

he'd run into a group of them on the Metro Before, he stood close, eyeball to eyeball, glaring. Three or four of them smirked and flexed and made ugly, low comments but John stood his ground, daring. They'd just leave. Confronted, they fold. Fold. You hear that, civilians? You stand, you disdain, you drive them out. You don't tolerate.

Because, you bunch of spineless muffins, doing so proves you are weak and frightened, soft, jelly-like, lovely victims. And in caves and mines along the Hindu Kush, they smelled you out the way a dog smells a bitch in heat and they came for you and your weakness and vacillation and bumper sticker thoughts of world peace and harmony. They drove children into the sides of buildings and sprayed viruses and we fell by the millions and the debris of us lies scattered and rotting all over this well-meaning landscape.

John stared, getting more pissed off. Tattooed metal-posted assholes were breaking down his front door. And trampling all over Theresa's grave.

Mother. Fuckers.

Who were these guys? Raiders? Sure had all the earmarks except Raiders were a bit more disciplined and didn't go in for the garish getup much anymore. And why were they attacking him? He certainly wasn't worth such a commitment of force. Puzzling. He would have to leave one or two of them alive just to answer some questions.

The setup wasn't going to get much better than this. John fished into the bag and pulled out a grenade, shifted the shotgun and stood. All right, do or die time. The blast will take out the front porch and the shotgun, the rest. The survivors will flee. John will spend the rest of the night hunting them down and posting their bodies on various light poles around the neighborhood. And then he'd have to see about moving into another house, dammit.

One, two, three ... go.

He pulled the pin and plunged the grenade and threw it while stepping out. He brought up the shotgun and focused on two or three people standing near the big oak who had turned in his direction. He pulled the trigger, the recoil knocking him back and was rewarded with a scream but no time to gloat and he jacked another round and fired.

There were cries of rage from the porch and the scrum was turning away from the far side of the porch where the grenade had landed but then it went off, a blinding white hot flash; phosphorus, not fragmentation, but that's okay, because people were burning, as was the front of the house.

John smiled and swung the barrel and jacked rounds and it was glorious because they were running from him and he was Slaughter and Mayhem and Death ...

Something hit him hard, right across the back of the head. Damn, that hurt, hurt like hell. John hated bumping his head, no matter how slight; it always sent him into a paroxysm of cursing and crying and this was the mother of all head bumps.

He dropped to his knees and dropped the shotgun and grabbed his temples, "Dammit all to hell!" Had he been shot?

Wham! Something hard whacked across the top of his head and he fell forward, losing all control, face buried in the driveway.

He was sick, the world roaring in circles and a savage hard light searing his temples and skull. Rough hands were all over him; he felt the .357 stripped away and was yanked over and faces, painted and twisted and hard, were above him, whirling and whirling ...

23

Light, but not the pure and calming light described in all those near-death experiences. Flickering yellowish light, instead, so probably not Paradise where, for all eternity, he would sing the praises of God and drift in languor and joy through puffy white clouds. Couldn't be the Lake of Fire, either, unless it's actually a little colder than advertised.

So, not dead. How unfortunate. Probably will end up dead, but not before a whole lot of fuss and bother, and quite painful fuss and bother at that.

Have to focus, have to focus but, oh God, his head. John'd never had migraines, but he was betting this was a reasonable facsimile. A long time ago, he was helping a couple of tech agents install cameras in a drug dealer's room when one of the techs suddenly went down with a migraine. He was completely out of it.

John had to lay him down on the floor while the poor sap just gasped from the pain, tears streaming. The ER gave the tech a shot but he was still *hors de combat*. John now empathized. He could really stand an Anacin. Or a shot of whatever they gave that tech.

He was on all fours, that much he knew, and was staring at something odd. Couldn't quite make it out through his blurry and jumbled vision, which a little shake of the head would clear but, oh man, that was the last thing he wanted to do. Why did he feel so heavy? ... oh, right, got it, he was being held down. That wasn't good, not good at all, and John, old boy, you really

really need to get hold of yourself and figure out what's going on. He blinked, which hurt like hell, but he could see a little better.

The odd thing, glowing in very bright firelight, was a boot.

Big boot, metal tipped, with some kind of design, a dragon, yeah, that's it, a Chinese dragon, the kind that winds back on itself and bites its tail. How cute. John wondered if this was a matched set and looked over and, bingo, another boot, another dragon. Now, who made stuff like this, some ate-up martial arts company? John looked hard for edges or spikes but, no, just metal caps with etched grinning dragons eating their own tails. Must taste good. Only the most stylish of characters would wear such stylish boots and John just had to make acquaintance. That meant looking up but, oh man, he really didn't want to, not with his head screaming like this. God, where's that Anacin? John wondered how much time Dragon Boot was going to allow him to recover.

Apparently not much. One of the dragons moved, grew suddenly larger, and kicked him hard in the mouth. He reeled back and over, flame and moon and stars and faces cartwheeling as he landed on his back, gasping and spitting blood.

Well, wonderful, those partials installed several years ago were now all cracked and his lips had exploded. Add the migraine, and John was suddenly not in the best of moods. There was a cheer, loud and harsh and feral, real loud from a lot of people and John was startled. What the hell?

Forget the headache and the jaw ache and the general sense of unwellness. John snapped his mouth back together with one hand and looked around. Bright light from all the burning things, all *his* burning things, illuminated a crowd, a big crowd, a really big crowd.

About a hundred and fifty mohawked painted-face people, eyes, lips and teeth blackened with rouge, were screaming at him while kicking in his ribs. Damn, really going to feel that in the morning. They leered and mouthed in sheer animal triumph as they danced around him while dancing on top of him.

Ordinarily, being beaten to death by a mob was distracting, but John noticed something and squinted hard at the faces looming in and out of his vision. There was a feature on all the right cheeks ... what was that? It was a little hard to see because everyone's boots and fists kept getting in the way but John made it out. A symbol, some kind of tattoo, an ankh, yeah, that's it, reversed, daggers on the points, just like the one spray painted on the Cassell Center wall, next to the unfortunate Mrs. Alexandria.

Uh oh.

So, what do we have here? Some kind of murder cult, pagans, anarchists, what? All probably applied, since they were bent on stomping him into the earth. Better than what they did to Mrs. A.

John threw up his elbows to protect his head, almost laughing at the futility of it. He was going into pain overload and could no longer feel the rain of blows. Fine, fine. It was always going to be somewhere and some time when he least expected it, and right here on his front yard, well, that was kind of poetic.

He'd already lived far past the averages and had done some post-Event good, like taking out a whole bunch of these cretins. Not enough, obviously, but he made a dent and that might slow them down, give MPD a chance to subdue these assholes and then hang Dragon Boot from a tree. So he'd done good. An honorable death. Time to go.

"Enough!" someone roared out and the kicking and hitting suddenly stopped, although the shouting stayed about the same. Several eagerly evil faces bent down and jerked John rather rudely to his feet as every single inch of his skin screamed in protest. He did a quick inventory of apparent injuries – a few cracked ribs, some pretty good internal bleeding, his bad right shoulder was on fire and that damned headache just wouldn't go away. Oh yeah, his mouth and teeth. But, considering the circumstances, overall, not too bad.

"Bring him here." Hey, that was Command Voice. John was betting he owned the dragon boots.

There was a lot of pushing and shoving until a couple of people asserted control, grabbed John hard and duckwalked him back through the crowd. John looked at his escorts.

The guy who had seized his burning right shoulder was white, about 6'4", rawboned, wearing an open sleeveless vest, large dark circles painted across his eyes and had red stained teeth, like he'd been drinking blood. Nice effect. He leered at John and yeah, definitely nice effect. Probably one of the lieutenants.

John glanced to his left and then did a double take. It was a girl, about 5'10" and built. Must be a weight lifter because her arms and shoulders were bigger than his. Ugly as sin, face painted all white with crimson around the eyes in a teardrop fashion, crimson hair pulled back tight in a bun and held in place with razor wire. Mixed race, hard to tell with all the makeup but heavy features. The green ankh stood out against her white painted cheek and she was wearing a plunging leather vest (must be the uniform) that completely exposed her down to the nipples. Really, really built. She had two huge bowie knives in leather sheaths on either side of her huge breasts and she glared at him with the most hate-filled eyes he'd ever seen. Charming.

After a few steps, the two goons jerked him to a stop. John blinked to get his focus and stared at the person in front of him. A big, medium-toned black man. Not Schwarzenegger big, but close. Fascinating hair, a bunch of spiked-up dreads with a metal tip on the end of each, a medieval knight's mace. Quite an effort. Unlined faced, hairless, very pretty, actually – could have been a pre-Event model. He was wearing a pair of wraparound Oakleys, all for effect; you certainly didn't need shades in this unstable light. Shirtless, which was kinda macho on a cold night, and several gold chains, each one progressively longer than the one above, cascading down his chest. Mr. T. But, under those chains was something else, a tattoo, a big red one. The ankh, writ larger, very stylized, with those reverse dagger points. And, oh yes, the lovely boots.

This wasn't good.

Boots said nothing, just stood there, unmoving, intimidating. John felt a chill down his spine. The man was stanced for effect, preparing for a show with John as the main attraction, on the order of the Cassell Center with hooks and skinning and major organ removal, probably right from a branch of John's own pin oak, right over Theresa's grave. Going to take hours and be vastly entertaining to the crowd jostling and shouting behind and beside John.

Panic welled through him but he ferociously tamped it down. Don't give the bastard what he wants.

Because, John ole boy, won't do any good. You know where this is going – a meet-up with Mr. Bones, the grimmest of the Grim, the universal Reaper himself. John had been prepared for introductions long before now, cop work exposing him to more opportunities than average, so he wasn't worried. You come to terms early on or you go nuts.

He was fairly sure he met the basic requirements for salvation and would spend eternity strumming a harp or whatever you did up there. Eat ambrosia, stuff like that.

He and God would sit down for a little *tête-à-tête* over why the Great Big Plan required all this misery. Something to look forward to, so death wasn't a big deal.

But dying, well, that was different. Not something to look forward to, especially the method he was currently facing. This was going to hurt like hell and John was not a big fan of pain. He'd watched his dad dissolve from Hodgkins and chemo over the space of a year, burning up from the inside until only a paper shell enveloping a mass of agony and despair remained. He deserved a painful death, the bastard, but John didn't see why Mrs. Rashkil's little boy did, so, while watching dad, he'd resolved never to linger like that.

If John got news he'd boarded the cancer slow boat, then he was hopping on the Bullet-to-the-Head express. Fast and relatively painless, spare the family all the grief, but, more importantly, spare him a lot of discomfort. Spike Head here wanted John to experience a lot of discomfort, sort of a cancer cell personified.

No. Freakin'. Way.

John set his jaw. There's just no freakin' way. If John got even the slightest of outside chances, just the hint of an opening, then Dragon Boots and he were going to dance, dance hard. Boot's minions would kill him but not before John, hopefully, had killed Boots. John stared at the Oakleys.

Let's see what happens next, shall we?

Spike returned the stare, cocking his head a bit, still silent, letting the moment build. Suddenly, he broke into the most disarming smile John had ever seen on a dirtbag. "Hi," he said.

John blinked, a little bewildered.

Spike Head laughed and looked magnanimously around at his followers, then back at John. "You could be polite."

What's the game here? John glared, refusing to play.

Spike waited, eyebrows raised, and then shrugged and looked around in amusement. "Okay," he said, "Cool. You ain't feeling too good right now. It's been a rough night." The Oakleys bore down on John. "For all of us." He paused for dramatic effect and the cold chill resumed down John's spine. The fun was about to begin.

Spike looked quizzically at John. "Do you know who I am?"

Although John had resolved stoic silence, mainly because his broken teeth and lips made it hard to talk, some openings you just can't resist, "The artist formerly known as Prince?"

Spike stared a moment and then reared back, letting out a great big belly laugh without one note of true humor in it. John steeled himself. Spike came back down and looked at him, smiling. John couldn't help it; he smiled back.

Wham! John reeled, a savage ripping pain tearing across his cheek, the arc of his own blood flying across his vision. Spike's open hand was at the end of the arc, the razor embedded in the big gold ring on his third finger glowing in the firelight. Sonofabitch, what kind of prison yard crap is that? Probably opened John's face up pretty good. The crowd roared its approval and Rawbone and Xena shook him hard.

"Funny!" Spike screamed, about two inches from John's face, "real damn funny. You're just a real funny guy, aren't you? I'll bet you kept everyone in stitches, the cops and losers and straights," he spat that last word out with venom, "and you just can't stop being funny, huh? Make fun of me, do you? Mock me? Me? I am a god!" And Spike raised both arms skyward, throwing his head back and roaring, just roaring, a soundless maniacal note of hate and evil.

Blood flowing like a river down his face, John uttered a gasp as his knees grew weak from the sudden rush of horror.

Good God Almighty. This guy's insane, completely, irrevocably insane.

Breathe, breathe hard and deep, get control. John put steel back in his knees and ordered the horror away. His left eye was flooded with blood so he cocked his good one through skewed glasses and stared at the raving Spike. Where in the world did this guy come from? How in the world did such a freakin' lunatic amass this small army?

About ten thousand likely answers popped into John's mind, all running along the same course: imagine about fifty scared, hungry, disorganized and confused uber-lowlifes suddenly left to their own devices when the Event happened. Budding Bundys and Vandals, all, but not quite good enough to join the union.

At first they loot and revel and rape and murder, but, after a while, being the goobers they are, run out of resources, can't find food or good water, fight more and more among themselves. Some get taken by the CDC, some get killed by real Bundys or Vandals. Mostly, though, they rot. Not smart enough to be Raiders, at best low-level Vandal wannabes.

The lowest of the low, could turn the stomach of Mother Teresa, directionless, frustrated, resourceless *canaille* and lumpenproletariat mixed into one ugly and hateful mass, squatting in their own feces in some rat-ridden tenement. Lost, mad at everything but not know-ing why, fighting to divide the sewage not even a Bundy would touch. Cannibals, probably.

Then comes this guy, charismatic and beautiful, speaking to their frustrations, their arrogance. He brutalizes a few and organizes a few more and, suddenly, has a gang. He promises them power and control and riches and death to the Straights and the Man and everyone who ever kept them down, terming the event

"Divine Retribution."

He leads them in small battles among their own until other semi-leaders are vanquished or converted and, before you know it, they're a hundred. They spread out, organizing and fighting some more, and then they're two hundred.

Instinctive strategist, he teaches them how to fight as a group and they have their first successes against some periphery Raiders and they start feeling real good about themselves and he makes a symbol and puts it on them and suddenly they are, for the first time in their pathetic lives, a part of something. They grow stronger, challenging better Raiders, absorbing them, taking control of greater areas, finally busting out of their Northeast or Southeast hellhole, a full-fledged army, straight at MPD.

And here they are, on John's front lawn.

Who knew? Metro said nothing and the first hint John received was Mrs. Alexandria hanging from Cassell's ceiling. A bit late. All this time, blithely biking back and forth, shooting a random Bundy or two, calling Coll every night, thinking everything's fine in his self-contained little world of Magnums and pool water and redundant defenses and now, what? John stood before Klebold and his capering Harrises.

You dumb ass. If there is one thing you know, John, old boy, it is the fathomless depths of human evil. Yet, never considered this. Stupid.

Ankh Man stopped his roaring and dropped his head slowly, looking at John for a moment. He took a step away and made a grand gesture as the crowd stirred, excited. "Here he is, my children!" Ankh called.

Ah, yes, that Command Voice John had come to admire, deep and sonorous and penetrating, would have made a great game show host. John glanced around to see the effect and, oh man, he had them. A bunch of eager puppies eyeing mom's teats.

"Here!" another grand gesture swept the front yard and ended as a full-handed point right at John, "the last of them. The murderer, the one who brought death to our brothers and sisters, who hunted us while we were helpless and shivering and cold. You know him, my children, you have seen him! Riding his stupid bicycle, standing on hills, shooting us! Behold, my children, the butcher, the oppressor, the nightmare!"

The crowd roared, waving angry fists at John, the closest ones spitting and the farther ones hurling some of the debris from his own house at him. Bad throws, only one roof shingle clipped John's knees. Ankh raised his hands for silence and walked slowly around John, eyeing him.

I Am Legend.

"Do you see him now? Do you see him? Living here fat and sleek and rich while we starved, while we froze and cried and ran from him and those cops!" he spat that word, too. "No more! Never again, my children. We will take back what's ours!"

He spoke the last like bullets and raised both hands high again and the crowd, on cue, roared again and all John could think was, fat and sleek? More thin and wiry, thank you very much, but facts weren't at issue here. There's a myth to propagate.

Which is, no doubt, how he got to be Chief Maggot, scapegoating Metro and the CDC and just about everyone, including oblivious ole John himself. The gospel according to Ankh: John personally brought the Al-Qaeda Flu to DC then single-handedly drove all the poor innocent guttersnipes underground, sneering and laughing and killing off their mothers and raping their sisters. Spike, only Spike, could defy and defeat him.

The same old oppression fable – it's all society's fault, you are wonderful people held down by a hateful authority, so rise, strike off your chains and, oh, by the way, while you're at it, rioting and raping and murdering, make me your king.

John supposed he should be flattered. He was the Right Wing Conspiracy, the Elders of Zion, the Trilateral Commission, pick the cabal. Nothing like being demonized. Which, of course, begged the question how in the world did this group of slobbering morons gather enough Intel on John that Ankh could create this legend?

Just how long had these guys been watching, anyway? Had to be quite a while, and rather closely, too, so John should have picked up on it. Why didn't he? He was good at this, better than average and the screaming cretins around him were sub-average, barely normal. They didn't have the brains, the motivation, the cunning, or the skill, which spoke volumes about their Fearless Leader, didn't it?

John peered intently at the strutting Ankh. Who, exactly, was this guy? Geez, it's like Lucifer himself showed up ... John blinked. And chilled.

If you accept the notion of God, then you must accept the opposite notion that He has an eternal enemy, always near, a merciless, relentless being who does not share God's powers but uses those against Him. He invokes grace and Eternal Love and traps God into neutrality by His own Essence, mimicking omnipresence and omnipotence through excellent organization and doing whatever mischief to God's Plan he can manage.

You cannot have God without him, no Yin without Yang, no good without evil, because those qualities are known by their opposites. So if God is there as the beacon of good then standing right beside Him is the beacon of chaos.

Chaos is powerful, the anti-good, living in the shadows that the light of good always casts. So, even in the most benign of times, there is no safe place, there is no safe hour, there is no peace save what you construct out of God's grace but there is, even in that, a glaring and profound weakness which you cannot see because the good blinds you. The eternal enemy can, though, and he sits at it waiting for that pure, strategic moment then, *wham!*, the black dripping claws go ripping through the chink and you are down and gasping and looking up as the eternal enemy holds your blood-blackened and still beating heart in triumph over his head.

As you go into the darkness, you see him take a bite of it and sneer at you through your own blood and you ask God, "Why?" and He shrugs and says, "That's the way it is. Now rest," because the only rest is death, whether high civilization remains intact or the world crashes into rubble.

The circle remains unbroken. John will die horribly tonight, and the Chaos Lord will gibber and scream orgasmic joy while the ashes of civilization spiral upward, the sparks fly ever upward while stirring out in the dark, somewhere, God nudges a reluctant Gideon to raise armies and put chaos back in its box.

Wonder if it'll be Collier?

Ankh dropped his hands and lowered his head, morphing into a picture of sorrow. John almost laughed. The burdened leader, all the cares and worries for his beloved children on his shoulders, now having to make a much-regretted decision. And what, pray tell, was that? Well, to rip John apart, piece by painful piece, a much-regretted sacrifice to his children's frustration. Ah, the price of power.

Spike played it well, letting stance and posture convey the message. After some requisite dramatic moments, Spike stepped forward, inches from John's face, and raised the Oakleys. "Wanna hear something?" he asked in a low voice.

John, slightly taken aback and, no doubt, showing it,

frowned. His loving escorts tightened their hold as Ankh leaned in closer, "Well, do you?" he almost whispered.

"Do I have a choice?"

"Of course not," and Spike placed a paternal hand on his shoulder.

John held his breath. Now? Is it now? If he could shake off Rawbone and Xena then strike up hard and fast right into Spike's throat, hopefully hard enough to shatter his trachea, then jerk-o would die, screaming for air. Who'll be taking a bite out of whose heart, Beelzebub? He tensed but no, no, wait, not yet, hold up, it just doesn't feel right. John stared at Spike out of his one good eye. Seemed like the old boy was expecting it.

After a heartbeat, Spike smirked. Yep, definitely expecting it. Good thing John held off. Spike leaned, "I'm really going to miss you," he stage whispered.

John blinked. It hurt to do so, but how else do you react to that?

"Really, I am," the hand gently reached up and adjusted John's glasses, "Came to admire you, man. You were smarter than the rest, much harder to pin down. I thought we'd just shoot you in the back but, damn if you didn't turn the tables and get my guy instead. Well done. Well done. I tried some other ways but you picked off the watchers or the ambushes I set. Quality work. I could have used a guy like you. I thought I'd give you a chance, left you an invitation."

Huh? Spike looked at him expectantly, like a teacher waiting for a reluctant student. John blinked. What's this guy talking about? "Invitation?"

John wasn't at his sharpest right now and he shook his head slowly, warily, not sure where this was going, "I don't know what ..." he started and then it dawned on him. "Mrs. Alexandria," John said quietly.

Spike clapped him hard on the shoulder a few times and beamed at Rawbone and Xena, "See, I told you this was a real smart guy!" He came back to John, "And you didn't get it?"

"Not exactly the type of invitation I'm used to," John said, dryly.

He shrugged, "Yeah, maybe we went a little overboard, but we had problems with her and her group and the children needed to vent a little. But if you'd been doing your job, found her earlier, then you'd have known and you could have found me and submitted. Or cleared out. I figured you'd never join so I really wanted you to leave. You earned it. But, no, you screwed up. Took too long. A little better work and all of this," he gestured around with his chin, "wouldn't have happened. Your fault."

"You never studied logic, did you?"

Spike laughed and wagged a finger at John, "That's not very polite. Just take it. My children gladly take the discipline when they screw up. But you probably won't be glad." His smile hardened, "Not glad at all."

Oh, Lord. John felt his spine turn to jelly and it took will, pure will, to remain standing. The game was clear: prolong the terror, sweeten the torture, like tasting the sauce before cutting the steak.

Spike loved the pain, it's what moved him, the infliction, slow and steady and stretched over long hours. The "children" didn't butcher the Mrs., he did, while the children watched and were cowed as he slashed and dissected the screaming, hanging helpless piece of meat for hours.

A cautionary tale. John was next.

Not if he could help it.

"You going to keep me in suspense?" Anger-driven strength returned to John's legs and he straightened and squared. Xena muttered something and moved in a little tighter and Rawbone picked up the cue, doing the same.

Ankh just smiled, "In time, in time. Don't you wanna

know what happened first?"

"What?"

"To your friends, those Alexandrias. Don'cha wanna know? Put up one helluva fight, they did, almost as good as you. Didn't matter. We killed all of them 'cept for her, saved her for you. Well, saved her for me, really, she was kinda cute," and he leered at John. "Oh, wait, my mistake, we didn't kill all of them. A couple of the kids saw the light and joined us. You know what's funny? You got one of 'em, just now, in your living room there." He paused, "See what you caused, man?"

What he caused. John eyed Ankh and had a sudden flash, the Alexandrias, especially the Mrs., solemn and earnest, red haired and blue eyed and regarding him with a wish to trust but the times didn't allow it, standing next to her man with the kids arrayed behind them, all talking about something. Hung up like a pagan offering, reduced to a screaming bloody lesson.

John couldn't equate the hope in her, trying to rise to the surface, with that thing hanging from the ceiling. It's just not the way she should have ended. She was one of the good guys.

No reason for it. Hoisted up a ceiling beam, raped and flayed and tortured, for no reason at all. She died forsaken, no purpose, no expiation, just pure, howling pain. Fruitless, pointless, everything she and her family were trying to do, up in smoke.

And, really, why'd they even try? There was no civilization, no refinement anymore. No vulgarity, either, no barbarism.

Things just are. Things just happen.

One thing became ascendant, then another. The Dark Ages took hold, then the Enlightenment, no real reason, just happened that way. You can't say one is bad and the other good because bad and good things happened during both, so the only important thing is act, and act is successful only if you're satisfied with it.

Mrs. Alexandria hung from a meat hook, John in the clutches of Satan and about to do the same but it didn't matter. They'd just lost, that's all. Coll will win or lose in whatever life he has left, based on act alone. Forgotten after a time. Unremarked. Postmodernism wins.

That really sucked.

Couldn't have picked a worse time to abandon all your premises, could you, John ole boy? If there was one thing he needed right now, it was some philosophical base, some structure, some mental template to overlay the world so he could see method. But, *phffft*, gone, and the only thing in his mind was act, pure act. He looked at Ankh, his satisfied smirk just inches from John's bloodied eye.

Act. Definitely going to act.

He wasn't going to hang from a tree limb and be rendered for the amusement of sewer rats, that he knew for certain, and it was calming. Maybe that's real meaning, preparation and resolve leading to the act, something for God to watch. We're television for divinity, but live TV, unpredictable. Maybe He applauds spontaneity. Then John should have Him pounding palms here in the next few minutes.

Ankh clucked, "Really too bad. We've got plans, you know. I mean, now that you cops are no longer a threat, we're going to finish off the black-market gangs. The Gangs, you know? Going to take a little bit, but I think they'll listen to reason, join us, you know? Think we're big now? Damn, man, we're going to be the new fucking army! Get bigger and stronger then, watch out, man, we're busting loose. There ain't no government anymore, man, no Man, man. I'm it," and he leaned back, proudly jamming a thumb in his chest.

What did he say? "Waddya mean cops are no longer a threat?"

"I mean they're no longer a threat. They're gone. We did 'em."

John stared at him. Oh, come on. Yeah, you may have driven off the checkpoint and stood toe to toe with an MPD squad or two, but a couple of skirmishes don't win a war. There's no way this undisciplined rabble would prevail against an organized, heavily armed paramilitary like MPD. No way. John smiled derisively, "Right. You wiped out MPD. You and the French Army here."

Ankh smiled back just as derisively, "Ain't nothing impossible when no one's looking for you. When they think you're just some street gang, don't take you seriously, it's easy to get the jump. They didn't pay the right attention, see? They were too busy looking like they were in control, saying they had the District 'cause they shot a burglar or two. They didn't have shit. It was all show, anyway, something one faction or other could lord over the other, keep 'em in line."

"What are you talking about?"

"I'm talking about those wannabe cops. What, you thought they were real? They weren't real, you're more real than they were. Somebody in the government put them together to get over on some other part of the government. I don't know who, I don't pay attention to that crap. All show, scare the others into thinking they had control. Weren't no control, not really, they just looked like badasses. Didn't mean they were."

Well, that fit, but he still wasn't buying it. "There's no way."

"There's always a way. If I had time, I'd take you back over and let you see where we stacked 'em up, from their commander on down, got piles of little blue pigs burning. They're my street lights," and he laughed out loud, which made Xena and Rawbone and, well, just about everyone else in earshot, laugh in response. Funny guy.

"But, I ain't got the time." He bored in on John, "I gotta settle you first, then I gotta get ready for the rest of this place."

"You're going to take on the Zone." John couldn't keep the incredulity out of his voice.

Spike shook his head, "I've already done that, just some details left. I'm taking on the Outside."

John laughed, short and contemptuous but appropriate for the situation, and deliberately looked around, taking in the cretins. "With this? You're going to hit the walls and the ZGs and the military with this. What are you smoking? The air force alone will take you apart. You won't last five minutes."

Spike smiled, "Maybe. That could be. But, I'll tell ya, I'm going to last a lot longer than you." And he stopped smiling and there it was, dark and dreadful, relentless purpose and overweening pride twisting Spike's face into a mask of pure implacability.

John's guts turned to ice. Talk is over, playing is done. The cat has tired of the game and it's time to rip the mouse apart.

Panic hit hard at John's brain but, even in that, a calm spot formed, resolved to act. He stood, little tremors of fear throwing him off balance and threatening to overwhelm, but he kept a laser focused right on Ankh.

Ankh nodded to Rawbone who let go and stepped up, handing him something. John couldn't really see what it was and Rawbone moved back to position but wasn't holding John anymore. Xena moved off a bit, too.

Crap. Not good.

Ankh looked down at his hands and John followed his gaze. Ah, his tanto and .25. Wondered what happened to them. No .357, though. Damn. Someone must have claimed it.

Ankh held up the weapons. His hands were surprisingly thin and tapering, almost delicate. "Yours?" he asked.

John said nothing. He was wary and tense while desperately calculating. He was free, had a bit of room but if he broke to any direction right now, they'd be all over him. Got to wait for the right moment, the right circumstance.

Ankh regarded the .25, turning it a bit in the firelight, then sneered, "Piece of shit," laughed and dropped it. Dropped it. John almost gasped, swore he heard an angelic chorus hit a note of "Aaahhh!" as he watched, out of the bottom of his eye, where it landed.

"But this," Ankh cradled the tanto, "is definitely not a piece of shit." Slowly he drew the blade, glowing yellow in the firelight, love in his eyes and John had to admit the man had taste. Ankh stared at it then dropped the sheath. He turned it over and examined the edge, ran a finger over it, his eyebrows rising at the sharpness. He held the tanto up, pointed at John's face. John braced.

"Bow down and worship the true god," Ankh spoke it softly then his hand snaked out like lightning. John felt a red-hot searing along the side of his head, a liquid warmth and a clean slicing where his ear should be. He grunted with surprised pain then *wham*! someone clubbed him across the back of his knees with what, he didn't know, but it was big and heavy and hurt like hell and the grunt became a yelp as he fell and then the real pain, the sizzling as someone applied a torch, probably a piece of wood from his own house, to his already blistered back.

John screamed. Anyone would.

The crowd roared its approval and threw more things at him but that was tickling compared to what preceded. John was seared and all he could think was, My back, my back. Nothing else in the universe but that screaming fired pain. He was ripped and the agony flowed to where his ear used to be and it was quite disconcerting to hold two areas of agony at once, trying to reconcile them. No, three, because his legs were pulsing and swelling as the blood clots gathered behind his battered knees.

John couldn't get his breath. All this pain drove it away. He was dead, here, dead and lost and Collier will never know and was now anchorless but, Coll, Coll, you must hope, you must cling to it even in the horror you must, you must, or you will die. Like your father. Right now.

All right, all right. Regain, center, pull in, Collier's out there.

Focus.

John's tears flowed freely and wasn't he now the craven little spectacle? Back on all fours, the dragon boots in front again, he looked up, glasses canted at a crazy level. How were they staying on?

Lucifer stood tall, gloating, fire-lit Oakleys and a sneer distorting his very pretty face. He held up John's ear, or what was left of it, raw and bloody and the crowd roared again, sensual, lustful, waves of sound that were rape. Ankh smiled, feeding on it.

You sonofabitch, you fuckin' butcher bastard. Drakul, the undead, Impaler, every murdering piece-of-crap sadist in history, that's you, Ankh. John was suddenly very very tired, unwilling to put up with one more second of this utter and complete BS. Who in the hell do you think you are, you cockeyed tattooed mace-headed bastard? And right then John knew, with all the reflexes of some Neolithic ancestor still screaming in his blood, that this was the moment.

Because, you see, Ankh had made a time-honored mistake: forgetting about his opponent. Like too many armies and nations in history, he didn't finish his enemy while he had the chance.

Attila reeled drunkenly before the gates of Rome, Hitler danced at the edge of Dunkirk, and Johnson dithered while Charley slipped away. They all forgot resolve was universally shared. You may be convinced of your own power and invulnerability, but so was everybody else.

That's why Zulus threw themselves on British rifles, North Koreans on the barrels of American tanks, Iranians under the wheels of Humvees because, no matter the odds, no matter the apparent superiority of the foe, no one's going down without a fight. The Zulus overwhelmed Rourke's Drift, the North Koreans besieged Pusan, the Iranians stalemated the Zagros mountains. All Pyrrhic, all, ultimately, failures, but they scored, drove in the knife, took plenty with them.

Surge. John felt it rise from the belly and caress his ravaged back. Kali swelled his heart and he stared at Nosferatu above him. That's it. Going to shove a stake through your bloodless and rotting heart, cut off your abomination of a head and stuff it full of garlic. Time to cast ye down, Lucifer, Son of the Morning Star, time to, once again, assert that you may have dominion over the Earth, but not over its dwellers.

John never lost track of the .25, despite getting half his head carved off. He marked it again, some inches past Ankh's triumphant boots. "Tell me," he gasped to those same boots.

Pause. Lucifer bent down, "What?"

Stupid. And perfect. The Neolithic ancestor was right.

"Can a god die?" John looked up as he asked it, Ankh's Oakleys a few inches away, and then moved like water, flowing and supple, snaking up Ankh's arm with the same lightning that had taken John's ear. Rawbone and Xena stood frozen. They anticipated John making a break for it. They never thought he'd go right for Ankh.

Surprise.

Reacting, Ankh made sudden resistance at the wrist.

Good. John's years of hapkido reverse-arm training kicked in, muscle memory roaring back. John knew, just knew, at what point resistance became advantage, and that was right now. He twisted around the fulcrum of Ankh's wrist and was suddenly behind him, bringing Ankh's arm back as he moved.

Ankh was very fast, testament to his reflexes, and tried to counter against the pressure but that only helped John sweep, in one continuous motion, the tanto out of Ankh's hand, grasp it with the blade reversed, reach over Ankh's shoulder and strike hard. A little lower than he wanted, but no matter.

The Japanese have a different philosophy concerning cuts; they go from the inside out. John had always liked that. The tanto entered just above Ankh's left hip, about where the soft part of the belly met the pelvis, and John drove it to the hilt. He pulled back hard and fast, ripping the tanto up towards Ankh's right shoulder and cut out just below the ribcage. He then hammered the blade home just above Ankh's heart while bracing his other hand behind Ankh's neck. All in less than two seconds.

John stepped around Ankh's shoulder to view the results. He eyed Rawbone and Xena but all they did was stare, completely astonished. Excellent. A little time to savor the moment, and John fixed on Ankh.

A Japanese cut done right first shocks then kills and yes, there it was, deep, deep shock transfixing Ankh's beautiful face. He didn't feel the pain yet, just the surprise and consternation: Ankh couldn't believe it. He was a god, invincible, and this vanquished pipsqueak pathetic middle-aged piece of police crap has just done what? Where did John get the temerity to even raise a hand? Oh sure, kill Ankh's minions by the dozens, but not him, the untouchable, the unapproachable, inheritor of all things dark, unassailable.

Yet, assailed.

Ankh tried to step back but John still held his neck. There was a warm liquid rush down John's legs and he shifted out of the waterfall of black blood and offal cascading from Ankh's stomach. Waddya know, disembowelment. Ankh's lips formed a frothy bloody bubble as he stared at his own Niagara, managing one word, "Oh."

John pushed him away. The firelight was beautiful now, revealing everything, the tanto stuck in Ankh's chest, his intestines and stomach pouring out. He looked at John and his mouth worked but a gout of blood chunked there, obscuring what he wanted to say. Must have gotten a lung, too.

John stood tall and clear because he wanted Ankh to see, take one last mental picture with him on that black journey down to his wretched master. You looking, you craphead? Good. Then remember this: and John smiled at him.

A collective gasp took the crowd as Ankh dissolved into sausage. Impossible. He was omnipotent, invulnerable. No doubt he'd miraculously escaped death a few times while consolidating power – some rival's blade got caught in his sleeve, a bullet ricocheted off a piece of metal in his shirt, that kind of thing. With the proper encouragement, those events morphed into the supernatural and the minions bought the whole "I am god" line, turning Spike into that Flagg character from *The Stand*. So they were just blown off their feet. Like Xena and Rawbone. Hmm. John should probably take advantage of that, even though it was quite delightful watching Ankh die.

Move. Now.

John swept up the .25 and cycled it as he spun into the Weaver, seeking a target. Shoot something, anything. And that would be Rawbone, who had finally come alive and was focused full on John, hate blazing his eyes and an ornately carved walking stick raised over his head.

So that's what hit John across the knees. Two shots, double tap, right in the face.

Not the most powerful round in the inventory, but good enough. Aim for a soft target, the eyes or throat, and go for shock. Yeah, yeah, the indiscriminate-shooting advocates who took over weapons training about ten years ago would have strokes. They wanted John to carry about 500 rounds of that pathetic 9 mm and spray the target area down with lead, always center mass, always. That was crap. One or two well-placed shots, regardless of caliber, does wonders. Like now.

Rawbone reeled, his face exploding in blood and that was quite satisfying but John didn't have time to gloat because Xena had the two bowie knives out and was advancing, screaming something unintelligible.

She'd ripped the vest completely off in her zeal and John took a half a second to admire that quite extraordinary rack before another double tap. A little hole blew in the middle of her throat and she collapsed, the knives flying off into the crowd. Good shootin', Tex.

All right, who's next? John scanned back and forth but no one was stepping up. Confusion reigned. There was a great roiling with a lot of the scum immediately surrounding John running and spinning and shouting, telling everyone in back what had happened.

John was, momentarily, not their concern and he took that opportunity to glance back at Ankh, who had fallen to his knees and was trying to shove his stomach back in, the effort becoming more feeble by the second. And then he saw something else.

Just behind Ankh and to the right, some leather-clad punk, turned to the crowd with his arms raised, silver bracelets cascading down his well-muscled forearms like a waterfall. That was lovely, but it was the M-16 hanging from the punk's shoulder that caught John's attention.

The crowd would recover and make John a hamburger patty eventually, say in the next two seconds, and he really should do something about that. He strode, back and legs be damned, past Ankh and the two or three tearful cretins trying to help him get that stomach back in, raised the .25 to the back of Bracelet's head, and fired his last two rounds. Bracelet's skull fissured and he spun away but John grabbed his shoulder and yanked him back, dropping the .25 and pulling the M-16 cleanly off. John looked at it. Yep, a real M-16. What variant, who knew? Wonder if Bracelet got it from Belvoir or Myer.

No matter.

Already on full auto so John stepped back, leveled it and pulled the trigger. It sang, just sang, and he cut a swath of tracer to the right and left with the first two or three bursts. Panic swept the crowd but John didn't have time to enjoy it as he blasted across an arc, overlapping the last rounds.

M-16s don't fire a continuous stream of bullets, only three-shot bursts with each trigger pull. The idea was muzzle control, good one because the 16 will rise something fierce. Still, a continuous stream of .223 would have been nice. John raked the crowd again.

The bolt slammed back, out of bullets. John held the smoking rifle and admired his handiwork, the bloodied and ripped bodies, the screaming, terrified mob. Might as well relax, the extraordinary luck that made the last 30 seconds so vastly entertaining had probably run out.

The firelight flared up nicely as flames poured out of the roof and the front bay window, illuminating the scene almost like floodlights. Damn, all his pictures and videos and books.

John took in a big breath. Be calm, just wait, get ready. It's all pretty much over, but at least you're going out with a bang. 'Bout all you can ask, that your death gets noticed. Ankh's crapheads sure noticed and John idly watched the spike hairs and nose bolts and leathers flapping and running and crying and fighting among themselves, forming eddies and currents of wrath and confusion while the more composed tried to drag bodies off and slap the others out of their hysteria ...

Ya know, John, nobody's moving on you.

He stood backlit against his own flaming house, quiet, still, holding an M-16 with muzzle suppressed while a tornado of scumbags whirled in hate and chaos and not a single one of these cretins was bothering with him. Yeah, several were gnashing their teeth and screaming something in his general direction but they were too busy with someone dead or spouting blood from a pretty good wound he'd just inflicted. The rest were pulling at each other, trying to reorganize, all focused on themselves and hoping Ankh would stand up and take control. Or Rawbone or Xena. Somebody. Anybody.

Run. Now.

His back was agony and giant baseball hematomas had formed up and down his legs but God damn the pain, he was getting the hell out of here. John shook the M-16 at the punks and scumbags standing behind him and they pulled back as he ran past. Idiots can't recognize an open bolt, he supposed.

He dropped to the side of the house and moved headlong across the wall, bursting through the knee-high grass and frantically pawing around to locate the short chain link fence buried in here somewhere ... yes! got it. It was dark, the fire not yet reaching this side, and he took a moment to get his bearings. Okay, cut to the right, locate the wooden privacy fence and then that big nasty thorn bush marking the safety lane through the Claymores. Don't screw this up.

Someone shouted behind him and there were answering shouts of control and fury from the front of the house. Damn, they've woken up. And were after him.

Go.

His charred back duly registered a protest as he fell over the metal fence and John yelped. Running feet and shouts gathered in the dark behind him, guided by his cry, but they were stumbling and confused, hitting the tall grass and then the chain link as John frantically pawed along in the dark no more than five yards away, feeling out a path until his hand brushed the wooden fence. He swung his arms and a sharp pain lanced his little finger. There, the damned thorn bush he'd battled every summer before the Event. He could kiss it now.

"Bring some light, bring some light!" someone shouted and John heard bodies dropping over the chain link. They'd be on him in seconds.

Desperate, John probed with one foot behind the bush, trying to locate the rocks and gravel and other crap he dug up and laid along the zigzagging safety trail through the Claymores. He'd been pretty clever with it, making a pattern unnoticeable to the casual glance but which he could easily find ... uh, in daylight, calmly, without being pursued. Not so clever now.

Panic. John kicked around harder but he couldn't find the trail and more people were dropping off to his left. Fortunately, they were going straight down the hill to the neighbor's back door, figuring he'd beelined for it. They're going to catch on quick, though, and someone's going to bring torches or flashlights or, worse, night vision, and they'd have him. Got to get out of ...

Clunk. A rock.

"Wazzat?" someone shouted out and all the movement over the fence and down the hill paused for a moment and then started in John's direction. Crap. Distraction. Now. He grabbed the end of the M-16 and hurled it high and hard towards the neighbor's and it landed with a very loud and satisfying crash against something wooden, probably the deck.

"There!" someone shouted and it was Dien Bien Phu, everyone opening up with whatever they had, 16s, Tecs, pistols, shotguns, bazookas. The neighbor's house exploded in glass and siding, accompanied by screams because the morons were cutting down the guys who'd gone ahead. John balanced on the rock and stepped a bit, feeling for the depression in the grass. All right, good, found it. While they're busy shredding the neighbor's and each other, let's make tracks.

The trail was below grade about a boot length wide. Overgrown now because, yes, he'd neglected it but, hey, not a problem. The difference in level was apparent. He took about five steps and hit another rock. Perfect. John stepped off that, feeling real cocky, and then immediately froze, the cockiness gone because the level changed – he was off the trail.

Oh crap, how close were those Claymores? Crap, crap, crap! John gritted his teeth. Get. It. Together. Stupid. This isn't a straight shot down the hill, it's a zigzag, so zig. But he was disoriented, not sure of direction.

He straightened, locating the sky glow of the burning house. Okay, reoriented, and he placed a foot back against the rock he'd just left and toe searched. There, trench reacquired and he took a step along it but lost his balance and quickly dropped to all fours, hugging the trail. He braced, waiting for the snap of a wire and subsequent clickbang of an igniting Claymore. Nothing happened, though, and he rewarded himself with breathing again.

The firing stopped and John could hear a lot of confused movement around the back of the neighbor's house. Ah, they're searching for his body. Good thing he fell because it put him below line of sight. He mapped the trail with his fingers, angling down and to the left.

That's good and bad, because he'd avoid blowing himself up (_inshala_) but he'd also head back toward the searchers. Keep low and start crawling, bubie.

Which quickly became agony. He had absolutely hated the Low Crawl through the obstacle course during basic training. It came up after he'd already run a mile or so, swinging on ropes, climbing over logs, jumping over ponds, then, lookee here, a 30-yard pit of sand covered with a lattice of barbed wire about a foot off the ground that he had to crawl under while fake explosions went off all around.

It had almost killed him then, when he was studly; now, with the added discomforts of a ruined back, a ruined ear, one eye and knotted up legs (and stoved-in ribs, don't forget those), it was downright murder. He was gasping about five yards into it and was still only halfway down the trail, very close to where the cretins were searching. He sounded like a train pulling out of a station and fought for breath control.

Somebody shouted, "He's not here!" and there was a shifting of movement around the neighbor's yard. John stopped, wary. They were spreading out, getting close, damn close, and John tried melting into the ground. He prayed the grass and creeper and debris from an old shed would discourage them from walking over and stepping on him. Better, stop them from triggering a Claymore and blowing every single person in a fifty yard radius, including little ole John, to hell, although that might be a blessing since he was too beat to jump up and fight them. Like he had any weapons for that.

Heavy thrashing, not more than twenty feet away, someone kicking through the grass, and in mere moments …

"Wait a minute!" one of the cretins called out and everything stopped.

Relief flooded through John and he resumed breathing although he didn't dare move. Were they giving up? Maybe heading off down the hill? Please? He saw something then, not sure what, and blinked hard but couldn't make it out because of the sweat flooding his one good eye, the bloody one practically useless and, on top of that, his glasses (still with him, God be praised) were fogged. He risked a quiet brushing of the lens which only re-arranged the dirt and crap but at least he could squint. Something bright, quick ...what the hell? Then it dawned on him.

Flashlight beams.

Crap.

Got to get out of here. Got to, otherwise, they're going to pin him down.

The beams were converging in the yard and the thrashing resumed and John reached out frantically and located the depression, stretching out as far as possible to see what direction it went and then crawled to that point, stretched out again to feel the distance, crawl, stretch, once more and the trail angled off sharply to the right, good, because that meant moving away from them and he was now in the middle of the Claymores and the noise the cretins were making covered the noise he was making and he reached out again ...

"Hey!" a yell behind John and suddenly the world was white and bright and stark. A flashlight beam had him. "What the hell's that?" another yell.

Oh, just your average Ankh-stabber hiding in the grass, fellows, nothing to worry about. The beam jostled off him as they shoved around to get a better look. John considered taking advantage of that.

Like right now.

He jumped up and ran, back and legs protesting but gotta go, gotta go. The beam swung on him, actually a good thing because it lit the sharp turn ahead which cut back from the house and there was just one more turn

260

after that and he'd be away. If he lived that long.

"There he is! There! Shoot, shoot!" several voices called out at once and the gunfire started, the ripping sound of automatics, both low and high caliber and the thrum of shotguns and the snap of pistols and there was a hailstorm ripping up the ground and the air and he was dead, dead, dead.

Not from the first volley because that's the amateurs, the ones who just blasted off rounds in his general direction while holding their weapons gang style, more likely to hit each other than John. No, from the shooters, the three or four of them up there who knew what they were doing, who were getting sight picture, were locked, holding breaths and leading John just so and will squeeze about ...

Now, and he hit the turn and cut hard to the left.

A bullet plowed through his side, taking a pretty good furrow out of the left ribcage and spinning him around with the shock and fire of it. He grunted and lurched but kept his balance. Another round sang past his head, merely cutting his shoulder, the first guy's shot obviously disrupting the second guy's. Thank him later. More beams trained on him, lighting the world including the path and he bolted down it, praying the bullets tearing around him didn't set off a Claymore.

John's side was burning and wet and crying for attention and he really, really needed the medical kit stored in the safe house. Let's go get it. He shifted hard at the final turn.

Wham! Something hot and heavy smacked into his left knee and John staggered. Whoa, don't do that – one deviation and it's going to be the Fourth of July. His leg suddenly went numb and, dammit, he was going to fall, transfixed by several light beams. Seemed like a good time for a final, desperately futile act so he gathered himself and jumped from his right leg, a flying leap over the tackles and across the goal line, clearing the trail but pretty sure his now-floppy left foot would snag a trigger wire.

It didn't.

He landed hard, the wounds in his side and knee, his burnt back, missing ear and clubbed legs forcing a scream as he hit the tall grass and debris and rolled to get out of the lights which couldn't follow him in the overgrowth, although bullets still cut around and above. He burrowed into the crap, making as small a target as possible.

Unbelievable. Made it.

But, probably not. There were several yells of triumph as light beams played up and around his location. They knew they'd hit him and were just trying to fix his position before they came down and finished the job. About ten of them up there and John wondered what the rest of them were doing: running around the front yard confused, trying to revive a cooling Ankh, fighting over leadership, looting, whatever.

Not important, as long as they stayed there and didn't wander around the back to give the posse a hand. If one of the ten hits a Claymore, the remaining nine might be sufficiently discouraged to stay away and John might actually escape, actually live through this.

He chuckled. Please, live through this? A platoon of raving maniacs had him covered, Claymore or no Claymore. All they had to do was wait him out. If he moved, they'd shoot. If he didn't move, sunrise would reveal him and they'd shoot. More likely, sunrise would reveal his bled out corpse, sparing them the need for any shooting. Just hang him in the front yard to rot.

So it goes.

For the second time tonight, he was in need of a cigar. Would be fittingly stoic to light one up and puff away. Help the boys up there pinpoint him, of course, but may elicit a few seconds of admiration for his John Wayne attitude. Could go one better and just stand up, wave his arms, yell some insults, and let them blow him apart. Why not? It's pretty much the end, only a miracle could save him and God hasn't been doing those since about 70 AD. It'd be pretty ballsy. He might even get mentioned in some future epic.

Well, hey, why not? Let's do it.

John actually pulled his beaten-all-to-hell legs together before he hesitated. Wassamatter, afraid? Not really, what's one more little pain at this point? Pissed? Yeah, definitely, after all his careful planning and effort, here he was, John Rashkil, the world's main purveyor of the everything-is-fucked philosophy, lying in foot high grass and crap about to get his head blown off. Should have known better. Ought to stand just to teach himself a lesson. So, what's stopping you? Stand the fuck up!

He didn't, and didn't even call himself a wuss. Some atavistic clinging to life, he supposed. No matter how painful or craven the existence, it is existence, so hang on, desperately. John flashed on Dad, dissolved, agonizing, all hope lost, but still demanding the very chemo that killed him. In his case, it was the fear of facing a very deserved judgment. So what is it in your case, bucko?

Collier, for one. He'd hate for Collier to hear, someday, that his brave and stalwart fighting-against-all-odds Dad just gave up and let the enemy have him, although standing up and giving the finger would be pretty choice. For two, it was the sense that God owed him some kind of help here and standing up might obviate the first miracle since 70 AD. He'd stayed loyal through some things that would turn St. Peter agnostic so, Big Guy, how 'bout it? Thunderstorm, maybe? Legion of angels? Either would do. He'd keep expecting that help right up to the point where they shot him in the back of the head while cowering in the grass, going out like a loser instead of a hero. Humiliating.

Eh, let's just see what happens next.

John settled down and let the pain wash over him. Ah, man, can't believe a person can hurt this much and still be alive. He probably wasn't, so let nature take its course. No one seemed in too much of a hurry to come down and finish him so if he just eased from this world through the simple act of bleeding to death, well and good.

He was probably past the drop dead point where a miracle would make a difference anyway, and his shattered leg obviated the urge to stand and give the finger, so take a breath, relax ...

Whoom! The ground shook and there was a searing white flash of light and concussion that drove the breath from his body. A wave of dirt and debris rolled over him. *Whoom*, another one, and *whoom*, damnation! another! What the hell? John brushed debris out of his face and peered through the grass and there was a flash of lightning and concussion and he was covered with crap again. Good God, the entire Claymore field was going up! They were like miniature atom bombs. Air pressure and debris slammed into him harder with each second and John realized the Claymores were stepping their way down to him.

Got to get out of here but it's death to stand with all the ball bearings machine-gunning through the air. So he started rolling away, crashing into rocks and wood and junk and tearing his already torn back to pieces, driving his smashed knee harder into the ground and the bullet deeper in his side but hey, it beats getting shredded.

The world was coming to an end. The heat and light were overpowering and the air was just slapping the hell out of everything. *Whoomwhoom*, two more in quick succession, coming nearer and nearer, and John couldn't hear anything else but the booms and concussion so he had no idea what was happening to the freaks, but could sure guess. If the pressure wasn't rupturing every organ in their bodies then the bearings were zipping through them like air hammers. Must be a bloody mess up there. And, if he didn't get a couple of blocks away in the next three seconds, it was going to be a bloody mess down here, too.

Of course, naturally, right then, John rolled into something, a fence or a pile of logs, who knew, and stopped dead. He couldn't be more than five yards from the end of the Claymores, and that was just too damn close. He struggled but whatever he'd hit was angled too high and he couldn't roll over it and he was too smashed up to go around and sure as hell couldn't stand. Stuck, and here it comes, *whoom, whoom, WHAM!*

He lifted off the ground, held there for a moment's inspection, and then whatever was controlling the laws of physics decided he wasn't worth the trouble and tossed him aside. He rode a wave of superheated air and concussion, like a dynamited roller coaster, and it took forever to drop, or, actually, slam, into what felt like a pile of concrete. His head bounced hard a couple of times and, mercifully, all went black.

24

John's senses slowly turned back on, and not the good senses, either. Pain, first. His knee, side and back roared into full-blown agony, competing with a whole bunch of other seared, bruised, and ripped body parts; more, John suspected, than the average human actually had. Crowning all that was a terrible headache, so he must be alive unless God took wounds along. In that case, hey, Gabriel, he could really use an aspirin.

Pain was quickly followed by smell – mostly cordite and heat and some underlying things like the rusty odor of blood, which, for it to be so clear, must be his. Made sense. You don't feel this bad without bleeding some-where.

Hearing, next. There was a rising sound, something burning to vapor and then slowly fading. Aftermath, it sounded like aftermath. There was some shooting, too, but far away. John didn't understand that.

The parts of him still intact felt itchy and soft, so he was still lying in the grass. Oh, please don't be poison ivy. That would just cap everything, wouldn't it?

He opened his eyes, or rather, eye. The blood over his left one seemed to have congealed into cement. Light, but irregular and distant, so no flashlight directed in his face, thank God, and he blinked a few times. Everything's really blurry ... oh, man, his glasses were gone. Great. Feebly, he felt around in the grass but, dude, stop, they were probably blown halfway to Lorton. Moving hurt too much, anyway. He squeezed his right eye shut and opened it a few times but that wasn't a cure for nearsightedness so John just stared at the fuzzy world.

Still nighttime. The irregular light was fire, not dawn, obviously his former house eating itself. What time is it, three in the morning, Four? Could be 10:30 last night for all he knew, just a simple hour since he'd talked to Coll. Doubt that. Time zips by when you're in the middle of a war so it's after midnight, at least. Of course, it could be three days later.

John squinted at what had to be rising smoke, about five to six columns of it, ghosts against the cheerful glow of firelight. What could those be ... ah, got it, they marked the last location of recently discharged Claymores. The columns were the only things he could see in that direction. Everything else was blurry ruin.

The shooting continued and he could hear shouts but they seemed distant. Wonder how long they'll remain distant? Eventually, Ankh's pals are going to come back here looking for the posse and find hamburger, instead, which just might irritate them. He should get goin' while the goin's good. John sat up.

What a bad idea. His punctured side screamed, as did his back, and the headache suddenly went uber-migraine and he vomited all over his legs. Wonderful. There was a copper taste so he must have thrown up blood, which was definitely not good. He felt a little better, though, even if disgusted. He looked around, turning his head slowly as red-hot ball bearings rolled around his brain. Nothing. A lot of unrecognizable smashed things intermixed with a couple of knocked down trees, but that was about it. Jesus, what were those Claymores, anti-tank? Anti-aircraft carrier? Next time, read the freakin' label.

Standing was an adventure because he had absolutely no control over his left leg. He found a piece of something, fence or tree, who knew, and hauled himself up with it. The makeshift crutch drilled into his armpit but he was numb and dead anyway, so, eh.

He turned down the hill and peered fuzzily, just able to make out Heather Court at the bottom. His safe house was located at the end, a huge brick palace with a monstrous bricked gate. The guy who lived there was a mason and apparently loved his work. John picked it as a joke because it looked like a fortress so thank God for a sense of humor, because he could only see the huge and grotesque right now. With a great gasp of pain, he placed the crutch forward. Move. Just move, there's sanctuary, there's medicine, there's rest.

That is, if he can get there. If no one shoots him in the meantime. If the human body was more durable than he suspected, if will was everything, if God does help.

If.

25

FIVE YEARS LATER

"Sergeant Rashkil?"

Christ. All. Mighty. Who the hell was bothering him now? Collier kept his eyes loosely shut, feigning sleep, which by God he was getting two hours of, no matter what. He didn't care if right now the whole Red Army was pouring through a breach in the Rancocas. Fuck 'em. Sleep.

"Are you Sergeant Rashkil?"

Jesus, persistent little bastard, wasn't he? Collier didn't recognize the voice, so not a sudden bug-up-the-ass request from the L-T to check out a warehouse or go get some supplies or shoot a couple of deserters. No, this was worse, some Battalion thing, something from the Major.

He was getting very tired of being the Major's go-to guy. Yeah, that's one of the hazards of being her lover, Coll old boy, you're on her mind, but, damn, these recon and capture missions were getting old. Was she trying to get him killed? Maybe. That would end the rumors, wouldn't it? Collier smiled inwardly. All notions of chivalry have him dying for the woman he loves. Perhaps she's more chivalric than he thought.

There was a pause but Persistent Bastard had not gone away. He was standing there; Collier could feel him. Did not take hints, this one.

"Hey! Sergeant Rashkil!" the voice was loud and the hot breath drizzling on Collier's ear meant PB was now leaning over him and shaking the hammock.

Shaking the hammock? Collier moved, clearing the leather holster he always wore, sleep or no sleep, and jammed the .45 underneath persistent bastard's chin while grabbing the back of his persistent little head. He opened his eyes, "You know you can get killed sneaking up on people like that."

Collier was looking into a pair of bright blue eyes, startling, like neon lights, big and wide and expansive and regarding him with coolness.

"I didn't sneak," Blue Eyes retorted from a thin slit of a mouth, red and set like an angry zipper beneath the squashed ruin of a nose. Lots of fist fights, this one. "I called out at least twice. You heard me. You ignored me. Now, you gonna shoot me?"

"I haven't decided." Collier pushed him with the .45, not hard because he had a sudden liking for the pissed off little bastard, and sat up. Two or three privates the next lane over stared at them – sullen, resistant, typical fuckhead draftees they were getting now. Collier glared and raised the pistol and they scurried away.

He turned back on Blue Eyes, who was sheathing a trench knife. Hmm, pretty fast. "Were you going to stab me?"

"If you shot me."

"Take me with you, huh?"

"Fuckin A."

Collier chuckled, "This a promotion move?"

Those gigantic eyes narrowed and Collier saw true offense in them, "I don't do that, Sarge."

"Hmph. That would make you unique," Collier observed and saw the offense turning into belligerence. Touchy guy, dressed in pre-Event jungles, good quality stuff, so must be vet. Short, no more than 5'6", making him one of the many people over whom Collier, in his 6'2" (and ½) loomed. Corporal stripes, worn and frayed, so corporal for a while, so a promotion move was not out of the question. But he had a Transportation Command patch, which made such a move odd.

"Is that how you made staff?" the corporal regarded him.

Collier shook his head, "I don't do that, either." He reached over to his blouse hanging on a peg and fished around an upper pocket for an elusive cigar while casually dropping the .45 to his lap, keeping the barrel pointed at the corporal. Somebody could have hired him to make the move. But, then, why didn't he just stab Collier in the hammock?

"Hmph," Corp bleated back at him, whether in derision or agreement, Coll couldn't tell. Every word out of Blue Eyes' mouth was probably a combination of derision and something. That might explain why he was still a corporal. "So, are you Collier Rashkil?"

Collier stiffened, but didn't show it. That's why no hammock stabbing; not sure of his target. His patron couldn't save him if he killed the wrong man.

"Possibly. Why you asking?" Collier's trigger finger tensed a bit. Who's doing this? Jonesy? He's the only one up for it, but Jonesy was vet and they'd saved each other's asses too many times for coincidence and you don't waste the guys who keep you breathing, so no, not Jonesy. A lateral from another company then, which was stupid because the Major would promote Jonesy before allowing an interloper and Jonesy would kill the bastard anyway. So, a moron from another company. Had to be Eliot.

The corporal stared hard for a second and then went red, "You know, I don't have to do this." He reached fast under a strap and shrugged the backpack off his shoulders.

Shoot him, Collier's reactions commanded and he moved the barrel off his knee and felt the tension and waited for the surprise of recoil but the corporal hunkered down and opened the backpack while muttering and dug around in what looked like a change of clothes and you just don't take your eyes off the man you're about to kill so maybe …

Collier held.

"Just doing a goddamn favor … treated like shit, shithole front … what the fuck? … advantage of my good fuckin' nature, bastard sonsabitches …" The corporal uttered this in various iterations and Collier couldn't help smiling. What a funny guy.

"There!" the corporal proclaimed and snapped straight up like a gravity knife, holding a big stuffed manila envelope, stained and dirty and torn on one corner and obviously of some weight. He shook the envelope at Collier, "Are you Rashkil or not?"

"Yes."

"Then fuck you," and the corporal pitched the envelope next to Collier, who flinched, waiting for the subsequent explosion. Take out him, the corporal and about five or six others, too. No witnesses and no payoffs. Not so stupid. Couldn't be Eliot, then.

A few seconds went by and nothing blew up and the corporal, still red-faced and now breathing hard, stood fists ready with a make-your-fucking-move expression. Collier didn't even glance at the envelope. Instead, he deliberately broke eye contact, slowly de-cocked the pistol and then laid it back on his lap, still available. "Perhaps I have misjudged you."

"Fuckin' A."

"So who are you, Corporal?" Collier stayed on the obviously perturbed dwarf, fighting the urge to go for the package. One issue at a time, one target at a time, don't be distracted by all of them. You get killed that way. Sometimes a grenade or an M-14 took care of a lot of threats simultaneously, but each action as it comes. The package seemed benign. The corporal didn't.

The corporal glanced at the package, some puzzlement on his face, but he played along. "Corporal Henry Price, Sarge, 3rd platoon, A Company, 2nd Battalion, 98th Truck, ATC."

"98th? I thought you guys were in the Valley."

"We are. Right now I'm not." Price stopped talking and regarded Collier, a challenge in his eyes. Collier resumed his search for the cigar, finally locating it and placing it between his teeth. It was a good one, a panatela, Maduro.

He had found four of them wrapped in a plastic bag behind a sofa in one of the houses on the main street of Pemberton. How the earlier scroungers missed it, he didn't know. Another sign of how sloppy things were getting. No bands on the cigars but they were high quality, dry, of course, but still smokable, probably some Cuban-seeded Dominicans. He had smoked half of this one already and now seemed as good a time as any to finish it. He fished around for his lighter.

"The Valley," Collier spoke it as he flashed on cerulean skies and cold air and blue mountains covered with snow and woods, the Shenandoah coiled around and through it all, mother and protector, always there, a guide, the way home. Home. "You going back?"

The corporal shrugged. That could mean a lot of things. Either Price was legit, doing some kind of supply run which made him one brave (and crazy) SOB, given their situation, or he wasn't legit, a deserter, which was odd because the last place a deserter showed up was back at a Reg unit. Deserters went into the mountains or headed West or jumped sides, believing that Red horse-shit about brotherhood and workers' paradises. No sergeants in the Red Army, brother, no officers, we are noble and equal and fight the oppression of the masses. No five-year-old MREs, either, we eat fine rolls and drink good wine and make our plans in a big circle and then

273

hug and screw each other up the ass …

Collier chuckled to himself. Amazing how many people actually bought that crap. And it was crap. The Reds had shown iron discipline, and you don't get that from team building exercises.

Collier found the lighter and fired up the foot, puffing hard to get the spark going while keeping an eye peeled at Price and a hand ready to grab the pistol. Hard to draw, blockage, but what can you do? He peered at the corporal through the smoke.

Price was watching with interest, a longing on his face. A cigar man too. That's a plus. So, doing a job or not, maybe avoiding some kind of reorg which involved a lot of promotion moves, maybe pissed off his sergeant. Maybe a lot of things, with the temper this little bastard apparently had. Collier decided to leave it alone.

He savored the roll of the smoke along his tongue and throat before leaking it from the side of his mouth. Collier tipped his head towards the package, still keeping the danger eye on Price, "What's this?"

"It's a package."

Collier chuckled. "Okay, funny. What's in it?"

"I don't know, Sarge, it ain't addressed to me. It's addressed to you."

Collier blinked. Not surprising the corporal didn't snoop; he seemed an honorable guy and mail did hold some kind of sacredness, even these days. But, who would send him a package? Who did he still know in the Valley? All the Fishburne guys were dead or scattered. None of the syphilitic skanks he'd bedded in Waynesboro would send a postcard, much less a package. Odd and odder.

He took another slow puff, "Who gave it to you?"

"Some guy in a refugee camp."

Collier's heart stopped. Everything stopped. He held the cigar about halfway to his mouth. Refugee camp? No way, absolutely no way.

"Sarge, you all right?" Price's eyes narrowed and a look of actual concern crossed his face.

"Describe him."

"Short fat white guy. Fat guy in a refugee camp, you believe that? Said his name was Bill."

The sudden hope blew out of Collier like a puff from the cigar, but he didn't let his disappointment show. Okay, so, not Dad. Did you really think it could be, you simpering little girl? Knock it off. Hope is foolish, a distraction, gets you killed.

Dad would never agree with that – *au contraire*, Dad would be aghast, say without hope there is no reason for anything and even false hope keeps you alive. Wrong, Dad, wrong. Hope does not keep you alive. Murderous rage does.

Collier gestured with the cigar, "Go on."

"You know, Sarge, you could just open it."

"I could, but humor me."

Price shrugged, "Okay, have it your way. I did duty at the camp about a year ago, down near Bristol. This guy Bill was some kind of engineer, did a lot of work around the place. Kept him out of the tents, I guess. Anyway, he was always doing us favors, fixing radios, giving us old CDs, that kind of thing. Scrounge, but a good one. He asked me one day if I knew you. Said no, and he asked me to take the package, if I ran into you to give it. Said he was doing a favor for someone else."

Bill, short fat engineer … something tugged at Collier's mind, a hint only, but he couldn't wrap a clear thought around it. "Who was the someone else?"

"He didn't say."

"And you didn't ask."

Price shrugged again, "Wasn't my business. Figured you could open it and find out all this shit for yourself." He made a meaningful glance at the package.

Collier ignored that, "Why you?"

"I'm a nice guy."

Collier laughed, "So you been carrying this thing around for a year just waiting to run in to me, huh?"

"Not a year, six, eight months, tops. And, like I said, I'm a nice guy."

"Still doesn't explain why he picked you."

Price frowned, deep and ugly, stirring Collier's hand slowly back to the pistol, "I get around a lot."

Ah. Now he understood. Blackmarket hire, running favors for one officer gang or another, messenger and assassin, immune to desertion or travel restrictions, handling merchandise and collecting debts. Collier stared at him. "Okay," was all he said.

Price visibly relaxed. Man in his position didn't brook a lot of questions. Collier took one more puff while eyeing him and then reached over and grabbed the envelope, one of those thick padded ones, definite quality, definitely pre-Breakout, hell, pre-Event. It was heavy. 'Collier Rashkil' was inked across the front in a spidery thin hand almost obscured by dirt and water stains. Nothing else, no address, no rank, not even his Division, just the name. Collier blinked. Bill, Bill ... there was something, but it evaded him.

"You gonna open it?"

Collier looked up. Price hovered, a look of expectation on his face. Like a kid at Christmas.

"You got some stake?"

"Just want to see the end of it."

Collier nodded. Reasonable. Price didn't do a lot of favors without some payoff and this was probably as good as any. He holstered the pistol and drew his boot knife, a thin bladed Airborne he traded a can of coffee for a couple of years ago, and ran it carefully along the top. Didn't feel any wires, but you never knew. He also kept the blade pointed at Price. You never knew about him, either.

The blade was true and made a thin perfect cut along the top. Collier eyeballed Price to see if he needed a thin perfect cut along the neck, then pouched the opening and peered inside. What the hell? Some kind of metal box. He pulled it out and set it on his lap, sheets of paper dragging out with it. Price craned his head around but Collier held the papers so only he could see them.

Really good paper, definitely pre-Event. The same spidery hand that addressed the package covered one side. He read:

Dear Collier,

You do not know me, but I saw you from time to time when your Dad visited the Gate. I was the guy running it. This is a box your Dad wanted me to pass on to you.

"Holy shit," Collier breathed.

"What?" Price asked and moved closer but Collier ignored him.

Be damned and blown to hell. The things that happen, that just come out of nowhere. Here, right here in his hands, a gift from Dad. Freakin' unbelievable. He went back to the letter:

Your Dad came to the Gate about 4-5 years ago.

Collier looked for a date but there wasn't one. Okay, have to puzzle out the timeline later. He continued:

He was hurt real bad, suffering from gangrene. I do not know how he made it. He got here on some kind of electric scooter. The docs had to take his leg off, I am sorry to tell you.

"Sonofabitch." God, Dad, not your leg.

"What is it?" Price got a little more insistent and moved even closer but Collier shoved him away.

I tried to call you, but I did not know where you were, all I remembered was you were somewhere down south. Your Dad was in and out of consciousness for a long time and could not help. Sorry.

Before he could recover enough to tell me how to find

you, Breakout happened. I barely got away. I do not think your Dad did. I am really, really sorry. He was a good man.

Collier stopped breathing. Dad. That iron ball of grief he'd been holding in the pit of his stomach for years stirred and knocked against his heart, surprising him. He thought all those sentiments were pretty well secured but, damn all the angels, who expected this? A looseness trembled up his chest and quavered, setting the iron ball rolling. He had never truly mourned, had he? No reason, really, until just now. He felt like something was breaking, a rickety dam overwhelmed by a sudden unexpected tide. Too much, far too much.

"Sergeant," Price spoke softly and Collier looked at him. Price was wearing the expression everybody did from time to time, no matter how tough or inured you were – shared grief for dead friends and the never-had families and the war and the loss, just the sheer loss of the last ten years.

No matter the coldness of the heart or the crimes committed, the grief was there ready, at times like this, to surge. It made them all brothers, was gang sign and tattoo, the whip scar they all bore.

So he shared with a whip-scarred brother. "It's a letter from that guy, Bill. He knew my father. He's telling me what happened to him."

"Oh, man," Price rocked a little and stepped back, re-spect for a hard moment, memory of his own.

I ended up in a Valley camp farther south after run-ning for a while. I had managed to grab a backpack out of my tent just ahead of the hordes because I kept a lot of emergency supplies in it. I also kept this box in it. Your Dad had given it to me almost first thing, before he would let me take him to the hospital. He made me promise to get it to you. See, he thought he was going to die any minute and he wanted you to have it. Best I could figure out from his fever raves, he got into some big fight with the guys who did Breakout and they ended up burning down your house and he dug it out later. If you saw what kind of bad shape he was in, you'd know how much he really wanted you to have_this box to spend his strength getting it out. I have no idea what's inside. He said you'd know how to open it.

I do not have any more time to tell you anything else. They are packing us up for Atlanta right now

"Bill went to Atlanta?"

Price nodded grimly, "Yeah, they sent all the refugees there, thinking they could get some new cure out of them for the Phase Two."

Collier shook his head. Atlanta wasn't there anymore.

and I am writing this letter real quick so I can give it to Price. He owes me a few favors and gets around a lot so I figured he has the best chance of finding you. I figure you have your Dad's genes so you survived Phase Two, and I figure you are in the army, like everyone else. At least I'm hoping you are still alive because I made the promise and I want to keep it.

I have to go. Best of luck to you. I really liked your Dad.

Bill

Price stood quietly while Collier read the letter again and then pulled the box to him. Flat black metal with four buttons and a switch on the top. Portable gun safe. Dad's old portable gun safe, obviously, the one he kept under the bed and over which he threatened to dismember Collier the one day he caught him playing with it. "This is serious stuff, Coll, not a toy. You treat it with respect."

Was a bit banged up, but secure, and smelled a little of burning. Dad had never showed him how to open it. "When you're man enough," he'd said, an event pre-empted by Collier's going off to Fishburne, one step ahead of truancy and juvy. How he'd cursed Dad as the

279

old man had packed Collier up and driven him south and left him at Fishburne's gate. He thought his life was over. Turned out his life was saved.

But for what, Dad?

He fingered the box. It had a series of buttons on top, pressed in a sequence to release the latch. He had no idea how to open it, despite what Bill wrote. He supposed with a crowbar …

"Christ, Coll! You memorized the entire script of Ghostbusters! This should be easy!"

Like a bullet, Dad's exasperated phrase went through his head. "Sonofabitch," Collier said, softly.

"What is it?" and Price craned to get a better look at the box.

Collier held up a hand to silence him, to get the thought, to remember … "Two times at two and four, once at three."

"Say it," Collier whispered.

"Huh?" Price blinked at him, puzzled, and Collier spoke to the box, "Two times at two and four, once at three."

You'll know when you see it.

Collier punched in the combination, twisted the switch and the box lid popped. Price crowded closer and Collier pushed him back, again. He opened it.

Gold coins. Diamonds, other pieces of Mom's jewelry. Worth a lot and he noted Price's eyes widening. A folded piece of paper was lying on top of something square and he unfolded it. A map, of all places, American University, with a red 'X' drawn in the center of what looked like some kind of field. Dad must have buried something there for him to find but, fat chance, Dad, the Reds stood between, and he picked up the paper and underneath was a book …

He gasped. *The Little Shepherd of Kingdom Come.* "Un-fuckin'-believable," he said.

"What?" and Price moved in, staring at the gold and jewelry first and making instant calculations and maybe he'd make an offer, fine, but it was the book Collier held up.

"Un-fuckin'-believable," he repeated, shaking his head.

"What's so special about the book?"

"My dad loved it. He found it in a thrift shop one day and went ballistic, said it was one of his favorite books from being a kid. He read it every year, on his birthday." Collier stared at the cover. Red cloth binding, badly stained, spine broken and barely holding the pages. Old book smell. Dad's smell.

"What's it about?"

"An orphan," he said, quietly, and gently stroked the cover. "Don't really know. Never read it."

He thumbed the book gently, seeing one or two illustrations like old books had, some hillbilly boy with some dog. "Schmaltz," Dad had said, but there was a pleasure in his eye when he said it.

Collier turned to Price, "I owe you. I owe you big. Anything, don't care." He pulled out one of the cigars and handed it to the corporal. Price savored the bouquet, nodded, slipped it into his upper pocket and, without another word, grabbed his backpack and left. Collier watched him go. Be seeing him again, no doubt.

Collier slipped the book and the jewelry and letter back into the safe, locked it and stuffed it in his backpack. Amazing there was room. He slung the pack, grabbed his helmet, the cigar clamped between his teeth and stepped outside the warehouse, pausing to survey the area first.

Troops walking by, most of them blouses out, some with no blouses just T's, ripped pants, sandals, and no haircuts, a very few squared-away in the mix who Collier promptly ignored. They weren't a problem. The ragged ones, though ... Collier scrutinized them. No visible weapons; that was good. Only patrols got weapons these days and always under the watchful eye of some vet. But you never knew if someone had squirreled away a 9 and everybody had at least a knife, so look.

They barely gave him a glance but imperceptibly shifted away, not so much because he was there but because it was A Company housing and they had a troubling reputation. Recruits never knew when some vet was going to storm out the door, grab somebody and haul 'em back inside for some kind of amusement. Collier shook his head. That wasn't his thing. He tried to be fair to everyone, like those fabled pre-Event non-comms, but he had stripes and was standing on the Company's porch and that was enough to make the field wary. Big brush tarred us all.

Nothing threatened so he stepped all the way out, paused, took in a large, luxurious curl of smoke from the cigar and let it flow in the March breeze. Not a bad day, clear skies, cool but not uncomfortable. Fighting weather. Railroad tracks rusted about fifty yards away, coming around a ramshackle building that only needed one firm breeze to collapse it. This used to be some kind of construction site where they made doors or frames or something Before, but was long abandoned. As was everything.

He stepped off briskly, heading for the Pemberton-Ft. Dix road that became Hanover Avenue once it crossed the railroad tracks into town. A right at the broken asphalt and he was heading up the hill into Pemberton itself.

Battalion was located in a three-story town house on the next corner above Paul's North End Bar, or at least what used to be Paul's, according to a rusted sign lying in a trash heap in back of the parking lot. It was the armory now and a couple of corporals on guard there eyed him and gave little waves as he strode by. He waved back. They were good guys.

Pemberton. How ironic. He took in the two- and three-story Dutch saltboxes, most still intact, marching up the hill that protected them from Red artillery. You're home, Dad, he thought, and slapped the bottom of the backpack a couple of times. He didn't know exactly where Dad had lived in town because they'd breezed through here only two or three times while on their way to Uncle Art's, and that at 60 miles per hour.

Dad usually stayed on 206 and had detoured this way just to take a rare quick glance because Mom hated the place, for reasons Collier never found out. Collier had been too young to remember much, anyway. Dad had gestured at some apartment complex on the north side but all that remained of it were piles of shelled rubble. Collier's grandmother had lived somewhere on this street when she was a little girl but he had no idea where.

About the only fixture of Dad's life still around was the high school out towards Ft. Dix. It was an artillery park now. Collier had gone through the trash-strewn halls, picking his way over racked out gunners while peering into classrooms, trying to imagine Dad, 18 years old, carefree and young and vital, running through these halls with his best friends and Mom. Couldn't really picture it; Dad was always an old man.

And what gods of coincidence had decided that this, Dad's hometown, was going to be the last stand of the Blues? Collier shook his head. He did not believe in gods, or God, for that matter. Demons, maybe, but they were not raving red-colored creatures making little girls throw up pea soup. They were, instead, the inexplicable way people behaved, so ridiculous and illogical there had to be some external, malicious prod to it. People's stupidity was all the evidence of demon existence Collier needed. He'd seen no concomitant evidence of God. In this world of hate and murder, God was irrelevant.

He smiled to himself. Dad would be apoplectic, but Dad's world had known moments of peace and good so he could afford to seek God. In Collier's world, God was not sought because good simply didn't exist. There was just survival.

And precious little of that. Here they were, battered and chased and beaten across Virginia and Pennsylvania and brought to heel behind Rancocas Creek, the water and its impenetrable woods serving as screen and flank protection. The Reds stood across the water, thousands of them, seemed like millions, and they roared and chanted and shelled and murdered them. The Blues stood here, desertions increasing, discipline decreasing, individual acts of cruelty substituting for leadership, colonels and generals more interested in personal fortunes and getting away than making a stand, and they were supposed to be the good guys?

Collier snorted. We have failed you, Dad. Right here in Pemberton. Ghost town now, Dad.

Collier peered up the street as he climbed Battalion's front steps. Lots of soldiers coming and going from left to right, avoiding the top of the hill and a silhouette that invited rifle fire, but all that activity was just surface, a big intrusion. Moldering skeletons draped in every house, rot and rust and rats, a few houses burned down, the Methodist church just short of the hill's crest half gone, its bricks spilling into the street, the implements long since looted. Post mortem. The Flu had hit this place hard, and Breakout had pretty much finished it off. The Reds were doing their damnedest to destroy what was left. Uncle Art's house might be intact but it was over on the Red side so he couldn't go look. Not that he expected to find anything or anyone, just curious. Collier carefully stubbed out the lit end of the cigar and placed it back in his shirt. It was a pretty town once. It was a pretty country once.

One of Jonesy's guys was on duty and had already moved the M-16 away so Collier could gain the door. He nodded to the private and stepped into the foyer, which had a gigantic set of steps immediately going to the second floor. A corporal peered down at him with a leveled M-16 but raised it when he recognized Collier, gesturing for him to come up. He clomped his way to the corporal, "Hey, Swift."

"Sarge," Swift was laconic and bony and given to an off-world stare, but he was an absolute barbarian on the line and Collier always took him on missions. Swift loved missions and there was an eager light in his glance. "We got something?"

Collier shook his head, "No. Is everyone in?"

"Yeah," Swift, no longer interested, went off-world again.

Collier shrugged and moved past him. Swift lived only for payback. Collier had lived for it too, in the beginning, but raged and slaughtered a lot of it out. Oh, he still wanted more, get past these goddamn Reds and finish off the 'Slams,' but the urgency was winking out. Far too much fighting left before reaching any sense of satisfaction.

He stepped down the very narrow walkway heading to the last door on the left side, keeping a hand on the railing overlooking the gigantic stairs. Bad choice, this house. It was too weirdly built, long stairs and very narrow walkways. Hard to get out if a shell hit, since the walkways let only one person by at a time. You'd have to jump the railing, end up breaking an ankle. Easy to defend, though, one soldier per landing could hold off a coup attempt. Maybe that's why the Colonel liked it.

Making the hard climb to the third floor commander's office discouraged visitors, too. The Colonel definitely liked that.

Collier knocked on the door and someone inside yelled, "Enter." He turned the handle.

The specialist at the desk scrutinized him, "Sergeant Rashkil." It wasn't a question and Collier didn't like the way he said it.

"Awbrey," flat response to convey that dislike. "Is the Major in?"

"Did she send for you?"

Note that he didn't answer the question. Collier felt a slow burn rise in his chest. "No, she did not."

"Oh, so this is ... personal?" A nice little insinuating pause.

Collier shook his head. What did you expect? This was the army and you can't keep secrets.

But this was the army and he was vet and non-comm and didn't have to take any crap from some skinny little acne-scarred maggot, either. He leaned both fists on the desk and pushed his face into Awbrey's nose. "The nature of my visit is none of your concern. Go tell the Major I'm here to see her, or I'll throw you out the fucking window."

Awbrey blinked and made a squeaking noise as he scuttled over to the inner office door. Since Collier had, on a few occasions, thrown insubordinate lunkheads out of windows, it wasn't an idle threat.

Awbrey knocked then glanced back with some insolence before going inside. Voices were exchanged and then he sidled out. "The Major will see you, but she's not very happy."

Well, thanks for that bit of unnecessary news. Awbrey slithered to the desk, his look containing a smirk that invited a breaking of the little creep's nose. Temper, temper, Coll old boy; one more Article 15 and it's the stockade.

He marched in, closing the door behind, hit attention and held the salute, "Sergeant Rashkil requests to speak to the Major."

She frowned at him from the desk, returning the salute. "Did I send for you, Sergeant?" The official voice, filtered with rank and strength and authority but he

286

could hear the silk tones in there, the tenor that made his heart tremble and always laid a warm chill on his spine.

Major Rosa Vasquez de Alemeida Arce. Her name was poetry. Eternal brown eyes stared at him from the light coffee of her skin, liquid and caressing, all their nights together blended into one passionate, powerful image in his mind, far more than just lust and desperation of the chance – a giving, a complete giving. It made him yearn, the rarity of it.

She was elfin and slight, diminutive features and frame easily mistaken for small and last time we checked, Dad, your son was basically a prisoner and the world was a giant concentration camp, but she was true steel and ice, an Aztec warrior who astounded him with her ferocity and brilliance, and who possessed him soul and body. Soul, body, heart, and mind. Everything. He loved her.

"No, ma'am."

She arched an exquisite eyebrow and her look became guarded, "Well, then?"

He couldn't blame her. It was odd enough that she called him directly for missions without going through the Captain or L-T, but she was G-2 and her missions were classified and need-to-know so she got away with it. No one noticed when he responded to her summons anymore, and, of course, no one knew about the extra rendezvous they planned after the missions. Practically everybody suspected because their dual absences were often noted, but she was good at subterfuge, so was he, so they had not been caught.

Yet.

But him showing up without summons, that was different, that was really odd and would be noticed. He saw the doubt in her eyes, wondering if he was about to do something truly foolish, declare his love openly, demand they be together, desert, leave this crazy war like they had often pledged in those secluded, dark, after-passion moments, but that both knew would never happen. Unless one of them, he, for instance, had just gone insane.

He smiled slightly at her discomfort and watched a light panic rise in her eyes. Her mouth parted slightly and he knew she was about to ask him if he had, indeed, gone insane so he held up a hand to calm her, "I just need some time, that's all."

She was puzzled, "Time?"

"A few days. Uninterrupted. No more than two."

She frowned, "Are you asking for leave?"

"No, ma'am, I know I can't get leave. Just, respite."

She regarded him. "Am I working you too hard, Sergeant?" There was a hint of devilry in her question and a spark of comedy in her eyes.

He suppressed a smile, "No, ma'am, not hard enough, I think." She cast a lidded, coquettish look at him and it was all he could do to keep from rushing forward and taking her in his arms, laughing out loud and startling Awbrey, who probably had an ear glued to the keyhole. "That's not it. There's something I have to attend to."

"Explain."

"May I show you something?" she nodded and he slipped off the backpack, pulled out the safe and extracted Bill's letter. He gave it to her, "I just received this."

She took it, frowned, read it. She looked up. "Collier," she whispered.

Whip-scarred brothers and sisters. She was from New York City and was an actual Survivor, the only one of her family – mother, father, three sisters and six cousins, all gone. She had some distant relatives in Texas.

So did Collier, for that matter, but Texas was a million miles away and, last they heard, overrun by Phase Two and Mexico. You made your families now from who you could find, and some of them worked but most didn't, the pretense eventually succumbing to the stark reality or,

288

more likely, the thousand forms of death. You then became a short-lived bandit or a short-lived soldier, Red, Blue, whatever, substituting a cause for a life and burned with the false passion of it because there simply wasn't anything else. You slaughtered to express that passion, convince yourself of human commitment. And, if you were lucky, you had a rare opportunity to meld with a kindred soul, one hurting as much as you but one who complemented your hurt with healing balm and you, too, could heal her, before the thousand ways of death or the ten thousand ways of separation asserted themselves.

"Rosa," he breathed.

They held each other's gaze for a long, long moment, and if it were anywhere else and any other time and Awbrey wasn't pressed to the door, they would have run to each other and clung and never let go. But they held their separate distances and let the glances serve as an embrace.

"What's the extra time for?" she asked. Grieving? she didn't ask and wouldn't because grief now was a moment or two, not a couple of days. "This," he said, holding up the book. She looked, didn't understand, but saw sufficient need in his eyes. "All right," she spoke softly. She gave the letter back and he put everything inside the backpack.

"Just a couple of nights," he pleaded, "that's it, then ..."

"All right," she underscored it and there was nothing more to say. The iron ball swung at his heart and he felt his chest go weak, felt the tonnage of the last several years fall hard and he dropped his shoulders and swayed a bit, eyes swimming, amazed that the sorrow was such a live thing.

He saw it mirrored in her eyes and the way her hand came to her cheek. "I'll let you read it." She nodded and her eyes swam, too, for him and for Dad. Relationships were immediate these days.

He saluted and turned and grabbed at the door hard and fast and had the pleasure of seeing Awbrey almost fall over as he hastily stepped toward a cabinet, pretending he was filing something.

"Awbrey!" she barked with her steel voice and Collier chuckled inwardly. She had seen, too. He went out the door as Awbrey, shooting Collier an expression of loathing, shuffled in for a major (no pun intended) ass chewing. Collier grinned at him. Tough shit, corporal. Stop your damned eavesdropping.

He nodded to Swift and trotted down the stairs and out, stopping on the porch overlooking the street. A couple of rare trucks lumbered by, filled with troops heading out of town away from the front. Wonder where they found the gas? Bandages were clearly visible on various arms and heads and legs. Collier didn't know them and they didn't wave and neither did he. Line soldiers on five-day rotation. Back to Division at Wrightstown, medical and rest and resupply, and then back here. Each time, different faces.

The Forever War. Collier remembered that book. Dad had given it to him when he was what, 12 or 13? He didn't think much of it, that being his hate-everything phase, especially Dad, not so much Mom, but definitely school, and everything was fucked because he had to do homework and clean up his room and he and Daniel just wanted to be left alone to play computer games day and night.

He shook his head as he watched the last truck disappear from view. How trivial that all seemed now. Dad had tried to warn him – things change, always, and in ways you never consider. Understatement. Daniel was dead. So was Mom and, obviously, you too, Dad. So, come to think of it, was he.

He took the steep hill up the block to the ruins of the

church. A jeep pulled out of the side road across the street, driven by a private. Some L-T he didn't know was in it. Of course. Wasting precious gas being squired around, huh, jackass? Collier pointedly ignored him as the jeep sped by. Move on, boy. Johnny latecomer, son of some Colonel or General or Congressman, commissioned by influence, not battle, the way Rosa and the few good officers were. Here to pick over the bones. As petulant, insolent, and incompetent as the recruits they got now, but add to that a sense of entitlement. Smarmy worthless bastard.

Better, he supposed, than the smarmy murderous bastards actually in charge of the army, the ones throwing them to their deaths solely to exercise some ego burst or make some kind of HQ political point. He wondered if the Reds suffered the same thing. Not bloody likely, given their success. They seemed to be more on mission.

He stepped around a pile of bricks and up a pile of cement and jumped over some rebar onto a little trail cutting through the top of the rubble. Balancing himself, he crouched low and stepped hard over the pile and slid down the other side. Safe. Stand up there too long and you invite sniper fire. He paused a moment to light what was left of the cigar. Good, good, better draw now and he puffed luxuriously. Gonna miss the one he gave Price, but it was well spent. He absently patted the backpack. Definitely got the better end of that deal.

He was up against a waist-high wrought-iron fence and clambered over it, gingerly avoiding the spikes. Gravestones and obelisks marched away from him up a little crest, their even pattern disturbed by broken stones and fallen monuments, the shells doing enough damage here. The stones were moldy green but startling white where broken, and you had a sense of ancient ruins interposed with modern construction, an apartment complex falling down among Stonehenge.

The chiseled names dwindled in the distance, the Forts and Bushes and Haines, all the good South Jersey families. They had lived some kind of traditional life, then fell by some traditional means, illness or accident, attended to by survivors and pastor and flowers, buried then forgotten. Their descendants now rotted in the houses they had passed down, not buried but still forgotten. Collier took a puff. He wondered if they knew.

There were lots of hiding places here and some trick of sound insulated it from outside noise. He and Rosa had already discovered that. No one else seemed to come here and it remained undisturbed except when they cut the air with their muffled cries, trying to hold it down so as not to arouse any curiosity from passersby, hard to do with the passion between them.

Must be some kind of symbolism, he and Rosa restoring life among the dead, but no, no, that wasn't it. It wasn't poetry. They were simply two lovers stealing moments before one or the other was stolen by war. Violating the rules about officer/enlisted fraternization made it dangerous but they were just rules and had no moral force, especially with what lay so powerfully between them.

Screw the rules.

He took a deep puff. The only life he saw, the only hope, was the fleeting glint of her eyes by moonlight. The best reason to fight, so they could love. They could war for another twenty years or twenty minutes, he didn't care as long as, at the end of it, they walked away hand in hand, out of the sound of guns and men. Maybe that was poetry.

He stepped over one fallen stone and picked his way through others, an obstacle course of prone and upright markers until he was in the middle of the cemetery next to a green encrusted tomb, still intact, the lettering long faded so he didn't know whose it was. The ground here was soft with moss and damp earth and he and Rosa had laid a blanket here many times.

He settled down, dropping the backpack and savoring a long pull on the cigar. He watched the smoke cloud above him, lifting gently into the air and dissipating. He had about an hour right now, then he would have to go back and tend to roll call and assignments and maintenance, then maybe another twenty minutes in the hammock before somebody bothered him about something that would take a few hours, then it would be lights out and he could slip away and come back here for maybe an hour or so undisturbed.

All told, it would take about two days to finish the Shepherd, what with his slow reading and the poor light and the time he could steal. The major had the two days covered; after that, somebody would get suspicious. But that should do it. That should.

He pulled out the safe and emptied the contents on his lap. He pawed through the jewelry, examining every piece and trying to remember the last time Mom used it. He read Bill's letter again. Then, he began to read Dad's.

ABOUT THE AUTHOR

D. Krauss is a former USAF officer residing in the Shenandoah Valley, Virginia. He has been, at various times: a cottonpicker, a sodbuster, a librarian, a surgical orderly, the guy who paints the little white line down the middle of the road, a weatherman, a door-kickin' shovegun-in-face lawman, a hunter of terrorists, and a school bus driver. He has been married for 38 years to the same woman, and has a wildman bass guitarist for a son.